CATHERINE CARSWELL

(1879-1946) was born in Glasgow, one of the four children of George and Mary Anne Macfarlane. She attended classes in English literature at Glasgow University, but could not in those days be admitted for a degree. Thereafter she visited Italy and studied music for two years at the Frankfurt Conservatorium.

In 1904, after a brief engagement, she married Herbert Jackson. When, in 1905, she told him of her pregnancy, he tried to kill her. Declared insane, he spent the rest of his life in a mental hospital. Catherine returned to Glasgow where her daughter was born, and worked, first in Glasgow and then in London, as dramatic and literary critic for the *Glasgow Herald*. In 1907 she began legal proceedings for the annulment of her marriage. She won the case, making legal history.

Her friendship with D. H. Lawrence was kindled by her favourable review of *The White Peacock* (1911). They began corresponding and their relationship lasted until Lawrence's death. In 1915 she married Donald Carswell, with whom she had one son, and in the same year she lost her job at the *Glasgow Herald* for praising *The Rainbow*. Soon after this the Carswells moved briefly from London to Bournemouth. She became an assistant dramatic critic at the *Observer* and continued working on the novel which would become *Open the Door!* (also published by Virago). In 1916 she and Lawrence exchanged manuscripts of *Open the Door!* and *Women In Love*. Her novel was completed in 1918 and won the Melrose Prize on publication in 1920. Her only other novel, *The Camomile*, was published two years later and she then devoted herself to *The Life of Robert Burns* which made her name in 1930. This was quickly followed by a biography of Lawrence, *The Savage Pilgrimage* (1932), a number of anthologies and a life of Boccaccio, *The Tranquil Heart* (1937).

After her husband's death during the black-out in 1940, Catherine Carswell lived alone in London. She worked with John Buchan's widow on his memorial anthology, *The Clearing House* (1946) and on her own autobiography which was published, incomplete, as *Lying Awake* in 1952. Her friends included Vita Sackville-West, Edwin Muir, Rose Macaulay, Storm Jameson, Hugh MacDiarmid, John Buchan and Aldous Huxley. Catherine Carswell died in Oxford at the age of sixty-six.

VIRAGO
MODERN
CLASSIC

NUMBER
261

CATHERINE CARSWELL

THE CAMOMILE
AN INVENTION

WITH A NEW INTRODUCTION BY
IANTHE CARSWELL

Published by VIRAGO PRESS Limited 1987
41 William IV Street, London WC2N 4DB

First published in Great Britain by Chatto & Windus 1922
Copyright Catherine Carswell 1922
Introduction Copyright © Ianthe Carswell 1987

British Library Cataloguing in Publication Data
Carswell, Catherine
The camomile.——(Virago modern classics)
I. Title
823'.912[F]   PR6005.A749

ISBN 0-86068-873-9

Printed in Great Britain by Cox and Wyman
of Reading, Berks

CONTENTS

'The camomile, the more it is
trodden on, the faster it grows'
1 Henry IV. ii 4

INTRODUCTION

Why *The Camomile*? A humble little creeping plant with a pleasant scent seems to have no connection with any aspect of this book—D. H. Lawrence thought that if Catherine Carswell had chosen a different title, the novel might have sold better. He wrote in a letter to her, 'So they don't like your Camomile at all! It may be the name, you know. Perhaps if you called it *Gingerbread* they'd sup it up like anything.' And later, to her husband, 'If only she had called it *Rose-hearted Camelia*, they'd have supped it up.' The clue to the title is given half-way through the book when the heroine's friend and mentor says of her writing, 'I see. It is like the camomile—the more it is trodden on the faster it grows.'

The Camomile was published in 1922 only two years after Catherine's first semi-autobiographical novel *Open the Door!* which won the Melrose prize and attracted much praise. Catherine, like Ellen in *The Camomile*, absolutely needed to write but started her career as a musician, not as a writer. Again like Ellen, she left her home in Glasgow to study music for two years in Frankfurt and this experience had a formative influence on her life. Her parents did not impose strict disci-

pline on their four children, but their acquaintance was circumscribed; the one important book
in the house was the Bible; the only novels allowed
were those of Scott, and Catherine's parents had
no interest in 'the arts'. But Catherine had an
essentially artistic temperament and great natural
good taste, so that when she left Scotland for the
first time and was introduced to a whole new world
of culture in Germany, she was able to respond
with deep feeling and appreciation.

When she returned to Glasgow, instead of
teaching music, Catherine began lecturing on art
and writing articles. After the brief interruption of
her disastrous first marriage, which was later
annulled, she became a dramatic and literary
critic for the *Glasgow Herald*. This was unusual for
a young woman in 1906 and there is much
evidence that her reviews were well thought of,
though sometimes assumed to be written by a
man. She had been writing for the *Herald* for nine
years when her contract was abruptly terminated
because she gave a favourable review of D. H.
Lawrence's novel *The Rainbow*. This was considered shocking by the editor and it was only
published because she managed to smuggle the
piece to the printer without the editor's approval.

Catherine's daughter was born only a year after
her marriage, but by that time her husband had
been certified insane and he never saw his child.
Catherine left Glasgow for London with her little
girl in 1912 and she supported the two of them by
her journalism. She also started her first novel,

Open the Door! (republished by Virago in 1986), by this time being totally committed to writing, not only as a career, but as the activity for which she felt a kind of inner compulsion. She did not find writing easy, or particularly enjoyable (except for letter writing). She told a friend that she rarely wrote a first line without crossing it out and starting again and again a dozen times before she achieved the exact nuance she was seeking. She would force herself to persist until she was satisfied. Catherine wrote in one of her notes:

It's a great shame and mystery that I am driven by so strong an urge to intellectual and literary pursuits for which I am ill-fitted (so that I am always trying to escape them) and that I cannot give myself up to some kind of manual work at which I am by nature apt enough and in doing which I could give rein to my inveterate disposition to dream and to think without trying to find words for my thoughts.

But in another note she uncharacteristically boasted, 'If to have expressive words and balanced phrases ringing in one's head is to be a writer, then I am one.' And also, with certainty, noted, 'I love, if not writing, having written. Writing interests me more than any other activity.'

Not long after coming to London Catherine's daughter died of pneumonia. She was only eight years old and although we know of Catherine's grief from the rest of her family, she never referred to it in her published writings and no comparable experience occurs in her fiction.

However, by the time of her daughter's death, Catherine's charm, her beauty and her gifts were making her many interesting friends in the literary world. This congenial life was shattered for her, as it was for everybody, by the First World War. I remember Catherine telling me at the beginning of the Second War that she hated going to Victoria station because her memories of farewells there during the First War were still unbearably poignant. In 1915 she married her second husband, Donald Carswell, who fortunately was never sent to the Front. Three years later their only child, John, was born and when the War ended, Catherine had a family and a home to look after. She took her domestic duties seriously.

Ellen in *The Camomile* rents a secret room for writing and says, 'I fly there as I imagine a lover might fly to his mistress.' In real life Catherine had also discovered that the only way she could escape from the demandss of family and friends was to have a secret place where she could write alone and undisturbed. In a letter to a friend she described her pleasure in that secret room in almost the same terms as those used by the fictional Ellen. In 1929, about three years after my family and the Carswells became friends and we were living in adjacent roads in Belsize Park, Catherine rented a room in Keats Grove opposite Keats House. Every weekend John (whom I married much later, in 1944) used to go with me and my brother to spend most of the day on the Heath and we had to pass the end of Keats Grove.

None of us had any idea that John's mother was writing in a room a few yards up the street.

Rooms in the Keats Grove house were let out and Catherine realised that if the Carswells had two lodgers, they could just afford to rent the rest of the building. This was probably the most attractive home they ever had and Catherine would have been astounded to learn that her delightful house was recently valued at nearly half a million pounds. But by moving there she lost the secret room which was so necessary to her. She couldn't manage without it, and found another in Windmill Street, off Tottenham Court Road. John never went to her writing rooms and believes that his father didn't either.

The Camomile is written in the form of letters and a journal. The letter form was used by Richardson for his two most famous novels, *Pamela* and *Clarissa Harlowe*; by de Laclos in *Les Liaisons Dangereuses*, and very recently by Alice Walker in her enormously successful novel *The Color Purple*. In all these books, as in *The Camomile*, the letters are ostensibly written by women and one wonders why this should be. Is it supposed that women have, or had, more time for writing letters? In Catherine's life letters were extremely important, and although she constantly revised and took endless trouble over anything that was to be published, she wrote letters easily and fluently and spoke airily of writing '10 or 12 letters today apart from all my work'. It is tempting to think that she chose to cast her novel in the form of letters because consciously or unconsciously she was influenced by her own habit and facility in this form.

She belonged to a generation for whom letters were a far more important means of communication than they are today. When she was growing up there were no telephones and no motor cars and unless friends were within walking distance, friendships were maintained by post most of the time. Moreover, a letter cost only one penny and was delivered the following day to almost any address in the British Isles. Even I can remember when local letters posted in the morning were reliably delivered the same afternoon.

Catherine's correspondents reflected her extraordinary range of friendships; they were famous and unknown, old and young, from Lady Tweedsmuir, the widow of John Buchan, to Jim who helped in her garden in Essex and was almost illiterate. But the core of her correspondents was a group of Scottish women, friends who included Dr Isabel Hutton, an early psychiatrist; Phyllis Clay, a sculptress whose graceful statue of Catherine holding her baby we still have; Dr Maud McVail, an early woman Medical Officer of Health; Hilda Bonnavia, an artist; Flos McNeill, the writer on Scottish folklore and cookery, and Maggie Mather, a musician and singer who studied with Catherine at Frankfurt. Most of these friendships dated from Catherine's youth and persisted until her death, for she was the first of the group to die.

Catherine had some male correspondents of

whom the most important was D. H. Lawrence. His letters to her, of which she kept nearly two hundred (all now published), are generally agreed to be among the most interesting he wrote. In almost the first of them he says, 'I must tell you I am in the middle of reading your novel [*Open The Door!*]. You very often have a simply *beastly* style, indirect and roundabout and stiff-kneed and stupid . . . But it is fascinatingly interesting. Nearly all of it is *marvellously* good.' What a mixture of disparagement and compliment! The criticism was not on one side only. Lawrence had a great respect for Catherine's literary opinion and sent her an early draft of *Women in Love* for her comments. This resulted in his making some alterations at her suggestion.

Unfortunately Lawrence never kept letters, but about three years after his death Catherine learnt that her letters from him had a commercial value. At this time the Carswells were particularly short of money and threatened with bailiffs. The letters were sold for £210 which was enough to avert financial disaster. After this Catherine prudently kept letters from those of her friends who had become well known, such as Vita Sackville-West, Storm Jameson, Neil Gunn, Hugh MacDiarmid, Rebecca West and Rose Macaulay. We still have these, done up in small bundles, with a touching little note in Catherine's handwriting 'Might be sold'.

The letters in *The Camomile* are very feminine, there are several good descriptions of clothes, as well as of young and older women and their relationships; but these are ultimately subordinate to Ellen's more serious concerns about the purpose of life and fundamental values. In spite of being very much in love physically, Ellen finally rejects the conventional life expected of her, in order to be true to herself and not deny her talent for writing, which for her would be death to hide. Integrity is an important theme of the book as it was in Catherine's life, and in her own letters to Flos McNeill, whom she advised about writing, she said:

In an autobiographical novel of the kind you are trying to write nothing is any good until you get somehow a stage *removed* from the self of the story, outside of that self, cool, critical, perhaps even hostile, having exchanged *human* sympathy for that very different commodity artistic or literary sympathy towards your characters. During this process it is true you need to face yourself . . . it is only by then—if one must and has the impulse—standing off and telling one's story firmly, unfalteringly, as clearly as one can that one retains in absolute secrecy and possession and privacy whatever secret inner truth there may be in one's experience.

She also condemned 'intellectualizing' and in this she was surely influenced by Lawrence. He could have written the following passage which is actually taken from one of Catherine's letters:

To *think* for me is entirely different from to 'intellectualize'. One can and should *think* with all one's being—thought to be real must be linked up with the stream of the blood. The intellectualizing business uses *other people's* experience and borrowed stuff and is a sort of cutting off and cowardice.

Catherine was severe in her condemnation of those who accepted other people's opinions and at the end of the novel Ellen acts against the expectations of her family and friends, as Catherine would no doubt have done herself in the same situation. She was always sympathetic to people's behaviour if it was true to themselves, but she wrote to my own mother, who was a close friend, criticising her for a love affair which she considered was not deeply felt and was unworthy of her. I was surprised to read this letter after my mother's death and to realise that it in no way damaged their friendship. Catherine was deeply honest and deeply loyal and she endowed her heroine in *The Camomile* with these great qualities. They are a source of difficulty and conflict, but lead Ellen, at the end, to feel confident in her decision to let writing be her first priority.

Ianthe Carswell, London, 1986

PRAELUDIUM

25 BLANDFORD TERRACE, GLASGOW,
Sunday, September 2, 19—.

MY DEAREST RUBY,—We got back from Loch Sween
last night.   It was still raining there when we left,
and we reached home in a downpour.   To-day it
rains steadily.   A wet Glasgow Sunday !   In spite of
Eliza's efforts to have everything ' nice and bright '
for our return, I don't like this new main-door flat
of ours in Hillhead.   Aunt Harry says it is 'nice
and cosy,' but Ronald and I would both far rather
be in the dingy, roomy old place in Blythswood
Square, where even Ronald thinks he can remember
Father's last visit to us, and of course I do in every
detail.   I suppose, though, that I ought not to com-
plain, as the flitting was forced on Aunt Harry by
my going to Germany.   At least so she says, which
makes me all the more determined to start earning
money at once.   To-morrow I begin with my first
private pupils — two children of six and eight,
daughters of a shipowner called Lockhart.   I shall
go to their house, which is said to be very grand—
all carved oak and tapestries and coloured glass in

the windows. Reverence enters the voice that speaks
of it. All the same, Mrs. L. tried to beat down the
fee printed on my cards (three guineas for twelve
lessons) to four guineas for the two girls. Then
on Wednesday morning, immediately after nine
o'clock prayers at a cranky sort of private school
near here, I'm to give a first 'Music Lecture'—a
ten minutes' talk with illustrations at the piano—
to the assembled pupils. Your Ellen is the latest
new-fangled notion of Miss Sutherland, the headmistress. Anyhow this should help me to keep up
my practice.

Not bad, you say, for a beginning ? Perhaps not.
But, Ruby, I feel ' *that* nair-rvous,' as we say here,
and, what is worse, a fraud. What if I have no gift
for teaching ? It is very funny to notice how impressed, yet how sceptical Aunt Harry is. If she
has read my professional card once, she has read it
fifty times, but I'm sure she believes no more than I
do that I shall really be paid money for my
lessons.

In spite of the rain I did like being in the West
Highlands again, and it was lovely having Ronald
away from his friends, even from Mungo Fleming,
and all to myself. Yet I was glad to leave yesterday. It is high time I made the plunge here. Three
months already, Ruby, since we left Frankfort ! And
to me it seems much more. Ronald is sitting beside

me now, clearing his desk, and he keeps shoving
packets of my Frankfort letters across the floor to
me with the point of one of his crutches. He says
he kept them all, thinking they might interest me
later. Here is a bit of one that will amuse you, as
it tells of our first meeting that day of the *Prüfung*
almost exactly three years ago. The letter is dated
solemnly.

' My Nineteenth Birthday.
' c/o Fräulein Bruch,
' Feuerbach Strasse 21a,
' Frankfurt-am-Main.

' . . . I have gone through my *Prüfung* at the
Conservatorium to-day and come off not so badly.
Also I think I have made a new friend, one as
different from Madge Bruce or Laura Sterling as you
can imagine. Probably neither Laura nor Madge
could stand Ruby (that 's her name—Ruby Marcus),
but then my friends never were very good at standing
one another. While I was waiting to be heard I sat
with a lot of other new students in an anteroom.
Next to me on one side was a short, square girl in a
sailor dress that scarcely came to her knees. She
had a big pale face, big hands and feet, and beautiful grey eyes, very steady, with heavy lids. Her black
curls must have been done with papers, I think, for
though most of them only reached her neck, the bits
that had been missed out were dead straight and

hung down to her shoulders. She was got up to look about nine, but told me she was fourteen. She chatted away like anything, speaking in an attractive voice but with an ugly accent. Her name is Dobbin and she comes from Leeds, where she has played at festivals since she was six. Her father is blind and very poor, and a rich widow is putting up the money for her musical education. Laura would have called her common. But though on my other side there was a pretty London girl whom Laura would have liked, with a lady-like expression and a beautifully cut white serge dress, I felt sure from the first that Dobbin was a genius and this other, so far anyhow as art was concerned, just trash. Perhaps genius is a part of the " reality " you chaff me so much about and for which I 'm always searching?

'To get on about my new friend. While Dobbin and I were talking and laughing and the girl in the white serge kept drawing herself away as if we were not the sort of thing she had come to Germany to cultivate, four other new students came into the room. I stared eagerly at their faces. There were three American boys with their hair brushed back, and one very dark, untidy girl, wearing an orange-coloured silk blouse. "This one too," I thought, "is probably a genius. It 's a pity she looks so Jewessy." And just then her eyes met mine, and I felt myself giving her a friendly grin. Though she smiled quite faintly back, her face lighted up as I'm sure only the faces of clever and sensitive people can. When she came straight to the chair in front of me I was as pleased as if I had been given another birthday present. She asked me, " Is this chair free ? "—as if I should know any more than Dobbin or the genteel one on my other side—and I, blushing idiotically, said, " No, the charge is ten pfennigs an hour ! " while Dobbin giggled (she's a fearful giggler) and the genteel one stared coldly into the distance.

' We had not more than two minutes to talk before Dobbin and I were called and my heart seemed to stop. Ruby did just tell me, though, that she was going to play Rachmaninoff's Prelude (the hackneyed one) as her *Prüfung* piece, and I guessed from that, rather to my relief, that she knew the ropes even less than I did. Miss Rory had *insisted* on my playing Bach for the *Prüfung*, but of course it isn't every girl that goes to the very Conservatorium where her teacher studied.

' Dobbin and I marched into a not very big room where the Direktor sat at a table covered with papers, and all the masters stood about or leaned on two grand pianos placed side by side. They took Dobbin first, which gave me time to look round, though my hands were cold and my knees knocking together with fright. Knopf and Zilcher I picked out at

once.   Knopf, who is considered by far the best piano
teacher in the place, had been pointed out to me in
the vestibule an hour before.   He is a slight, shab-
bily dressed man with a fair beard going grey and
extraordinary eyes, bright blue and piercing.   Zilcher
I recognised by Miss Rory's descriptions.   Unlike
Knopf, he is well, almost foppishly dressed—a dark,
fattish man with a moustache and a kind, indolent
smile.   Miss Rory told me he was Frau Schumann's
favourite pupil, but here they say that label is worn
by every one that ever had a couple of lessons from
the great Clara.

'Dobbin launched out into the Hummel Concerto
with Knopf at the other piano playing—at first very
carelessly—the orchestral part.   Ronald, I could have
knelt down and kissed her ugly feet!   Her touch is
like a man's for tone and strength, yet one feels that
only a child could have such perfect simplicity of
expression.   She is of course a prodigy.

'Miss Rory had warned me that as a rule one movement of a Sonata or Concerto was all they would hear
at the first *Prüfung*, but with Dobbin Knopf simply
turned over page after page, playing better and more
carefully himself every moment.   When they were
finished no one uttered a word of praise.   Knopf got
up, put his hand on her shoulder, pressing every one
of his fingers into it (I caught the look he gave her—
such a look out of those sapphire eyes!) and said, "Das

geht, meine Kleine. Du bist zu mir!" And though it is the rule for good students to choose their masters for themselves, not a soul interfered. Only Zilcher winked one of his black, rogue's eyes at the Direktor, who pretended not to notice anything.

'The odd thing is that instead of being made more nervous by Dobbin's performance, I lost at once both fear and hope. Nervousness became an impossible affectation. I knew I could not compete with Dobbin; all I could do was my best, and even if I did my worst, those half-dozen men had newts' ears and could judge pretty accurately of my powers. That, you see, is why I ask if genius is Reality. If the girl in white serge had played before me, I 'm certain I should have been governed by the nervous desire to impress the masters beyond my deserts, to deceive them if possible by doing even better than my best. But after Dobbin, I no longer wanted to aim above all at being highly thought of. I simply wanted to let those musicians see me as I was, so that they might the better judge and help me.

'I played my Bach (Prelude and Fugue in E major) neither very well nor at all badly. They let me go on right into the middle of the Fugue, when the Direktor waggled his white beard and growled, "Genug, danke, Mees Car*stairs*," and to

Zilcher, who stood near him, he muttered as if in a temper the cheering words, " Es giebt ein ganz hübsches Talent, auch Geschmack," whereupon Zilcher stroked his moustache and made eyes at me. This meant that I was given leave to choose my master and could have Knopf if I liked. Naturally I was dying for him, but when he turned from talking to Dobbin and looked at me as if, just to oblige me, he was willing to gobble me up without so much as chewing me, something in my Scotch blood rebelled. Then and there I forced myself to say I wanted Zilcher, and when Zilcher opened his eyes very wide and wrapped me round, as it were, in his warm, cuddling smile, I felt glad. It certainly looked as if such a thing had never happened to Knopf before, and though I don't for a moment suppose he cared, the other masters were clearly amused. The Direktor's white eyebrows fairly flew up his bald, bright red forehead.

' Afterwards I waited about in the street for Ruby. Poor thing, she came out with tears in her eyes and looking very pale and dazed. They had stopped her after those three first tedious notes of the Prelude and made her play scales instead and read out some Mozart, after which, without offering her a choice, they handed her over to Zilcher. When I told her about myself and Knopf she could hardly believe her ears, and thought I had made a mistake which I should regret later. Still, when I came to explain, she understood better than I had myself. She thought it had probably had more to do with Dobbin than I had realised. " It must have seemed," she said, " rather like offering yourself as a concubine to one who had just married a true wife." Don't you think this was clever of her ? She lives in London with a crowd of sisters and a mother who is literary (but successfully so, not like ours). She doesn't much like her home, which is in West Hampstead, and I think she rather envies me for being a proper orphan, also for having a brother. Fancy, she has never in her life met a missionary ! She seemed surprised when I told her that Father was one. Her mother is a widow, but might easily marry again, a thing they all live in dread of.

' In the end we rejoiced that we were to have the same master, and planned how we might share lessons, as here they always take two pupils at a time for the *Instrumentstunde*. We went for a walk together right into the country, talking hard all the time about ourselves and everything, especially art. We came to a *Milch Kur* place and drank huge glasses of special milk, and later ˌwe found a bank covered with purple autumn crocuses—so lovely ! We picked a bunch each, and Ruby thought she could leave her rooms, which are not very nice, and come to Fräulein Bruch's if it isn't full up. She told me that, though in a schoolgirlish way she had been several times gone on women older than herself (like me with Miss Rory), she had never yet had " a real, great friendship." Remembering Laura and Madge, of course I couldn't say quite the same, which a little distressed her. But I do think this between me and Ruby is going to be my first sober, grown-up friendship. It is wonderful how I find my vague ideas clearing up and changing into definite thoughts while I am talking to her. I am still full of the mists and fogs of the North. She has the pitiless clearness of the South. And even when she shocks me a little, I feel as if it were doing my mother's daughter good.

'Now after this long, exciting day I must go to bed. I have my piano (hired for 12 marks a month) in my bedroom. My bed with its high puffed-up *Bettdecke* is like a little snow-covered mountain. How happy I am! I am not in the least homesick. I know now that in Glasgow I must nearly always have felt homesick—sick to get away from home to some place where even the beds are different! Perhaps this is not quite so heartless as it sounds. Perhaps it comes from my having lived those first four years of my life in Constanti-nople. Everything that is foreign I greet with rapture like an exile returning home. The more foreign it is, the more it seems to remind me of some golden, forgotten time. You, Ronald, are the only thing in Glasgow that I really miss. . . .'

Does this, I wonder, Ruby, recall to you as it does to me that first day? How young we seem, looking back! I meant only to send you the parts about yourself, but when I started copying it out, it all seemed so remote, so *dreamlike*, that I couldn't help letting you have the whole. Perhaps for me Frankfort was never very real. Do you ever feel that? It was lovely of course in its escape and freedom. But wasn't there something a little operatic about it? Something of *La Bohème* with the tragedy missed out? This may not have been so for students like Boris Fabian and the Dobbin, who had so much more than our 'hübsches Talent' for music. But—though it took us so long to realise it fully—you and I were both there under false pretences. You were there because you loved all the arts and had to escape from West Hampstead, I because I loved all the arts and had to get away from Glasgow. And though we had both been buttered up by our silly music-teachers into the belief that because we had general artistic taste music was our gift, I think we always 'knew in our souls,' as Boris used to say, that nothing comes of choosing an art; the art must choose you. I daresay it was partly this that made us such friends right from the beginning.

Meanwhile here we are, both back in the places we worked so hard and lied so stoutly to escape from, both faced with the necessity of justifying our brief escape by giving music lessons for money. It all seems very strange to me.

Do you remember that fair-haired, sentimental girl from Bristol—I never could remember her name—who played the fiddle so badly, was so terribly in love with Knopf, and always cried at Solfeggio? She used to say she longed to escape from 'the dreary realities' into 'a world of dream and fantasy.' My trouble is the other way. I am for ever straining after Reality with a capital R, and life seems to fob me off continually with something perfectly fantastic — like Aunt Harry, for instance, like Frankfort, like Glasgow. Do you find West Hampstead any more real than the Feuerbach Strasse? I don't of course know what reality is, but I do hope some day I shall. I suppose getting married and having children would bring one face to face with it. But then that may never happen to me. Anyhow not for years and years.

Do let me know how your pupils get on. You say so little compared with these screeds of mine. Yet I am driven to write at length to you. Instead of so many letters I may try to keep some kind of a journal and send it to you in batches. The more I think of this the more I believe it would help me. For one thing it would act as a safety-valve and might prevent other scribblings. You know my fears in that direction. This might direct my unlucky inheritance into a safe channel. Tell me what you think. — Ever your loving friend,

ELLEN.

THE JOURNAL

I

GLEE FOR FEMALE VOICES

GLEE FOR FEMALE VOICES

Sept. 5.—Glasgow is like Frankfort in this, that you can hardly go out for ten minutes without meeting half a dozen people you know. But whereas in Frankfort one's acquaintance was practically limited to the students and the masters, here it is unbounded. There are, to start with, the members of our congregation, and Dr. Sturrock's church is both large and well attended. Then there are Aunt Harry's friends, boys that were at the Academy with Ronald, old men that knew Father, all the girls from my school, and heaps of other people besides. I am surprised if I pass two dozen people in the street and don't know at least one of them, and on getting into a tram-car the first thing I do is to look round, see how many of the passengers are acquaintances, and decide which one I shall sit by. Because of this I at times feel almost incapable of leaving the house, but if I *must* go out, I invent all sorts of ways to avoid having to see and to be seen, or at least spoken to. I stop and stare into shop-windows, find there 's something wrong with the catch of my bag, bend to retie my shoe-

lace, or dodge down a side lane. Even so, as likely
as not some one who knows me too well will come
up and regardlessly waylay me. How splendid it
must be in London where it is really quite unlikely,
when you go out, that you will meet any one you
know! To be able to walk in the crowded street,
secure in the knowledge that you need have no
companion but your own thrilling thoughts! I'm
sure I should welcome that, even if just at first I
sometimes missed the other from habit.

Sept. 10.—Had tea with Madge Bruce to-day.
Laura Sterling was there too. At such times I do
realise quite sharply that I have been three years
away. I am, I think, as fond of them both as ever
I was, but what painful limitations there are in
these intense schoolgirl friendships that begin with
terrific emotional enthusiasm! I should never, for
instance, be able to sit down and write this kind of
journal to either Laura or Madge. Laura would
certainly say that my remark about early friendships
was 'disloyal.' 'Loyalty,' 'sacred,' 'honour,'—
these are terms Laura uses very often, and she looks
very angry and beautiful with them on her lips.
But to me they have come to mean the very negation
of true friendship. I have come to prefer the words
'honesty,' 'private,' and 'decency,' in their places,
and I don't care what any one says to the contrary,

the vocabularies employed in such matters mark a vital difference between one state of mind and another. Not only 'by their fruits,' but 'by their words you shall know them.' With you now I feel I can both hear and say anything of genuine interest. I know we can hurt one another and have often enough quarrelled. The point, though, is that we do not take offence at one another's hands. There are no Bluebeard's chambers in our talk.

Whereas take Madge. Almost all the time I am with her I am acutely conscious of how easily, by saying certain things which I honestly feel, I could at once and for ever wreck our friendship. Like so many Scotch people, Madge identifies herself with a dozen things that are quite beside her own personality. That is to say, you cannot say a word in criticism of her family, her house, her church, her quarter of the town, or even of her town itself, without her taking it as a personal affront. This means, for me especially, that I must at all costs avoid hundreds of topics, from the colour of her drawing-room wall-paper (salmon pink, 'watered'!) to the bad manners of her eldest brother Willie, in case she should fly into a passion and declare that she will never speak to me again. With Laura it is different—less crude but far more excruciating—because Laura for some reason considers everything about *herself* as Sacred. While I was in Germany

she got engaged to Wilfred Dudgeon, a Glasgow
boy whom we have all known as long as we can
remember. But do you think I dare ask Laura
when she fell in love with Wilfred (for she always
used to laugh at him cruelly) or whether she is in
love with him at all? No. If I did, there would
come about a terrible, offended closing up of her
sweet face, and I should know I was shut out from
her kindness. She would not show it like Madge.
She would keep up the outward appearance of
friendship, and I should know that I could always
count on her 'loyalty.' But the inside would be
gone.

Sept. 14.—Four lessons I have given now, and
two 'talks' to the girls at Miss Sutherland's School.
And already I begin to feel like an old hand. When
the time came I did not feel nervous after all, nor
particularly fraudulent. I merely realised that all
set teaching of any art (unless perhaps by a very few
individuals born with the rare genius for imparting)
is in the nature of things bound to be three parts
fraud. One comforts oneself, therefore, by the reflection that where there is no choice one must make
the best of it. Later on some entirely new way of
teaching may be discovered, though I don't see how.
For the present let us at least not deceive ourselves
but rather other people (our pupils and their parents)

if we can! I tell you, Ruby, this has thrown a perfect flood of light over my own pupilage! Tricks of Miss Rory's, tricks of Zilcher's—I have found myself trying them, each one, so far as in me lies, on my pupils, found myself noting the invariable results. Broadly speaking, the art of teaching music is identical with the art of seduction. Get your pupil to fall in love with you. Your pupil will then work hard, trembling before your wrath, enraptured by your least good word, and the odds are that considerable advancement will be made. This, with a little simple technical direction, and of course demonstration, is all the teacher's business. No wonder my dear Zilcher was fat.

Do make haste to get pupils and tell me if you have a similar experience. You seem these days to think of nothing but drawing, but as you say yourself, before you can attend that School of Art you will have to earn the money for your fees, and how else are you to get it but by teaching?

For my 'talks' I have begun with some dance rhythms—the Waltz, the Mazurka, the Minuet, and so forth—giving classical illustrations. I don't know if this is what Miss Sutherland wants. The girls certainly love it. And their ignorance, for people who have had hundreds of expensive piano lessons, is beyond belief. They have been taught to play 'pieces.' Of musical forms they have not

the most rudimentary knowledge. Here is something that can without deception be taught.

Sept. 24.—Laura interrupted my journalising
this afternoon by coming in to consult me about my
dress for her wedding. I am to be her chief bridesmaid and have not decided on the colour I want, but
as she is not to be married till February I can't see
what the hurry is. While we talked I kept feeling
that perhaps I had given you an unjust idea of her
by not telling you a lot more. She is very, very
interesting, beautiful too, you must remember, and
in spite of that spiritual touchiness of hers it is
impossible not to love her if you know her well.
Many people—Mungo Fleming for instance—find
her cold and not specially lovable, but she and I
have been friends since I was ten and she was eleven.
It is eight years now since Mr. Sterling got into
dreadful business trouble and died very suddenly.
All Glasgow knows the truth, but to this day the
Sterlings keep up the fiction that their father's
' heart-failure ' was not self-induced. I 'm not sure
but the younger girls are really ignorant of the
whole thing. Laura certainly knows that I know,
that her father's partner, old Mr. Dudgeon, knows,
and perhaps one or two other people ; and this,
with her own knowledge, has cast a shadow over her
life since she was fifteen. But the mere idea of her

sacred family affairs being public property (as of course they are) is so intolerable to her that she has, I honestly believe, persuaded herself that her secret is safe.

Laura is the eldest of five, all girls, and all golden haired, milky-skinned, and very handsome. When I first knew them they lived in a great house overlooking the Park, did everything in fine style, and were envied by the rest of us at school because they went riding, had French governesses, and used to go to places like Brittany for their holidays. The night Mr. Sterling killed himself (he was a jolly, hearty sort of man, quite different from his silly little fretful wife) I was sleeping at their house after a big children's party, where we had a conjurer, a magic-lantern, and the most scrumptious supper. Early in the morning Mrs. Sterling rushed into our bedroom in a fearful state, woke us up, and told Laura that her father was dead. Laura went with her, and I waited where I was for what seemed several hours. (It certainly must have been a good while, for in it they had got the doctor and done all kinds of things.) When at last Laura did come back she told me rather coldly (it was not till some weeks afterwards that she broke down and confided in me) that her father's heart, *never strong*, must have given way suddenly after the way he had jumped about, pretending to be a grizzly bear to please the smaller children at the party. I would have done anything to help or comfort her, but she absolutely repulsed my affection. The only thing to do was to get into my clothes and run home as fast as I could. I remember I was dreadfully hungry.

The next afternoon Ronald came back from school and said the boys were all talking of Mr. Sterling's suicide, and of how he had left the firm of Dudgeon, Sterling & MacInnes in an awful hole, the way he had been carrying on for years past. At my school there hadn't been a word of this, but Wilfred Dudgeon had blabbed to another boy in the Sixth Latin who had a brother in Ronald's class. It wasn't, of course, in the papers, for there are no coroner's inquests in Scotland, and the whole thing, Ronald said, would probably be hushed up by old Dudgeon with his well-known fervour for Christian work. (Mr. Dudgeon was a leading elder in our church, and a very rich man.) And people, Ronald said, will always forgive a man and help his family, no matter what he has done, if he has paid the utmost penalty like that, of his own free will.

When I remember what a little idiot I was over that business it makes me laugh and feel hot at the same time. Think what I did, Ruby! In spite of the boys at the Academy, I was so impressed by the way Laura had deceived me that I got it into my head old Mr. Dudgeon might be deceived too. Then, if he knew only of the business disgrace and not of the suicide, he might not be kind to the Sterlings after all. I lay awake a whole night thinking it over, and next day I went to Mr. Dudgeon's office to make sure that he knew!

Of course it was a fiasco. To begin with, Mr. Dudgeon is one of those pompous Christians with whom I defy any one to be quite human and natural except by committing homicide without delay. When he meets Aunt Harry he asks in mellifluous tones, ' And *how* goes the Work ? ' And when he meets me he asks, smiling very sweetly and falsely, ' And *how* is your dear Aunt ? ' That afternoon at his office, when I said I was Laura Sterling's greatest friend, and wasn't it fearfully sad that Mr. Sterling had killed himself and left them all penniless, he simply cleared his throat and said he *had* heard certain rumours that were current, that certainly the death of so *worthy* a man as his late partner was ' a sad business, a very sad business,' but that his advice to kindly disposed young ladies like myself was not to put too much faith in idle gossip. The only sign that he was in the least upset was that when he said good-bye he repeated the question of his greeting, ' And *how* is your dear Aunt ? ' instead of asking, as he usually does at parting, ' And *how* is that brave, good, clever brother of yours ? ' Ronald, in spite of his crutches, once thrashed the younger Dudgeon

boy Bertie, who used to waylay and bully little boys
of the Lower School; and I always feel there is a
trace of spite in the way old Mr. Dudgeon always
will insist on Ronald's lameness every time he mentions
him. When I told Ronald about my call later, he
laughed till I thought he would be sick. He did
not think any one could have been so silly as not to
see that, quite apart from good feeling, Mr. Dudgeon
had no choice but to save his firm's reputation, which
meant that he must not only make good all losses to
his clients, but pension the Sterling family as well.
' To think of you,' he said, ' going to point out his
Christian duty to that *Creeping Jesus.*' I saw it all
then, and what a fool I had been. And for this
reason I did not think it would be fair to tell
Ronald that on my way downstairs from Mr. Dudgeon's office I had met Aunt Harry going up on the
same errand !

After that the Sterlings moved into a flat and
changed their whole way of living, but the girls did
not have to go to a board school as Laura at first
had said they would. I remember once when Mr.
Dudgeon's name was mentioned, she said to me,
looking like a fairy queen in a tragedy, that whatever her family might do, *she* could accept no favours
' at the hands of a man her father had *cheated* ' !
This, of course, was after she had told me the truth
about Mr. Sterling. What always seemed to me

strange and ugly in her was the way she dwelt on the disgrace and hardly seemed to think what agonies her father must have endured before he could have come to such a pass. For he, too, was an elder in our church and a great philanthropist.

Oct. 2. I have a *Room*! A room all to myself and away from home! It was originally Ronald's idea. I made it my own fast enough, you may be sure, but I'll never forget I owe it to him.

At home it is impossible to think in peace, much less to practise. It's true that after several distressing rows I can now count on holding the drawing-room for the few pupils who prefer to come to me for their lessons, but no sooner do I begin to practise or read or write than I am sure to be interrupted.

Scene. Last Saturday. It is 11.30. Ellen is playing scales in thirds, sixths, and tenths, and has just got to A flat minor in sixths. Enter Aunt Harry (always knocking first, which is enough to drive Ellen mad to start with). Ellen goes on playing but stares angrily round. Aunt Harry looks distressed, apologetic, but as obstinate as the devil.

ELLEN. Yes? (She begins A flat minor in tenths, increasing the pace and playing fortissimo. Up go Aunt Harry's hands to her ears.)

AUNT HARRY. Couldn't you stop just one moment?
I don't want to disturb you, but——

ELLEN (stopping dead). Well, what is it?

AUNT HARRY. The celery has been forgotten, and
I thought a little fresh air would do you good. You
know how fond your brother is of celery with his
cold meat on Sunday. (This after Ellen hád already
done all the Saturday shopping at 9.30 on her way
to a lesson. Of course it was stupid of her not to
have noticed there was no celery on the list. Ellen's
brother does love celery. Still——)

ELLEN. Well, why can't Eliza go, or Nelly? I'm
working.

AUNT HARRY. Nelly is doing the steps for Sunday,
and Eliza has that *frozen* feeling on the top of her
head. If you had been *playing*, dear, I shouldn't
have thought of troubling you. But as it was only
scales——

ELLEN. Go away now and I'll get the celery in
half an hour. (She begins to play C major pianis-
simo in octaves.)

AUNT HARRY. McGillvray's was all gone last
Saturday by twelve o'clock, and I didn't want you
to go to Barnet's. The second eldest Barnet girl
was so rude to me that time I took back the basket
of strawberries that were bad underneath. She
said——

Things are even worse if I am not practising.

'Still reading?' she will say in a pained voice. 'Just your poor mother over again.' And she will sit down on the very edge of the sofa to tell me the latest difficulty with Nelly, or how irritating is Eliza's new habit of whistling into her thimble while she is being given orders, and do I think she ought to be spoken to about it? It wouldn't seem so bad if Aunt Harry would throw herself comfortably back on the sofa. I suppose her sitting so uncomfortably on the edge is intended to convey that she isn't really interrupting me at all.

One day she found me scribbling away like a steam-engine at this journal. Though she tried not to show it, I saw horror in her face.

'What are you so busy with now?' she asked, attempting to smile.

'A letter to my friend Ruby Marcus.'

She looked suspiciously at the big ruled MS. sheets that I was using—as you know, I seize on whatever kind of paper comes handiest at the moment.

'So long as that is all, I have nothing of course to say,' she said, but in the voice of an unbeliever. And then almost at once she began in a roundabout way talking of Mother and of Ronald's lameness. As if I didn't think often and bitterly enough of these things myself. But I simply pretended not to know what she was driving at.

Of course there's my bedroom. But it is such a

small room, mostly filled up by the bed and the enormous walnut suite which belonged to the spare room when we had a bigger house, that I can hardly write there unless I'm actually in bed. I do my secret sewing there (trimming hats and things I don't want Aunt Harry to see), but even so she often noses me out, and anyhow I can't practise except in the drawing-room.

So, my girl, for one and sixpence a week I have rented a back bedroom, minus the bed, in Miss Sprunt's house, which is off the Byres Road, about ten minutes' walk down-hill from here! Miss Sprunt used to teach Ronald and me music when we were quite small. (Oh, those music lessons—'Good boys deserve fine apples' for the lines in the bass clef, 'Ellen goes by Dan's field' for the treble, and as I never knew anybody called Dan, I never could see why I should go by his field.) Poor Miss Sprunt has to support a terrible old mother, and she has a brother that drinks, which is the reason Aunt Harry sent us to her and has gone on taking an interest in her all these years. She still takes in cheap pupils. The outside of her house is depressing, the inside, without being actually dirty, is frowsty and poor.

Not an ideal place for a studio, you say! Yet I fly there as I imagine a lover might fly to his mistress, or anyhow as I should like my lover, if I had one, to fly to me. To think that no one else has the right to enter without my permission! I have hired a cottage piano and taken across a lot of music and some books. I find I can use the wash-stand quite well as a desk (Miss Sprunt was delighted when I asked her to take away the carpet and the crockery with the bed), but I am making it a rule that I must not even *begin* to write there before I have done at least one hour of practice. It would be grand if I could start right off to distemper the terribly floral walls and get the place to look workmanlike, but I'm resisting that temptation. I ought, don't you think, to have the strength of mind to work in any surroundings so long as I am free from interruptions? Let the frills come later.

The very first morning there (after practising with an effort!) I started writing a four-act play. I have such a strange exciting theme which I must not speak about yet or some of my interest might evaporate. I'll just tell you this much. The title is 'Influence,' and it is a tragedy.

Oct. 8.—You say Madge and Laura cannot be 'real, great friends' of mine after all. But I think they are. You see, for one thing *they* can say anything whatever to *me*, and they do, I can tell you. Besides I am really fond of them both, though I may have none of Laura's loyalty. It is true that

between you and me things have been different from
the first. Perhaps this was because we met away
from our homes. Then we are both fairly detached
from our families, and desperately, critically interested in ourselves, so much so that we are glad to
discover even the more disagreeable things. Our
cards are always on the table. That is why such a
journal as this is possible between us. Already,
though I have scarcely got well started on it, I
begin to see how much it is going to mean to me in
my life here. You know my dread of any literary
tendency in myself. When I think of Mother and
of her writings that she spent so much money on
publishing, I feel a horror of all that is vague,
mysterious, or even imaginative. It is this, I
believe, that makes me long so ardently for what I
call reality. I want to get a grip of things and
never to lose it (as she did, poor darling!) for
shadows, however exciting. To do this I must keep
my eyes fixed on life itself, most of all on the life
that is going on immediately around me. Then, if
I *must* write I shall at least be writing of what I
tangibly know. And here is where I think this
journal will help me. It will pin me down. Now
that I come to think it over, I daresay it was this
same fear and desire that made me fight so hard to
get away and study music seriously. The sheer
technical necessity of practising the piano seemed a

way of safety for me.   There was of course Miss
Rory's flattery besides, egging me on, and there was
my adoration of her.   She was the first really
elegant woman I had ever known, and from the first
lesson I had from her when I was thirteen she made
a pet of me.   What was perhaps even more, she was
the first person except Miss Hepburn, my English
teacher at school, whom I had ever heard talking
seriously of art.   How that went to my head!
What a revelation of the whole of life!   I now
think Miss Rory was positively naughty (in the
Shakespearean sense of the word) to overpraise me
as she did, and so easily to mistake general artistic
enthusiasm in me for the very particular talent of
music.   Especially when she must have seen how
madly I was in love with her.   But after all it is
silly to blame her.   She made me work hard and
got me those three blessed years of freedom and
study, and *you*.   Yes, I forgive her.   But for her,
Ellen Carstairs and Ruby Marcus would never have
met!

Oct. 13.—Two more pupils roped in this week.
One is a boy of twelve and *really* musical—anyhow
ten times more musical by nature than his teacher—
but unfortunately he is also clever at school and has
hardly any time to spare.   Here is where a girl like
Dobbin scored so enormously.   Music apart, life

itself was her only subject for study. What does a musician want anyway with education in the ordinary sense? My other new pupil is Sheila Dudgeon, who wants a course of 'finishing lessons.' The only difficulty about her 'finishing' is that she has omitted the formality of beginning. This I told her in the best approved Knopf manner during her first lesson, also that her performance of Sinding's 'Frühlingsrauschen' was less like the rustle of Spring than like pigs competing at a trough of mash. She was a little bit offended, but much more, I assure you, impressed. She is a big fat girl of seventeen with an exquisite complexion, but has white eyelashes and is rather like a young and pretty pig, which suggested to me the above figure.

This means that, not counting Miss Sutherland's school, I am now giving eight lessons a week, *i.e.* earning two guineas weekly from private pupils. It certainly looks as if I should get as much teaching as I want, and possibly a good deal more. At my own old school they have put my card up on the notice-board, so very likely I shall get children from there. In this connection a queer thing happened the other day. Miss Hepburn (I think I told you she was my old English teacher?) tore the card down and threw it on the fire, declaring in one of her sudden, scarlet rages 'Ellen Carstairs has no business with such genteel truck as pianoforte instruction!'

Poor Miss Hepburn is tone deaf except to the beauty of words, for which she has a most acute ear. I once took her to a concert and she left after one item of what she called 'that pretentious and expensive noise.' The worst of it is, I hear that this silly act of hers over my card has brought her own affairs at school to a head, so that she has been asked to resign at the end of the term. For the last year her temper has been getting more and more uncertain, and girls have been complaining at home. One thing is sure. They may get a saner, they will never get a more inspiring teacher of literature in her place. I must ask her to come one day and have tea in my Room, though probably now that she has this grudge against me she will refuse. You see when I was in her class she thought I was a genius, and she made up her mind I was to be a famous writer! I expect she will disapprove strongly when she hears that I am going to play Kate Hardcastle in some scenes from 'She Stoops to Conquer' that we are having for the next *Social* at school. This will be on breaking-up day before the Christmas holidays. You will have to advise me, Ruby, about my dress. Perhaps you could get me something on hire in London? Till the rehearsals are well under way I shall not say a word to Aunt Harry. Her disapproval will outdo Miss Hepburn's, though for widely different reasons.

Oct. 16.—What do you think of this for a quotation—not, alas! from my play?

     ' There sounds the trumpet of a soul drowned deep
     In the unfathomable seas of sorrow. . . .'

The idea of a trumpet, loudest and most rousing of instruments, speaking, but with its note made faint by the intervening waters of sorrow! This sends a shiver of appreciative ecstasy down my spine. I went down to the Mitchell Library to read, started on some Elizabethan plays, and came on this in one of them. Queerly enough, it made me think of poor Miss Hepburn, both of her voice and of her eyes. She has hazel eyes with long black lashes, and in the light-coloured irises there are dark specks that used always to make me think of shipwrecked men drowning. When she speaks, something in her deep voice seems to be signalling to you through an ocean of anguish.

Oct. 24.—The last time I ' grieved' Aunt Harry was yesterday—twice. First I told her there was ' too much of man' in our family worship, which might, I said, be the reason why Eliza so often made thin excuses to stay away, Eliza being a notorious man-hater. I should explain that ' too much of man' is a favourite complaint of Aunt Harry's when she hears a sermon or a prayer that is not evangelical enough. So she was greatly put out by my use of the phrase against herself. She was rather puzzled than comforted when I went on to beg her pardon, for what I had *meant* to say was ' too much of woman.' The fact is that I am driven nearly crazy twice a day by Aunt Harry's running commentary while reading the Bible, and by her general domestic review while we are helpless on our knees. One could put up philosophically with a chapter of Scripture and a decent prayer morning and evening. But when it comes to both being a mere excuse for Aunt Harry unloading herself on the assembled household, I for one can only keep still in my place by uttering a steady flow of curses in German under my breath. Once or twice Ronald and I have persuaded her to read the prayer out of a book of prayers instead of making it up in our Presbyterian fashion. This, though, only made matters worse, for she couldn't resist putting bits in, altering a word here and a phrase there and tacking a whole lot on at the end, Ronald and I, of course, always knowing exactly from the tone of her voice which were the made-up bits.

The second offence was at supper when Aunt Harry was telling us how terrible it was that Mr. Somebody-or-other ' had been found dead *in his own carriage* ! ' I could not help saying it was a mercy it was his own carriage and not a common cab—so much more comfortable for the poor gentleman,

let alone the cabman; whereupon Aunt Harry
came down upon me for blasphemy! What is so
wonderful is Aunt Harry's placing of the accent in
telling a story of this kind. It is as though we
ought to feel sad, not about the death, but about
the carriage, or perhaps about the extra tragedy of
death coming at all to a man who owns a carriage.
I remember once she looked up from reading something in some religious paper, and with tears in her
eyes told us of a lady who had died suddenly—
'such a beautiful creature, with all that wealth and
breeding could give her, and translated, literally
translated at her own tea-table!'

Oct. 30.—Like Robinson Crusoe (how I envy
him at times!) I have been making a list of the
advantages and disadvantages of my Room. Here
it is—

Advantages.	Disadvantages.
1. Latch-key.	1. Chimney that smokes in east wind.
2. Privacy.	2. Cats (many outside, one —not a nice one—inside).
3. One tree visible from window if you screw your neck.	3. Yellow lace curtains put up by Miss Sprunt out of kindness of heart.
4. Nearness to our house.	4. Convenience for Aunt Harry to send round messages.
5. Pleasure my presence gives to Miss S.	5. Miss S.'s pleasure attested by her 'coming in for a chat.'

Advantages.	*Disadvantages.*
6. A poor thing, but mine own.	6. Miss S. never far away.
	7. Miss S.'s mother never far away.
	8. Miss S.'s brother never far away.
	9. Miss S.'s pupils never far away.
	10. Miss S.'s furniture.
	11. Miss S.'s clothes in the cupboard.
	12. Cold.
	13. Carpet beaters in the back green.
	14. Boy in the lane with an instrument giving life-like imitation of cats.

Don't you agree that there must be something radically wrong with a civilisation, society, theory of life—call it what you like—in which a hard-working, serious young woman like myself cannot obtain, without enormous difficulty, expense, or infliction of pain on others, a quiet, clean, pleasant room in which she can work, dream her dreams, write out her thoughts, and keep her few treasures in peace?

Nov. 9.—The green lamp is lit, the mahogany clock ticks on the parlour mantelpiece, Ronald is doubled up over an architectural drawing that he wants to finish for the office to-morrow (I'm sure none of the other apprentices takes half the trouble

over office jobs that he does, yet he does more work
on his own than all the others put together), and I,
writing my journal to you, am equally intent and
peaceful. Who would think that a tornado had
swept through the house but a quarter of an hour
ago? Yet so it is. Aunt Harry has been gone
exactly fifteen minutes by the mahogany clock.
She is even now in the Berkeley Hall listening to
her beloved Tinker Marley ('the tinker evangelist
from Truro'), but shortly before leaving home she
was in a devil of—I mean a fury of righteous anger
with me.

This is how it was.

This afternoon, as you might see advertised in
to-day's *Glasgow Herald*, the Monthly Tea-and-
Prayer Gathering was held in our dining-room (not
in the drawing-room, because the piano is not so
suitable as the harmonium), and was addressed by
our dear friend, Miss Davida Jones, who has always
so many interesting things to tell us of Work in the
Zenanas. Last night I was kept busy writing post-
cards to members of the Tea-and-Prayer Gathering
just in case they might not read their *Heralds*
closely enough, and this morning Aunt Harry called
on as many of them as she could, lest, I suppose,
they should not have noticed my post-cards. In
Glasgow we are nothing if not thorough.

As a rule I play the hymns at the Gathering, and

help to hand round tea afterwards, and I take care to stick to the harmonium till tea-time, because in that way I can keep a book on my knee and read it without giving offence while Davida or another speaks. But to-day I was allowed to get off even this so that I might go and hear Dr. Sturrock's weekly address at 4.30. I really and truly meant to do this—Dr. Sturrock is always interesting, besides I'm a bit in love with him—but Aunt Harry's meeting begins at three o'clock, and as they sang their opening Psalm (a Miss McFie from our church dragging shockingly on the harmonium) I was washing woollies in the bathroom. At 3.30, never thinking any of the Gathering would leave the dining-room, as tea was to be served there, I hung my things on two towel-rails before the drawing-room fire, and having a whole hour to spare, thought I might as well go to my Room and finish my first attempt at typewriting (lately I have had to relax that rule about always practising first).

You know what mistakes one is always making at the beginning with a typewriter. I wasted heaps of paper, but I gritted my teeth and wouldn't stir till the thing was done. By that time it was a quarter to five, and I had a pain in my back, and Miss Sprunt offered me a cup of tea—all slopped over into the saucer, of course—so I gave Dr. Sturrock the go-by.

After drinking my tea I began to punctuate what I had typed and found a lot of it wanted rewriting, while cats yowled in the back green and one of Miss Sprunt's pupils (the daughter of our greengrocer) made even more distressing noises in the room below. Miss Sprunt's teaching fills me with so great an amazement that it is hard sometimes to concentrate on my own business. This pupil began a scale, ended quite casually on the leading note, and started playing Handel's 'Largo.' Miss Sprunt, having thus got the lesson well under way, went down into the basement on some mysterious errand to her brother or her mother, neither of whom ever appears above ground. On such occasions she leaves the door of the pupil's room open, I suppose to give the pupil an impression that wrong notes will be heard below stairs. But I'm sure I was the only person in the house that heard, after the fourth bar of the 'Largo,' the first bar of 'The Lost Chord.' And to think that this was my music teacher from the age of seven to the age of thirteen ! No wonder Miss Rory was heaven after that ! No wonder I was deceived ! The delicious thing is that I know Miss Sprunt loves me to practise when one of her pupils is there. Then she can say airily, ' Hear that ? That is an old pupil of mine ! '

Well, I got home late for six o'clock tea, and by entering the parlour full of virtuous questions about the Zenana Gathering managed to stave off the subject of Dr. Sturrock all tea-time. Ronald once began asking me, but I silenced him in German and thought all danger was past. I was wrong, though. Aunt Harry followed me to my bedroom afterwards to ask me 'all about it,' and when I told her I had not gone she stamped with rage and rushed into her own bedroom. I followed, persuaded her to unlock the door, and was so mild and regretful that presently she melted from anger into vociferous grief. It seems that some of the Gathering had gone into the drawing-room before Aunt Harry could spot my washing and hide it. 'They must conclude so little sympathy exists between my niece and me,' she mourned. 'To think that while we sang the first version of the Hundred-and-Second Psalm, you, Ellen, were washing your combinations!'

I kissed and tried to comfort her out of her own mouth, saying what did it matter what *people* thought, so long as God knew that there was love and sympathy between us. She shook her head at this, declaring that it was all very fine, but that we must not be the cause of others stumbling, and must avoid 'the appearance of evil,' otherwise it were better that a mill-stone were hanged about our necks. All the same she cheered up quite considerably in the end and went off in very fair spirits to hear Tinker Marley. She said she 'would much rather stay at home after being so sadly upset,' but that she was doing it for the good of her own soul and of mine. Poor Aunt Harry! As if we did not all know that she is head over ears in love with the bright-eyed Tinker from Truro!

Nov. 10.—To make up to Aunt Harry for yesterday, to-day I have been cutting out and sewing knickers for her. They are dark grey and very warm and strong, as she feels the cold terribly. I wonder if she has any idea how trying she is! It makes it all the worse that I am fond of her and can never forget how good she has been all those years to Ronald and me. Soon I shall have to tell her about the Christmas play at school, and there will be another scene. Sometimes I feel I shall not be able to endure this kind of life much longer.

Here is a song I thought of while I was sewing Aunt Harry's knickers, and afterwards I wrote it down, but I don't know if it is any good. It is meant to be set to music—Boris Fabian's perhaps?

A GIRL'S SONG

There will be golden dawns
And a woodland path to choose,
Where my love will bid me walk with him,
And I shall not refuse.

There will be days of rain
With soft falling dews,
When my love will wrap me in his coat,
And I shall not refuse.

There will be starlit nights
Too sweet and dark to lose ;
Then my love will kiss me on the mouth,
And I shall not refuse.

Nov. 14.—I was tremendously interested in your letter about your mother. Fancy your *envying* me Aunt Harry ! I don't think you realise how difficult life with her is. Yet perhaps I understand what you are driving at when you say my circumstances are better than yours. Your mother, being so very modern, leaves you free to do as you like, but just because of this you find it harder than I do to discover what it *is* that you like. Is this at all what you mean ? You say when I am hypocritical at least I know it, but that half the time you are a humbug without intending it. I'm not so sure about that. You seem to me very clear-sighted. And of which of us can it be said that there is no unconscious bunkum ? I do think there may be something in what you say, that by being *made* to do a certain number of disagreeable things one learns more quickly and more passionately to know the things that one would be at. It must certainly be awful ' trying to think ' of what you ' want to do next.'

I have just read your letter over again (how interesting it is, and how I love you for writing it!) and I am wondering if your mother is not just lazy. What you say of her looking in at your untidy bedroom, and, just because you were rude to her, not making you tidy it, or even speaking to you about it, makes me think she must be. But then she is beautiful and literary (dread word!), and knows heaps of interesting people (so many *men* too, lucky Ruby!), and she's your mother, not just your father's sister. I should have thought there was no comparison between your living with her and my living with Aunt Harry. There you are, though; you are unhappy I can see very well from your letter. Get happier soon. I think your drawing is the thing. Isn't it splendid anyhow that we can write so freely to each other? Imagine my telling *Madge* that her mother was lazy! Not that she is. *Gott bewahre!* Mrs. Bruce's solemn boast, made in the tone of a fervent believer reciting her creed, is ' I really think, my dear Ellen, that I may say you could not collect an egg-spoonful of dust in my house. Without boasting I see to it that the very pan in the servants' closet is kept like a dinner plate!'

Nov. 16.—Trying to be straight with myself, and

asking myself if I would rather have your mother or
Aunt Harry, I have decided in favour of Aunt Harry,
though at the same time I 'm not *convinced* that you
would choose her if you knew her. As usual you
have been cleverer than I, and have seen the truth
that in spite of the friction and difficulty one *should*
find a quicker road to one 's own reality with her
than with a character like your mother. For one
thing, Aunt Harry has really strong feelings, and a
noble idea of duty, so that however ridiculous and
annoying you may find her, you can never despise
her. For another thing, merely having to oppose
her forces a naturally lazy person like me to act with
the greatest energy. (Fighting *your* mother must feel
rather like boxing with a feather-bed.) Lastly, as you
yourself have said, Aunt Harry, without in the least
intending it, helps one to discover what one most
wants. All the same, Ruby, I 'm so terrified at finding out what it is I want that I hardly dare face it
yet. Again and again I am driven on to it. Again
and again I run away from it and try to plunge into
something else. It would not have mattered in my
eyes if Mother had merely messed up her own life, or
even hurt every one round her and created a scandal,
so long as her writings themselves were good or useful or very amusing. I believe I could almost (seeing
how perfectly happy and beloved he is) forgive her
for Ronald. But when I read those books of hers !

D

. . . A mere dip into one of them puts me off this
journal for a week at a time and sets me feverishly
practising. Yet what am I to do? I teach every
day now, am busy in a hundred ways besides, and
even so all I see and think keeps forming itself in my
head into words and scenes and even sentences which
I simply *have* to scribble down. The rate at which
I fill a notebook is dreadful. It is like a disease,
this craving to write things down, this terror of
losing a thought by not putting it at once on paper.
Only last night I made a bonfire of notebooks and
MSS. in the drawing-room grate, and this morning,
there being a strong east wind, when the windows
were opened the charred bits of paper started flutter-
ing about the room like a flock of birds with broken
wings. Eliza was furious. To keep myself from
crying while the stuff was blazing up the chimney last
night, I practised frantically at the Brahms Inter-
mezzo in G minor. With what a soaring, generous
melody it opens ! It set my grieving spirit free and
gave my soul great pinions. But what a state my
hands are in with want of practice ! To-day they are
aching badly after half an hour of Czerny. I can
just see—if I shut my eyes—how dear old Zilcher
would pick them both up, frown at them, give them
each a little smack, and then wink at me as if we
had kissed on the sly. You know, though I liked
him so much and it was the thing to do, I never

once let him carry on with me. At times now I
wish I had. Nothing kept me from it but my
upbringing, and my perhaps silly determination to
keep myself absolutely for ' him,' *i.e.* the imaginary
lover to be. My conscience had never much to
do with it. I didn't then, and don't now, think
there would have been anything *wrong* in it.
There certainly wouldn't have been any humbug.
We all knew exactly what Zilcher meant, neither
more nor less. He was a sweet man. Just to be in
the room with him made me feel warm and happy
and, oh, how feminine ! And now suppose ' he '
never comes along ! What a sell that would be !
I should in that case regret Zilcher most piteously.
For there are no Zilchers in Glasgow. None, none !
Why is this ? There is a Dutch musician here
who is probably the best piano master we have (I
sometimes think of taking a dozen lessons from
him to keep me up). He is quite attractive,
after the style of Frohwein at Frankfort, and of
course his pupils worship him. But from all
I hear, and from my own prolonged study of
his face, sitting near to him in the area in St.
Andrew's Hall at last Tuesday's orchestral concert, I fear that our Mr. Van Ryssen has long
since ceased to take toll of his pupils in the
approved manner. He has been in Glasgow more
than ten years, and something in the air of the

place has abstracted from him his beautiful and natural amorousness.

Nov. 25.—A stranger preached in our church this evening, and Aunt Harry thought the sermon ' wonderful.' Here are three extracts from it which I took down verbatim—

' A sleeping Saviour is often in the company of a stormy sea.'

' A trembling sinner needs a triumphant Saviour.'

' 'Tis worth while losing the mast to find the Master.'

Can't you see the little man sitting in his study rolling these *bons mots* over with his tongue? But can he possibly believe, think you, that such tit-bits can in any way help any living soul?

I was reading about Danton the other night. ' De l'audace, et encore de l'audace, et toujours de l'audace!' If only ministers would preach this kind of thing! Most ministers, if they searched their hearts and spoke the truth, would, I think, begin each sermon by quoting from the blind man's placard on the Kelvin Bridge—' Dear friends, I am totally blind!' Then in our churches we might possibly get somewhere.

Dec. 10.—All to day, and yesterday too, I have been labouring under an intense physical excitement

for which I can point to no cause except two days
of bright, very keen weather coming after a fog.
But as I have felt the very same on dull, muggy
days, I don't believe the weather is accountable.
I said nothing of it to Ronald, but to-night he told
me, apropos of nothing in particular, that he had
an attack of the same kind and felt inclined to
juggle with the stars.   He explains his by his lameness, which prevents his dashing about when he is
in good spirits.   Some days in March especially,
he says, he feels that with his not being able to run
and jump the racing of his blood will destroy him.
I told him that no matter how I tear about at
such times the flame goes on devouring me in an
almost painful rapture, and that I believe he gets
more out of it than I do because he puts it into
his work, whereas in my case it merely exhausts
itself and me quite fruitlessly.

The stars are lovely to-night. Ronald and I
stood on the door-step looking at them together.
How I love Ronald !

He is coming with his friend Mungo to see the
dress rehearsal at school.   I think I'm pretty well
word-perfect now, and I love my part.   I told him
you were choosing the dress and having it sent.
He is almost as excited about it as I am.

Dec. 18.—What extraordinary weather for this

time of year ! Is it the same in London ? To-day
was so sunny, so warm, so entirely beautiful that all
the time I was not teaching I kept inventing distant
errands so that I might be out walking.

I might also call to-day 'the day of the Dress.'
The box arrived in the morning when I was out at a
lesson, and when I came home, drunk with the sunshine and the precious mildness, Aunt Harry met me
with a terrible aspect and drew me into my bedroom.
She had been tidying my room when I was out, a
thing that makes me wild, and had come upon a
shop receipt for seven and sixpence lying about somewhere. As it happened, it was a joint affair between
Madge and me when we had been buying things
together, so I explained and that was all right. The
great thing was she had *not* found my new hat
which cost a guinea ! I have never paid so much for
one before, but it is really exquisitely becoming (the
milliner said she would like to have a photograph
of me in it as an advertisement for the new shop she
hopes soon to start in London). As I bought it I
vowed I would never pay so much for one again.
The milliner insisted it was dirt cheap, but I call it
a lot for a mere hat. Aunt Harry would think it
monstrous.

Naturally she had seen the box with the dress in
it, and I had a sort of feeling that she had undone
one end and peeped at it. I couldn't be quite sure

of this as it was tied up fairly well, but I judged it
unsafe to say, as I sometimes do in a like case, that
it was something come home from the cleaners.
How I longed to be alone in the room ! But there
stood Aunt Harry waiting with her hand on the
door-knob and such a queer, lovable expression on
her face, as if she were suddenly begging quite
humanly for my confidence. She had surprised me
some days ago by taking the news of the play quite
quietly. I think Ronald must have been there
before me.

Ruby, it is *lovely* ! All those frills ! And that
very bright rose pink ! How clever of you to choose
it ! I should never have thought of that colour for
myself as even a possibility, yet for some reason it
suits me marvellously well. Ronald himself admits
it, and in such matters he is hard to please. So
long as Aunt Harry was there I only held it up under
my chin before the long glass and said very quietly,
' Not bad. What do you think ? ' Though I
wanted to do high kicks I showed no excitement
whatsoever. Aunt Harry stroked it and fingered it
(I 'm glad it is so perfectly fresh and the silk such a
good quality. I was afraid it might be a bit tashed)
as if she couldn't resist loving it with her ' natural
man '—as indeed who could ? With her ' new
man ' she of course rejects it utterly. She holds
that it is a very ' loud shade ' for me, and she has

tried (unsuccessfully) to make me promise that I 'll wear a chemisette with long transparent sleeves under it. The bodice *is* rather low—that is, for Glasgow.

All afternoon Aunt Harry has been thinking of nothing but the dress, and going in every now and then to have a look at it where I have laid it on the bed to take the creases out. Sometimes she was smiling and admiring it, but oftener she was gloomy. Twice she shed tears over it. Once she said, ' I know I cannot expect Miss Dodds ' (the headmistress at school) ' to be a Fidelia Fiske, but still . . .' This was in connection with a call she once paid on Miss Dodds to ask why could not the girls meet and be happy, and perhaps read some nice, suitable Shakespeare play together, even taking parts, but without all this staging and dressing up and painting of their faces. At the time Aunt Harry had just been reading the life of Fidelia Fiske, and she took a copy to lend Miss Dodds. Luckily Miss Dodds has such beautiful manners that I know she must have been quite sweet and patient with Aunt Harry. She would understand my difficult position. But I shudder to think of such a call paid to, say, Miss Rory. Miss Rory, for all her charm, thought it funny to be rather rude to what she called ' Philistines,' especially if they were elderly, and if there was nothing she could get out of them.

To begin with, Aunt H. had said she wanted to
come to the performance, so I had an invitation sent
to her. Now she has refused this, and says she will
go to-morrow instead—that is to the dress rehearsal
—and that she will sit in a corner so that no one
shall see her face!

Later.—The end of the dress was that it was
covered up with dust-sheets so that Eliza might not
see it (you bet Eliza did, though!) and also so that
Nelly ' might not be led astray and seduced to love
the theatre.' By the evening it was safely out of
the way, for we had a rehearsal at school, and I have
left it there.

I wish I could do some *big* nice thing to make up
a little to Aunt H. for the vexation I have been to
her the last few days. If only it were not so difficult
to please her without being a hypocrite! Not that
she seems to mind my being hypocritical nearly so
much as she minds my being natural. What a pity
that is!

Dec. 20.—For once I am going to write in this in
the morning. Generally I don't let myself touch it
till night. But of late writing at night has turned
my head into a rookery, with ideas for the rooks, *caw-
cawing* by the hour, but never getting any farther,
and serving no end but to keep me hopelessly awake
when I want to sleep.

After playing at Miss Sutherland's school this morning and giving lessons to the very unmusical Lockhart children, I went to my Room meaning to practise. But the whole house smelt so fusty and steamy, with a washing going on just under my window, that I fled.

Now I am sitting in the Botanic Gardens. Though the puddles are frozen in the shade, you could sit out for ever so long in the sun without feeling cold. I like the Botanic Gardens in the morning. No one there but children with their nurses, and old men with pale, dreamy eyes thinking of nothing, perhaps wondering vaguely if they will hold on to see another spring. I am on a bench overlooking the Kelvin, and have been watching the seagulls. Whole flocks have come up inland from the Clyde. There are rooks too, very noisy and restless, deceived perhaps by the sunshine into thinking the winter is over. Sometimes one flies past me so close that I can see how the sun glorifies his feathers. Can any one ever have gone through life without again and again feeling a wild envy of creatures with wings? Think of what flight must be to a bird! And here are we, doomed, if we wish to move from place to place, to plant one foot before another interminably! I know it is lovely to tear downhill on a bicycle, but even this must be as nothing to the experience of floating and swooping on wings that sprout from your own shoulders. Being in one of the new aeroplanes (Aunt Harry says they are ' of the Devil, devilish ') comes, I 'm sure, nowhere near it.

Last night was the dress rehearsal at school and things went fairly well, though they must go better to-night. The curtain kept sticking, and once I had to spoil a dashing entrance to go and push the rings along with a pole. Why does an audience always laugh so much more heartily at such an accident than at something funny in the play itself ? I suppose it must be the sudden escape into unrehearsed realities. Would not the most thrilling stage scene go *phut* if the stage carpenter's cat strolled on and began to wash her face beside the footlights ?

Anyhow, there was lots of spirit in the acting last night, and we were much applauded by all the youngsters. Margaret Sterling, who is Laura's second sister, has turned out as Tony Lumpkin to be a real comic, and Jean MacDiarmid, a very kittenish girl with fluffy hair who has just left school, makes a splendid foil for me as Miss Neville. The other parts are taken by quite old girls (one has grey hair, think how awful !) who are experienced play-actors, two of them being specially good at men's parts. They said I was all right. Certainly I have got over my first self-consciousness.

All yesterday afternoon my hair was in curl-

papers. I even gave two lessons with them in, but
Aunt Harry made me wear a woollen hood over
them 'for the sake of the servants.' When I undid
them I didn't comb them out but only loosened
them slightly and bound them across with a bright
rose-coloured ribbon. You should have seen the
masses of bobbly corkscrews that came all round
just to my shoulders like the pictures of Nell Gwynn.
At school they thought I was wearing a wig! Aunt
Harry cried when she saw me; she said I looked 'so
dreadfully light.' There is no doubt that when my
hair is done and my cheeks rouged the pink dress
looks *wirklich zum fressen*, as Fräulein Bruch used to
say of us on the few occasions we got into evening
dress. I wear a large pink rose in the bodice (which
is just a wee bit tight round the ribs), and the *tout
ensemble* is greatly admired.

The dress rehearsal was really a performance for
the children who are still at school, and they did
some recitations and bits out of plays themselves
and danced afterwards. Ronald and Mungo both
came, and when our play was over I sat between
them and watched the others. The funniest thing
was a scene from 'King Lear' acted by the Lower
Third, with a very high-voiced, pink-and-white-faced
girl of eleven as the king in a long grey beard, and
a deep-voiced girl, twice as broad and a full head
taller, playing Cordelia!

I think Mungo must have been overwhelmed by my costume, for not a word could I get out of him. I couldn't resist teasing him. His face is so very expressive when he gets one of those bouts of shyness, and it just eggs me on more and more. Besides, I'm sure in a way he enjoys being teased, though he would run away if he could. I asked him, in the words of the play, ' Is it one of my well-looking days, child? Am I in face to-day?' But Ronald answered for him, also in the words of the play, though not quite—' I never saw a more *spiteful* (instead of " *sprightly* ") and malicious eye!' Mungo even refused to dance afterwards, though I know he can. All evening he sat beside Ronald discussing Free Will. Ronald says he has a very metaphysical mind and is the most brilliant man of his year in Philosophy. I like him very much, and I know he thinks there's no one like Ronald, but I wish he wouldn't wring his hands and bite his nails. These things make me so uneasy. He is going to be a minister. I can't think why, for he never seems one bit religious. I suppose he finds theology a kind of gymnasium where he can exercise his precious brains.

To-night there is to be a proper dance afterwards and every one is to be in fancy dress. Laura is coming as a nun, Madge as Boadicea. I expect heaps of the old girls will be there and lots of out-

side friends as well. Three other scenes out of plays
will be given besides ours. Stella Christie, who is
said to be the most beautiful girl that ever was at the
school, is going to do Hermione in 'A Winter's Tale.'

Dec. 21.—Last night was a success : one of those
successes that can never be repeated. My acting
sur*p*rised every one, most of all myself. There were
two hundred people there, and I felt as if I had the
whole audience in the palm of my hand. What a
peculiar but glorious experience ! I knew I could
make them laugh whenever I liked, and if it had
been a sad part I could have made them cry quite
as easily. I can't explain how this should have
happened just last night, for I have acted in things
before, but never felt like this and probably never
shall again. No sooner had I come on than the
absolute conviction came to me that my body and
my voice were perfect means of expression perfectly
in my control. *I* was somewhere far away looking
on at myself, exultant but cool, not involved at all.
This sounds cocky and exaggerated, but it is what
happened. Afterwards quite serious people like
Dr. Sturrock and Dr. Bruce (Madge's father) told
me I was a ' born actress,' and Miss Hepburn looked
searchingly into my eyes and spoke of ' this, your
new talent.' If I were a year younger, Ruby, I do
believe my head would have been turned. But a

year ago I could not have acted as I did last night.
Dr. Sturrock laughed like anything when I told him
how I rushed up a 'close' two days ago to dodge
him when I was out in my curl-papers.   He said he
had 'wondered greatly' what sort of a being it was
that had 'so palpably fled at his approach.'   I knew
before that he had beautiful eyes, but never till last
night had I looked deep into them when he was
laughing.   They are like the sea, blue by day and at
night almost black, and you feel as if you could
throw yourself into them, as into the sea, and drown
happily.   Yet his wife is rather like a hen, with a
nose that looks as if she might peck you with it at
any minute.   It seems impossible that he can like
to kiss her, yet they have such a large family that I
suppose he must at times.   I wonder what he would
have said if he had known the notion that was
passing through my head while we stood talking
there.   I was wondering what it would be like to
be secretly loved by a famous preacher like him.
Not a soul would know except himself and yourself,
and when he was with you he would be merely a
man and your lover, whereas all the rest of his time
he would have to be in the public eye as a pastor
and an example.   I imagined myself sitting in the
gallery at church, seeing his wife in the minister's
pew and all the people listening to every word he
said, and how I would whisper to myself, 'He's my

lover, I'm his beloved.' This takes a while to write down and looks silly when written, but it went through my head in that one second when he had been teasing me about my curls and stood smiling down at me. What's more, I know that every woman in our church, even very old ones like the Miss Clarks, have just the same kind of thoughts when Dr. Sturrock talks nicely to them. They would die sooner than admit it frankly like me. But there it is, and for this reason I will never marry a minister, however much he may win my heart's devotion.

Laura looked lovely in her nun's dress. It is of fine white cashmere with a slate blue cape and hood in one and white bands under her chin and across her forehead. I couldn't have believed she would have looked so perfect with all her hair hidden, but now I shall always see her as a nun. It is *her* dress : it suits her soul. Its only disadvantage as a fancy dress is that it is rather hot for dancing. Anyhow, she would hardly dance at all, though Wilfred Dudgeon was there and was always asking her. I do wonder what they talk about when they are quite alone. Last night they sat together nearly the whole evening, but each time I looked at them they were without a word between them. Madge was very splendid and large, though not tall enough, as a warrioress with a silver-paper spear, but the dress was not really becoming. Her singing was, in its own way, as great a success as my acting. I played for her, and revelled in the sensation she made, feeling for some reason like a young man. I never love Madge so much as when she is singing. Other people may sing as well and better, but there is something so *innocent* about her voice that it makes me laugh and cry at the same time.

Aunt Harry had stayed away, even from the rehearsal. She looked dreadfully vexed when I came home in my dress. She had not actually seen me wearing it before, and I was hoping she would not sit up, but she must have done so on purpose. When I was in bed, though, she came to kiss me good-night. She said then that she was sorry she had not been able to give me the pleasure of her approval and her presence, but she served ' One higher than man.' We parted very affectionately.

Dec. 23.—I find I have not told you the half about Friday night, so as this is Sunday I shall try to put some more down.

There is no doubt those three years away have made a difference to me. It does not always appear even to myself, but on Friday, ten minutes before my play started, I was peeping at the audience through a hole in the curtain, and it came to me all of a sudden that *I was outside* ! Once I had been a part of what I looked on. Now I saw

E

it as if I were the boy in the fairy tale who spied
from behind a rock at the seven cloud maidens.
At that moment there were about seventy of
our girls scrambling over the forms for places
and shoving past each other.   What a racket!
But I realised for the first time why men and older
people think nearly all girls attractive, and I wondered how I should look among the others if I were
there and some man instead of me at my peep-hole.
I watched four of them especially—Laura and Madge,
Isabel Christie, and Joanna Bannerman.   Madge
never stopped going off into little fits of giggling.
She couldn't resist giving quite a hard smack to the
bottom of any girl that happened to bend within
easy reach of her (Madge still retains that infantine
habit).   When they had settled down, Isabel sat
between Madge and Laura, and Joanna on the outside.   I tried to decide which was the prettiest and
could not choose between Laura and Isabel.
Joanna, of course, is by a long way the eldest.   At
school she was four classes above me (I was keen on
her when I was in the Upper Third), so she must be
at least twenty-six now.   To my mind she looks
more.   She is one of those that every one watches
and talks about without quite knowing why—
perhaps because she is the kind of person things
happen to.   It is some years ago since she very
suddenly married an Italian man and went to Italy.

But her husband died within six months and she came back to Glasgow. Her mother is one of our Tea-and-Prayer Gathering members, but doesn't get on well with Aunt Harry. On Friday I had a good look at Joanna. I wonder what her secret is! She is not really pretty—a longish, flattish face with the eyes rather too close together and a habit of looking down her nose—yet somehow without making any effort she has got the reputation of being a beauty. I never knew any one of whom so many other girls were jealous. Can it be her experience? Is it perhaps the hidden wish of many young females to marry at twenty and to be left widows at twenty-one?

Isabel Christie, I consider, has a beautiful face, though one is apt to forget it when her sister Stella is about. She was rather backward at school (in everything but drawing) and stayed always in the class below Laura and Madge and me, while Stella was in the class above us. Now she is an artist and teaches in Miss Sutherland's school, but our hours are different and I hardly ever meet her to speak to. Though she is dark and Laura so very fair, they have both the same kind of still, pent-up look. When you are with them you long all the time to unscrew something for them. But the difference is that you feel Isabel is longing to be unscrewed if only she knew how to set about it, while Laura deliberately, *passionately*, I believe, keeps screwing herself up tighter and tighter, using what she calls her ' sense of honour ' as the lever.

When ' A Winter's Tale ' came on we were all agog to see Stella. How can I describe her Hermione to you ? It was atrocious and it was exquisite, and the atrocity and exquisiteness were in equal proportions. I don't think I ever heard anything more discouraging than her voice. It was perfectly level and toneless with self-consciousness, so that not a word of Shakespeare's poetry made the slightest impact on the senses. Miss Dodds could have spared herself the trouble of cutting out all the improper passages, because after an effort or two one simply gave up trying to listen to her. But her movements, her poses, the way her lovely draperies (Isabel had designed and made her dress) fell into folds——these were things you could not take your eyes off for a second. It cannot, I think, have been entirely the mere force of her beauty, though this is great. She must have some gift for dumb-show acting, for her gestures were wonderfully and, one felt, *unconsciously* eloquent. It was only her voice that was frozen by her self-consciousness. In the scene of the statue coming to life she was quite perfect till she had to make her single speech. Even then it was not that her voice was unpleasant. It was simply colourless to a degree that terrified me.

But, Ruby, how soon I tire of being with, even of watching people! A single look into one human being's eyes, a few words, five minutes peeping through a curtain, and I have so much to think over and examine that I long desperately for solitude. After such a night as Friday sleep for me is out of the question. I live through it all again with every perception a thousand times sharpened. Why? What for? I don't myself know. At times I think I am trying to find a meaning in it. At other times it seems a case of struggling to absorb something too large and complex for my powers. After the dullest party I feel like a boa-constrictor that has swallowed an ox. And all the while there is an attempt to test my own inner world by all these new impressions from outside, as well as to discover by the light of that inner secret world what parts of the outward experience are important or useful to me.

Then, when at last I have sorted out my riches once more, the realisation of what it is to be alive in the world comes over me and makes me almost faint. Then I could run out into the street and call to the people to stop and listen to me. But what should I be able to say to them if they did stop? Nothing. Their eyes and faces would only excite me still more, and terribly strange thoughts would flock into my head, thoughts which if they were uttered would soon land me in Gart-navel (our local Bedlam).

All yesterday I felt strange and feverish and as if the least wind would blow me away like a little dust. The outlines and colours of things seemed clearer and very much brighter than usual. Now my head aches, and I would give anything to switch off the wheels of my being and sink into oblivion. If I had my wish I would drink a potion of forget-fulness and be laid in a great cool bed in a room with high windows thrown open to the sound of the sea and the salt smell of the sea. How I should sleep ! And how I should wake next morning, and stretch, and laugh with joy at being able to start thinking again of the wonder of being alive.

THE JOURNAL

II

STUDIES AND INVENTIONS

II

STUDIES AND INVENTIONS

Jan. 2.—How glad I am the holidays are almost over ! Somehow one does miss parents at Christmas, even when one is grown-up and, like Ronald and me, long used to doing without them. Aunt Harry doesn't much hold with Christmas festivities anyway. She prefers the good old Scottish Hogmanay (without the drink !) and says Christmas is ' tainted with Papistry.' So we do not give her her proper present till her birthday, which is at the end of February. All the same I had some lovely presents—an attaché case made of real morocco from Ronald, a Waterman fountain-pen from Laura, a copy of *Martin Chuzzlewit* from Madge, and a metronome (which I asked for, because if I don't ask she 's sure to give me a missionary book) from Aunt Harry. I have already devoured your *Return of the Native* (Aunt Harry was delighted seeing the title, and made sure it was an account of the Gospel being preached in the Congo), and I am determined to read as quickly as possible everything Hardy has written.

Though Christmas itself was dull with us, it just happened that on the following Sunday we had one of

those rare, delicious times which I suppose must come
to all families now and then.   The charm of such
times is their *absolute* character—I mean their being
unique to one particular family and in some essential way different from the special moments of any
other family on earth.   I should think one of the
great acts of faith demanded from a novelist is that
in describing something of the sort which is bound
to be a *peculiar* experience to himself he should stick
faithfully to the facts, believing that *just because of
their peculiarity* his description will ring true with
the reader, however different the peculiarity of the
reader's own experience may have been.   And this
must be equally true whether the novelist is tran-
scribing or inventing incidents.   Do you see what I
am driving at, I wonder?   It is hardly ever from
likely touches, nearly always from *un*likely ones, that
the reader gets that sudden, piercing sense of life in
a good book.   Yet at the same time it must never
be an unlikeliness which is contrary to nature.   That's
the difficulty.   It must be an eminently natural unlikeliness !

But I was telling you about last Sunday.   At
dinner in the middle of the day things had gone
badly, as they generally do on Communion Sunday.
Ronald was singing the many virtues of Mr. Murray,
the architect to whom he is apprenticed, and Aunt
Harry said she was sorry she could not approve of

him as she feared he was 'not an experimental
Christian.' Ronald is very rarely cross with Aunt
Harry, but at this, to my great satisfaction, he
fired up a bit, and for the rest of the meal things
were rather strained. At night though, for some
reason, Ronald was in wild spirits and Aunt Harry
couldn't resist him. She even let him juggle with
the cheese plates (he has always loved juggling and
has smashed a good many things learning, but is
getting good at it now) and he didn't break one.
Now and then when she recollected that it was
Communion Sunday she tried to reprove him, but
she went into fits all the same and really enjoyed it.
She never looks half so sweet as when she lets herself go with Ronald. Then Ronald did an imita-
tion of the way Aunt Harry had talked to Mungo's
mother and sisters the other day, always drawing
his chair nearer with every sentence. It was Aunt
Harry to the life. Eliza, who was clearing away the
supper things, laughed like anything, though always,
of course, behind her hand. Eliza has a new set of
teeth that make her more genteel in her speech than
ever. Lately she has become a perfect dragon at
the front door, only half opening it and actually
sending away visitors she doesn't like the look of.

On the last day of the year two young men, new
friends of Ronald, came to spend the evening, and
before tea Aunt Harry made us sit round and read,

each in turn, quotations from a missionary calendar. If I had been Ronald I couldn't have stood it, but he was quite patient, taking it as a joke. We had even to sing two hymns, which greatly surprised our visitors, who are English and are here to study engineering. Tea itself was such an uproarious feast that the elder boy had to leave the room once, he laughed so much. He lay down in the passage outside and turned quite pale so that I was frightened, but he came all right again. The wit that flowed from Ronald and me truly surprised ourselves. I suppose we felt we had to be extra amusing to make up for Aunt Harry. But it was Aunt Harry's being there that made the entertainment what it was.

When it struck twelve I ran to open the front door, and, Ruby, a man was there, standing quite close to me and perfectly motionless! I gave the most fearful screech and banged the door shut again. By the time the others came he was gone. Ronald said I should at least have stopped to look whether the man was dark or fair, and that by not doing so I may have spoiled my luck for the year, besides being very impolite. But can't you imagine what a fright it gave me? It was a dark, drenching night.

Sunday, Jan. 6.—These two days we have had

wild snow-storms. I'm seizing the opportunity of
the school holidays, which are still on, to go oftener
than ever to the Mitchell Library to read. It is
not a convenient place to get at—especially in this
weather—quite a long car journey to a dismal little
street full of warehouses and cranes that keep hoist-
ing and lowering piles of wooden crates full of
goods, so that one can hardly walk on either pavement, and the narrow roadway is blocked with carts
and horses—nor is it particularly nice to sit in when
you get there. The atmosphere is foul, partly, I
suppose, from the numbers of out-of-work people
who spend the day there reading advertisements.
But I must have books, and have them without
feeling that Aunt Harry is reading them over my
shoulder or burrowing among my underclothes for
them when I'm out. Besides, it is so difficult anyway to get the ones I want most out of any of the little
circulating libraries near home that I am tempted
to go on taking out books I don't specially want,
and wasting time and money reading them. As for
my Room, I have made it a rule that I mustn't read
there any day I have not done at least three hours'
work, either practising or writing (not counting this
journal). That means I can hardly read there
at all.

So I go to the old Mitchell, and from the very
distance and discomfort, and the fact that I can't

take the volumes home, I am *compelled* to pick out
only the books I vitally want. I find I have to
try on lots of dodges like this with myself. Do
you call it dishonest? I fear it may be the
inevitable result of my tolerating so many other
dishonesties (like teaching music and going every
Sunday to church) in my life here.

In the last few weeks, going down to the
Mitchell at odd times I have read the works of John
Davidson (a Greenock man), plays, poems and all;
Shaw's *Plays, Pleasant and Unpleasant*; the poems of
James Thomson (*City of Dreadful Night*, etc.); and
two of Hardy's novels (these since your present).
If only I could write as well as I can read, I
should be a good writer! You think any one can
say this! Not at all, let me tell you.

Jan. 7.—Still terrific weather—icy cold with
snow blizzards. This morning I bought myself a
dress (fawn velveteen) at Dymock's winter sale.
Dymock's is one of the smartest (and dearest)
shops in Glasgow. I had very seldom been inside
before, and then only to help other people choose
things. But, as Madge says, 'unlike the cheap-
jacks,' Dymock's *do* sell off their own goods at their
sales and so have real reductions. I had not
dreamed of buying anything when I went into
town, was indeed walking in to the Mitchell

partly to warm myself, partly to economise in car
fares.   But I caught sight of this dress in the
window, and it seemed so much as if it were made
for me that I couldn't resist going in to try it on.
In vain I thought of the books I want to buy, of
all the frightfully poor people Aunt Harry is
always begging for.   It fitted me so *perfectly*,
except that the skirt will want a few inches off,
that I simply had to have it!

Jan. 9.—Had the fawn dress tried on at
Dymock's this afternoon just for length.   I felt
bad about it, all the more that I'm not so sure
now if it suits me!   £5 is a lot of money, besides
I had forgotten yesterday about Aunt Harry's
birthday.   Ronald and I want to give her a fur-
lined coat between us.   She really needs one, but
nothing would induce her to buy it for herself.
(This is not stinginess on her part, but that, 'considering the sad and heathen state of the world
at present,' she does not 'feel justified,' etc., etc.)
That means I am pretty well cleaned out till next
quarter, for there is Laura's present as well, and
for that I have set my heart on a pair of old glass
candlesticks I saw in a shop in Cambridge Street.
My dress has a blue girdle of such a lovely shade—
a kind of turquoise.   It was this, I think, that
forced me to go in to try it on, and then I fell.

But, worst of all, I bought a hat too to-day, of exactly the same shade of fawn! The woman said it would be a sin to let it go. It cost twenty-five shillings! It *really* suits me.

Jan. 15.—A cousin of ours called Peggy Moncrieff died in Aberdeen yesterday. (No, I shall not have to go into mourning. That *would* have dished me!) Her husband, a very clever children's doctor, was supposed to be devoted to her, and no one knows what he will do without her. She was certainly lovely to look at, but 'unsuited' Aunt Harry says 'for married life,' whatever she may mean by that. Aunt Harry is going to Aberdeen for the funeral. She has told us she is going to be 'very careful' what she says, for she thinks that 'poor Peggy has only got to Heaven by the skin of her teeth, and because she had praying parents.' Ronald says that even if she hadn't had praying parents Aunt Harry would still have let her get to Heaven 'by the skin,' etc. For then she would not have had 'the opportunities with which we have been so richly blessed.' Ronald says that is one of the many lovable things about Aunt Harry—her theology is so elastic when it comes to the bit.

I myself think Peggy's teeth must have a pretty thick skin if she 'scapes Hell. She once said in

Ronald's hearing, when he was about ten, that he would have been 'better dead'; heaps of times she called me 'a cheeky brat' when I was nothing of the sort; and I know she refused to have more than one baby, though her husband adores children and wanted several. What business has a woman like that to get married?—unless of course she explains to the man beforehand, which I'm sure Peggy never did, she was always such a liar. I expect when they were engaged she pretended that she wanted to have a baby every year. But there you are. It is said that he worshipped the ground she trod on. She was really beautiful. I see that now, though when I was fifteen and she was twenty-five I wouldn't admit that she had any good looks.

Would you like to be beautiful? I can't make up my mind if I should or not. It seems almost like a profession in itself, and not a very interesting one so far as the beautiful person is concerned. Ronald says I've greatly improved in looks lately, and as he once told me not to worry because I had 'an air' I'm hoping for the best. But real beauty like Peggy Moncrieff's or Stella Christie's is quite another thing. It is by far the most important thing about them.

Aunt Harry will have to spend at least one night in Aberdeen (she *will* have to be careful!), so I'm taking the chance of having a special little supper party at home. What, though, if Aunt Harry changes her mind and doesn't go? This is the kind of problem with which I continually have to deal. I'm getting lines on my forehead with anxiety.

Jan. 16.—A 'Christian friend' of Aunt Harry's (Aunt Harry calls her 'Edith,' but I don't think she likes it) 'took advantage' of Aunt Harry's absence to sleep at our house to-night, so that little supper party of mine had to be postponed. The lady's name is Miss McRaith, but though she must be of Irish extraction she comes from England. She's not quite young, nor at all old, and, if she knew how, she might be rather pretty to look at. She does *not* know how. Her hair, when it is down, is lovely (she took good care to let me see that by coming to my bedroom door half an hour ago with it all loose round her shoulders to ask for a bit of ribbon to tie it with). It is much fairer and curlier than mine, though I stick to it that mine has richer shades in it, and personally I don't admire that terribly curly hair. It is about twice as long and thick as mine, being almost like one of those advertisements for *Harlene*, but it doesn't grow so nicely from the forehead as mine, nor go nearly so nicely when it is up, and that's what counts, isn't it? What's the use of a great lot of hair if it doesn't add to the beauty of the head it grows on? For me it might just as well be in a glass case at the barber's.

Aunt Harry has told Miss McRaith to regard our house as her 'second home.' Luckily this doesn't mean quite so much as it sounds. She is the Lady Missionary in Lord A.'s Settlement for ironworkers in Motherwell, so that when she comes in to Glasgow for a meeting or anything she needs a bed and cannot afford a hotel. The stupid thing is that we have no spare room now. This means either (1) that I have to clear out of my room and sleep on the dining-room sofa, or (2) that she comes when Aunt Harry happens to be away for a night. The first is nuisance enough, the second is something worse. Those precious nights when Aunt Harry is away!

Jan. 17.—The specially interesting thing ('noble,' Aunt Harry calls it) about Miss McRaith is that when she was converted, about ten years ago, she is said to have broken off her engagement with a man who was 'young, handsome, well-connected, and blest with this world's goods.' This was so that she might not be 'yoked together with an unbeliever.' Aunt Harry says she has 'suffered much for conscience' sake,' and that I should respect such suffering whatever views I hold. Poor Miss McRaith, she does look as if she suffers. But I wonder if she really broke off the engagement *herself*! If she did, her suffering must be at the thought of having played such a mean trick on any one. (Once I gave my word to a man in that way I'd rather die than take it back, wouldn't you?) But somehow the more I see of her the more I think hers looks like the pain of the jilted party. Eliza can't abide her, and utterly refused the other night to put clean sheets on Aunt Harry's bed for her. 'They did Miss Carstairs, so surely they can dae Miss McGraw,' she said. She will insist that Miss McR. is not English at all, but a 'ram-stam Irish,' and that her real name is McGraw. About the sheets, I was so vexed over my party that I could easily have been wicked enough to let things take their course. All the same, I sent Eliza off and remade the bed myself.

At supper I asked Miss McR. if she thought Shakespeare was converted.

'Not when he wrote his plays,' was her answer! Anyhow, she's more consistent than Aunt Harry.

But, oh, the relief when she is out of the house again! I take a long breath and spread my wings. She must know this, I think, for she gives nasty thrusts occasionally, trying to make me say something rude to her, while all the time, especially if Aunt Harry is away, I feel I have to be at least civil to her as a guest of the house. One day I

even trimmed a toque for her. She's no hand at
dress, poor thing.

Jan. 20.—Your letter about Boris Fabian arrived
this morning and all day I have thought of nothing
else. Decadent he may have been, as you say, but
he must have been *very* unhappy or ill, or both, to
have got the length of killing himself. For if ever
any one was gifted and quite soberly conscious of his
gifts, he was. Poor Boris! Poor lad! I wonder
what went so wrong. We shall never know. Do
you remember how horrified—and, let us now own,
excited—we were when Mr. Hermann told us he
was going with women of the town? Of course it
was because we had neither of us definitely known
that of any man before, but I feel rather ashamed, and
I expect you do too, of the way we waited the night
after that in the Theater Platz to see if he would go
home with any one when he came out.

Don't you agree that he was tremendously gifted?
I know he was lazy about practising, but then he
never intended to be an executant, and goodness
knows he had enough facility and technique for his
own purposes. To compose and to be Kapellmeister
at Munich, that was his dream. I thought his com-
positions very, very interesting and original. That
queer Nietzsche oratorio thing *Der Uebermensch* . . .
I know parts were a little comic, but parts im-

pressed me as being more than talented. The
Sunday I went with him to the Königsberg, where
he had rooms, he sang nearly all the vocal parts to
me in his husky, out-of-tune voice. This evening
I have been going over every minute of that Sunday.
He was not, though you always *would* think so,
seriously in love with me, but we liked one another
very much. I remember once he kissed my hand
after a talk we had been having, and with that
cynical smile twisting his small mouth to one side
(his mouth was certainly his worst point, so weak-
looking and small, almost like a fish's mouth) he
said, 'If only you good girls were not *quite* so
good!'

That day at Königsberg a terrific thunderstorm
came on when we were out walking in the woods,
and, as I had no wrap, when the rain came on he
gave me the cape of his coat, which was a kind of
Inverness with no sleeves underneath, so that, while
I was quite covered by the cape, his arms got
drenched through and through. He loved the storm,
though, and the wet and everything, and strode
along in front of me waving his arms and shouting
motifs out of *Der Uebermensch* at the pitch of his
voice. I was *furious* with him when I missed the
last train back to Frankfort owing to his watch
having stopped, and still more furious when he
doubled up with laughing on the lonely, dripping

little station platform.   But I went back to supper
in his rooms and we made a wood fire and sat talking over it till late, roasting chestnuts and eating
smoked salmon, for which he had a passion.   He
told me all about his ambitions then, and asked me
did I think I would ever give concerts in London.
I can't think what made me give the answer I did,
for at that time I had not yet realised how trifling
my musical powers were, but it was as if some one
struck a match in my mind, showing me my future
quite clearly.   'I shall never succeed at music,' I
said.   'In time I shall find a way of expressing
myself, but it won't be music.'   He looked at me
with those extraordinary dark blue eyes (even more
beautiful than Dr. Sturrock's) and that mixture of
inquisitiveness and extreme friendliness that always
made something melt within me.   'Do you mean
by love and bearing children?' he asked.   I had
not been thinking of that, but I stared back and
said, 'Perhaps that too.'   'And what besides?' he
went on.   It was then that, just as if some one else
was speaking through my mouth, I heard myself say,
'I shall write.'   It came as quite a surprise to both
of us.

He got me a room at the inn, and borrowed a
thick linen nightgown from his landlady, though he
said he was sure I shouldn't mind sleeping for once
in my chemise like a Russian girl.   Then in the

morning, so that I should catch the very earliest train back and avoid scandalising old Fräulein Bruch, who, if she saw me at breakfast, would never guess I had been away all night, he wakened me himself by throwing a great branch of apple-blossom in at my window. I jumped out of bed and looked down at him. It was a lovely morning after the storm, and in the sunlight his hair was like pure gold. And now he is dead.

Is it because he is dead that now, at this moment, and for the first time, I feel almost guilty towards him? How could things that night have been different between us? Neither of us was passionately in love with the other. And yet . . . it was *my* doing, *my* upbringing entirely that made me set aside the natural consequences of the strong attraction we both felt for one another and the circumstances that egged nature on. I daresay things were best as they were. I daresay I could not have acted otherwise. Yet I shall always feel there was truth in his reproach, 'If only you good girls were not quite so good!' How I wish things were different!

Well, Boris is dead, but I am still alive. And if I am to be true to that truest moment in his company when through him I *knew* what I ought to be doing, I shall have to hurry up and do it. It isn't easy.

Jan. 22.—

> ' It joys me that I ever was ordained
>   To have a being, and to live 'mongst men,
>   Which is a fearful living and a poor one.
>   Let a man think truly on 't—
>   To have the toil and griefs of fourscore years
>   Put up in a white sheet, tied with two knots.'

What think you of that for a quotation outside of Shakespeare? And what should we do without the minor poets that our good Dr. Sturrock despises so much? The other day I happened to mention John Davidson to him, and this is what he said, in a playful but condescending tone—' I fear that Browning has spoiled me for the *little* people'!

Jan. 25.—This morning I wrote in my Room without a fire till my right hand was stiff and blue with cold. Then I went in to the Mitchell, and walked all the way to warm myself. There was a bad fog on. Everything in town was filthy and choky, but friendly, as things are in a fog, so that in the common affliction you feel you can speak to any one and couldn't be offended if any one spoke to you.

I am in the middle of *Jude the Obscure*, but had forgotten the catalogue number, so I had to turn it up again before I could fill in my slip. As I stood before Vol. F-H of the Catalogue, a man I have long

ago nicknamed 'Don John' passed from Vol. A-C
to one on my other side, but something in the way
he glanced at my volume made me think it was
really the one he wanted. As it happened, in passing
behind me he knocked slightly against me, and he
begged my pardon in such a nice, surprisingly
educated voice that I asked him if it wasn't Vol. F-H
that he wanted. Somehow after that we got into
a conversation about Hardy, and I soon realised that
'Don John' was a scholar with a practised mind,
and that all my ideas were crude and schoolgirlish
to a degree. It isn't that he in the least *tries* to
make one feel his superiority. It simply emanates
from him. Now I wish we had spoken to each
other before. He is nearly always in the library, so
I expect he is writing a book for which research is
needed. He is quite middle-aged and looks poor.
He always keeps his hat and ulster on while he sits
or still oftener stands about reading. To-day when
he begged my pardon, he lifted his hat, and for the
first time I saw him for a moment without it. It
was rather a shock to see how bald he was. I don't
suppose we talked to-day for more than five minutes,
but for the first time in my life I knew I was talking
to a man for whom *books* really live and matter.
Even with Dr. Sturrock I get the feeling that books
are merely either useful to ministers or a kind of
general adornment to life.

Sunday, Jan. 27.—It would take a novel by
Henry James to set forth the subtle relations
between Miss McRaith and myself.   Probably Aunt
Harry has been talking to her about me, and I
rather suspect is *arranging* to go away for the night
occasionally so that Miss McRaith may try to
influence me for my soul's good, and afterwards
report on the result! Anyhow, I am most careful
not to contradict the lady. This disappoints her,
because it means that her tests have failed. She
must feel rather like a chemist who keeps touching
some stone with certain acids under the action of
which the stone should fizz or change. But no!
The wretched mineral shows no reaction whatever!
She is always devising new stratagems by which to
get at me. I, however, am a very alert stone
indeed! She and Aunt Harry and I went to a little
meeting (*intime*) where the speaker was a Converted
Actress (this apropos of my performance at school).
I had consented to go out of sheer curiosity to see
what a Converted Actress looked like, but the whole
thing was of course a farce. The C. A. can never
have been good-looking enough for the back row in
the chorus, and for anything more ambitious had
not yet learned how to speak. She talked about the
'droring-room' and 'religious idears,' and had no
notion of how to stand or hold herself. In fact, I
know of a good half-dozen travelling evangelists

(male ones especially) who were never on the stage but could give her points on her former (alleged) profession.

After the meeting the C. A., who had been watching me during the hymns, came up and said, ' Can you sing ? ' What she wanted to ask, of course, was, ' Why don't you sing the hymns with the rest ? ' But she merely simpered and asked, ' Can you sing ? ' No one will ever know the self-control that was needed to prevent my replying, ' No, can you act ? ' Actually what I said was, ' Yes, at times.'

Jan. 31.—You will say I am obsessed by Miss McRaith. So would you be if you had to spend any time with her. The wretched thing is that I can't help feeling sorry for her even when I most dislike her. She seems always to be saying ' *You* are having a fine time, yet *I*, who have given up all for the sake of Jesus, am grudged the few simple and innocent pleasures I might with a free mind enjoy.' This was how she looked when I showed her my fawn hat and dress. Her expression said, ' Though I am devoting myself to the poor, I like pretty hats as well as any one, but of course nobody thinks of that, and I have no time to trim them for myself.' Or, when she remarked on my morocco attaché case and I said it was a present from Ronald, she looked, ' How nice it would be if some one would give *me* a

present, but *that* is hardly likely!' So that you
feel quite guilty if you don't hand the blooming
thing over there and then! I wish I could be rude
to her as subtly and yet as effectively as Eliza.
When Miss McRaith conducts prayers (as she always
does when she stays here) Eliza either pretends she
can't see to read her verse in turn, or she reads it so
delicately that you would think she was playing
spillikins with her new teeth. It is quite extraordinary the contempt she manages to convey in this
manner. No one fails to understand it, and Aunt
Harry is furious but helpless.

Feb. 4.—Don John and I have had several more
talks, always quite short ones and only about books.
I ventured to tell him what a *dark* impression
Hardy's novels make, not so much on my mind when
I am reading them as in my memory when I recall
any one of them. Also how in the same way his
' stocks and stones '—that is to say all the bare
heaths, great rocks, and wind-driven trees that he so
peerlessly describes—are *in memory* so all-important
that they overshadow, and in time almost blot out,
the mere human characters of his stories. Don
John (he hasn't told me his real name yet) explained
this, wonderfully I thought, by saying that it was
because in Hardy's view the stocks and stones are
the primal things. Out of them his frail human

figures spring, but stay only for a moment to execute a few tragic gestures before being once more absorbed into the stony mystery. Don John finds this a fault as well as a quality in the novels but a pure virtue in the poems. He thinks, too, that in the novels Hardy uses the long arm of coincidence ' quite indefensibly,' and that many of the stories are marred by that ' wallowing in miserable accidents,' which I have often, I see now, resented myself without having been able to put my finger on the cause of my resentment.

For Shaw Don John will not hear a good word. He simply dismisses him with the remark, ' Shaw knows nothing whatever about human beings, so what he says about them, or makes them say, can have no permanent value.' He pronounces human as if it were spelt ' yuman,' which I think sounds so funny. Yet his voice and accent are both most beautifully English without being the least bit Cockney. Perhaps it is the right way to pronounce it—Yumanity ? But it makes me laugh.

I wonder if he will ever tell me anything about himself or the book he is writing ? He is beyond any sort of question a gentleman, but he gives the impression that it is rather a long time since he led a gentleman's life in any material sense. I feel he would be uncomfortable if I were to ask him home to tea. Not that I *can* as a rule, with any comfort to myself, ask people home. More's the pity!

Feb. 11.—A very uncomfortable, but I suppose flattering, thing happened to-day. I was playing to the assembled school at Miss Sutherland's, had just finished the Minuet from Bach's Third French Suite, and was in the middle of a Purcell Minuet, when the hall door opened and in stalked, of all people, Miss Hepburn. She had the dreadful suffused look that she gets sometimes, all over her forehead and eyes, and a big vein stuck out in her forehead like a root of ivy. Everybody stared at her of course, not knowing who she was or what she was after, and some of the smallest children, who sit at the very front, shrank back in terror. She is enormously tall and hulks forward in a curious way from the shoulders. She said nothing whatever, but just stood and glowered at us all, and Miss Sutherland looked inquiringly at me as if I were the person who should act. Though she is the Head, Miss Sutherland is a very timid woman. Besides, it happened that she knew something of Miss Hepburn's reputation, also of her queer sort of friendship for me.

So I got up and went to shake hands with Miss Hepburn, but she put both her hands behind her back.

'Do you want me for anything?' I asked. And with the greatest vehemence she replied, 'Yes, I want you, and the world wants you, for one thing only, and here you are frittering your strength away in rubbish!'

I saw then what she had come for. I think I told you that she had got it into her head ever since I was in her class at school that I ought to be a writer. She was angry when I first told her I was going in for music, but she prophesied that the musical phase wouldn't last long and might help me by way of experience. Since I have come home from Germany, though, and settled down to teaching music, she has been ruder and ruder to me with every opportunity, and now it has come to a head.

'We can discuss that afterwards by ourselves,' I said quite pleasantly. 'I still have to play a Chopin Minuet to the girls. Then I'll come with you.' And I asked her if she would rather wait where she was or go into the lobby till I was finished. I devoutly hoped she would go to the lobby, but she said she would stay in the hall, and she sat herself down right in the front row, the children there making more room for her than was quite polite.

When I had played the Minuet (very badly indeed) Miss Sutherland whispered to me that I could go without any more 'lecture,' so I made to take Miss Hepburn off with all speed. But before I could get her out of the place she let fly several loud remarks which every one must have heard.

'You are no musician,' she said. 'You are a *prostitute*, that's what you are. You are prostituting the talents God has given you.' And so on after the same style. I just caught sight of Miss Sutherland's red, shocked face at the word 'prostitute' as I dragged Miss Hepburn out of the Hall.

At first when we got down to the street, where it was starting to rain, we went for one another like a pair of fishwives, but I couldn't keep it up long. For one thing, poor dear, she is wrong in the head. For another, the rain soon cooled me. For yet another, cutting out such words as genius, or even talent, something within myself tells me only too clearly that about me she is essentially right. I *am* doing the wrong thing. I *am* trying to run away from my appointed work. What she does not realise is that I have such painfully strong reasons for so doing.

In the end we went to a shop and drank coffee together, and for the first time she invited me to her house. I'm to go there for supper on Thursday week, and to meet her old father who, she always declares, is a genius and has a wonderful library.

G

Many a time I have wondered why she has never asked me there before, but up to now she has only taken me out for tea in a shop.

Sunday, Feb. 17.—Don John smells a bit; as if he slept in his clothes, *i.e.* as I suppose Balzac smelt. I read in Balzac's Life that he used to go on writing without stopping to wash or change his clothes—merely eating at intervals and throwing himself as he was upon his bed to sleep—till he was fairly covered with vermin. What a thrilling and awe-inspiring power of concentration must have been his! Yet when I told Madge Bruce about it, she said it was so disgusting that it almost made her ' puke.' Myself, I don't think I mind dirt much if there is a good reason for it, like that or like poverty. Cleanliness is very good, and I'm pretty clean myself, having been trained up so and got used to it. Yet at times I think we lose something, and even cheat one another, by being so desperately clean. Certain blind men, they say, retain, or regain, the primitive sense of smell in its full delicacy, so that on coming into a room and meeting strangers they can tell by the mere aroma of each person, before any word has been said, whether they are going to like or dislike, trust or fear the new acquaintance. But surely people like Mrs. Bruce, Madge's mother, must quite wash away their individual aroma? I should not mind that myself (not being blind) if they were not so uppish about it, as if it were some great and solemn virtue in them. Then there is the other side of it. On a hot day Madge goes through real agony lest any one, particularly any *man*, should be aware that she is perspiring. One day, to tease her, I said a man once told me that at a dance girls with her colouring always smelt like steak and onions. I wish you could have seen her face! I went on to tell her that the same man said he would never marry a woman till he knew the smell of her sweat, and that it was quite possible for a man to marry a lovely looking girl and then to find, because he had omitted to take this precaution, that he didn't like her a bit. It was Boris Fabian—as I daresay you have already divined—that told me these things. And he told me too (what you and I had often wondered about) why that plain girl, Frieda Bünsen, was so frightfully attractive to all the men. 'Frieda,' he said, 'has such a strong and beautiful animal smell.' It is true, of course, that our Boris had a marvellous nose (I remember in the woods after rain he would get me to lead him along blindfold, while he would tell me, merely by their scent, which kind of trees we were passing), but he was so very sure of his explanation about Frieda where other men were concerned, that I can feel no doubt it was the true one. Well, I told Miss Madge all this and she blushed—as she does when she is truly scandalised —almost black. She said it was horrible, then that it was not true, and she asked who the man was that told me. I replied, ' A Polish boy who was a genius.' At that her face cleared and she began laughing. 'Oh, only one of your dirty Germans!' she said. 'What a relief!' As if, if it *is* true, it mattered whether the information reached her through a foreign or an English source! Or anyhow, as if anything Boris Fabian ever did or said in his life were not clean compared with the way in which Willie, Madge's eldest brother, pushes one's feet under the table at card games, when there is no means of retaliation or escape because his father and mother are present! But what is the use of arguing with provincials?

All this, however, ' of Smels and Odors,' as Montaigne has it, is off the point. What I set out to tell you when I was carried off my course was that yesterday at the Library Don John for the first time told me some things—very few it is true— about himself. He is a classical coach and goes there every day, partly to look through the advertisements. He also reviews books—mostly historical, foreign, and philosophical. And he *is* writing a book! It is to be a ' History of Free Thought in the Middle Ages.' (So perhaps he is himself a

free-thinker, but I have not asked him this yet.)
I truly do not think he eats enough. He is so
fearfully thin, when you come to look closely at
him, that the bones at his temples are as sharp as
the backs of knives, and the temples themselves
look like little cups. If I am ever at the Library
about one o'clock, I notice he pulls out a paper bag
and munches what looks to me like dry bread. One
day I exclaimed quite aghast, ' Is that all you take
for lunch ? ' But he only smiled (usually he is
rather grave), and told me he could not work on a
full stomach. He says that he goes out later in
the afternoon for a cup of tea. What coaching he
has seems to be at night.

I had already told him about my being an
orphan, about my music teaching, and about my
writing and Mother's. Of my writing he said, ' I
see. It is like the camomile—the more it is trodden on the faster it grows.' And when I asked him
who had said that, he smiled again and said, ' An
observant fat man called Falstaff.' When he smiles
like that he makes you long tremendously to tell him
every single thing about yourself and your troubles,
just to get his comments and to lay your soul bare
before his sad, sunken, truthful eyes. Surely it is
men like him that ought to be ministers ! He
gives you quite a different feeling from Dr. Sturrock.
I can't explain it, but there is something impersonal

. . . no one would dream of being 'gone' on him. I have told him about my Room, and perhaps he will come one day to have tea with me. But it would not be much fun in this cruel, biting weather.

Feb. 20.—Laura's wedding is the day after to-morrow. Dr. Sturrock is to marry her in church, and both Madge and I, besides Sheila Dudgeon and a whole squad of the Sterling girls, are bridesmaids. The thing is to be done in style and every one has been invited. *I* should not choose to be married so. But perhaps this is partly jealousy. Because after all it might not be bad to be the shining centre of such a wondrous occasion, and if you did the other thing (creeping off to the Sheriff, etc.) your friends might think you were ashamed of the bridegroom or something. Besides you could keep your secret just as secret between the two of you, perhaps more so, for all the people buzzing round and criticising. Then there are the presents. I don't see how any one in her senses can object to getting heaps of lovely things given to her. (When it came to the bit I had quite a struggle to part with my glass candle-sticks!) I don't know. I must think it out seriously.

Laura's is to be a pink and white wedding. All the bridesmaids are to be in deepening shades of

pink; the Sterling girls, being so fair, will be in a
very pale rose, but Madge and I, who are to stand
next to Laura, are wearing the same strong shade of
my dress in 'She Stoops to Conquer,' which every
one remembers as a success, and it should suit
Madge well too, as she is so dark (it was just
a kind of freak that it suited me). Laura's dress is
dead white, without a touch of what is called
'relief,' and she will carry white roses and lilies.
Madge and I carry pink roses. You ought to see
the presents! The Dudgeons being so rich themselves, people have all felt they must give things
that will bear inspection, whereas at the wedding
of a poor couple any old plated butter-dish will
pass muster! Laura may not be happy. She is
certainly thrilled. Her eyes are wonderful, and she
is perfectly sweet to every one as if she were going to
die soon. She keeps us all at arms' length, though.
Madge is disappointed at the lack of confidences.

Feb. 21.—The Hepburns' is certainly an un-
earthly kind of household. They live (without any
servant or so much as a visiting charwoman) in the
ground floor of an ancient but rather noble-looking
house off Cathedral Street, which is a windy, grey
hog's back hill running into the heart of the town.
I supped there to-night and met the old father.
Though Miss Hepburn keeps telling you that he is

a genius she treats him like dirt. I'm sure he was glad when it was time to get away to his newspaper office. He is a compositor.

But first I must tell you about the supper itself. We had roast fowl (I happen to know what fowls cost just now), *new* potatoes, and asparagus! We had a chocolate soufflé and the best of fruit and sweets. We had champagne! And in the middle of the table there was a bowl of wonderful hothouse flowers. When I was ill-mannered enough to show some astonishment at this really very surprising 'spread,' she said, 'Genius deserves the best, though it rarely gets it!' I had the feeling that when they were alone she and Mr. Hepburn had bread and cheese meals, with perhaps an occasional box of sardines as a treat, and that for a long time to come, thanks to this party, they would have to go without the box of sardines. But in the circumstances there was nothing to be done but to make believe as best I could that I was enjoying everything. This was not very easy, as old Mr. Hepburn made a mere pretence of eating and hardly spoke a word throughout the meal. Neither did he drink anything, and every time Miss Hepburn poured champagne into my glass or her own he pulled out a little green bottle of very powerful smelling-salts and took a deep sniff at them.

I must say Miss Hepburn made up for her

father's quietness by being more talkative than I
have ever seen or even imagined her. She fairly
shouted with laughter, throwing her head back
wildly, and drinking up the champagne as fast as
she poured it out. She told us more than once
that she had 'warmed both hands before the fire
of life,' and that now 'she must depart.' Strange
and rather reckless she nearly always looks, but
to-night I saw for the first time that she may well
have been wonderfully handsome as a young girl.
Her eyes are still fine and have a beautiful tawny
colour. I don't think she can ever have had a good
figure. Her bones are too big, her shoulders come
dreadfully forward, and she is too tall, rather like a
man dressed up in woman's clothes. Her father is
just the opposite. He is small and very white in
the face, almost waxy, with small hands and feet
and a thin faded grey beard through which his
pallid chin appears. His voice and manner are
very, very quiet. But for his beard he might pass
for a delicate little old woman.

In their love of books, however, the two are
united, though I think it is the actual volume, the
binding and paper and print, that he cares most for,
while she values nothing but the author's thoughts.
Ruby, what a library ! I was thankful when supper
came to an end and he showed me some of his
books. In Edinburgh he used to have an old book-

shop, near Parliament Close, and he says it was his
constant affliction that his 'pets' too soon found
purchasers.   He told me that what he has now is
'a mere remnant' of the library he would have
possessed if things 'had gone more fortuitously'
with him.   It was a delight to watch his small,
sensitive hands touching and turning over book after
book.   Robert Louis Stevenson came to his shop,
he said.

He became quite talkative, and so interesting
that I wished I could have taken down all he told
me word for word.   I asked him about Stevenson.
'Stivenson has the name,' he said, '. . . clivver,
not a doubt of it, though I nivver had much
notion o' thae essays o' his.   A bit silly, I aye
thocht, tho' some folk are daft aboot them. . . . I
mind him fine—a delicate-like lad.   He used to
look into the shop comin' back and forrit to Parliament House . . . a guid conceit o' himsel', I
thocht.   Mphm!   He bocht a book whiles. . . .'

'No, Henley nivver came my way, tho' I kent
him well by sight—a coorse lump o' a man. . . .
Edinburgh's a wee bit place—ye canna help seein'
folk.   Bein' Glasgow yourself, ye wadna like the
life yonder, Miss Carstairs—gey parochial.'

'There was Laurence Oliphant too.   He was
before your time, though.   I mind when he was
standing for Parliament.   A brilliant man, but

unbalanced, ye understand—got daft-like notions.
But ah! a brilliant mind, Miss Carstairs, a noble
mind!'

'. . . I aince had a first edition o't. I sold it
for thirty shillings—thirty pieces of silver, aye! I
wish I had kep' it. It's worth a heap more now . . .
I've Quaritch here . . . Ay, seven guineas at Sothe-
by's . . . that was in 1892. It fetches far more
now. This Quaritch is clean oot o' date. I keep
it, but it's very little use. It's like everything in
this house . . . I canna keep things up.'

When he had gone I helped Miss Hepburn to
clear and wash up, and she told me that her father
had lost his Edinburgh shop through 'drink and
drugs.' For years, she says, he used to soak his
tobacco in laudanum, and had such a craving for
that and for drink that she and her mother would
often go to their wardrobe and find that he had
pawned all their clothes. Then, when his books
had to be sold up, he suddenly reformed. Now he
does not even smoke, but when the craving for
drink comes over him he takes out his smelling-
salts and sniffs. When the smelling-salts were
explained I felt dreadful about the champagne, but
she was perfectly callous about it. Who would
have thought to look at him that he would have
had such a strong will? For the rest of the
evening Miss Hepburn and I kept off literary topics

as much as we could, and she showed me a great
collection she has of photographs of early Italian
and Flemish pictures. I had no idea that she had
travelled so much, but it appears that, being a
school teacher and having long summer holidays, she
scrimped herself in everything else so that she might
never miss a summer on the Continent. When she
kept exclaiming at supper that she had warmed
both hands before the fire of life, I felt it terribly
pathetic because I could hardly fancy she was doing
more than talking through her hat. But there was
something about her as she showed me her pictures
that made me think it was myself that was the fool.
And now I say, who knows? How strange and
wonderful, past finding out, is every human being!

Feb. 22.—Laura had a lovely, sunny, frosty day
for her wedding. Of the wedding itself what am I
to tell you?

It 'went off well' as they say. All the arrangements down to the last frill had been planned by
Laura herself, and our Laura is a bonny planner.
Almost everybody looked their best and said the
right things. Laura herself looked her most beautiful, but also her most nun-like. I don't know if
any one else had the same feeling, but all the while,
from the first moment of her appearance at the
church to the last, when she ran out of the house

in her grey dress under a blizzard of rice, I had the
impression that she was taking the veil.   I believe
it must have been this alone that saved the whole
performance from being, like most of the weddings
I have been at up till now, blatantly middle class,
and somehow a little disgusting.   She was very pale
and perfectly controlled, and her eyes shone marvellously, but with abnegation I felt sure ; with abnegation and its excitement, *not* with love.   She was a
lamb going of its own free will to the slaughter, and
by its own request decked for the sacrifice with
white roses.   But what matchless egoism is in this
lamblikeness !   I watched her, fascinated but observant, and I could have sworn that no single thought
of her bridegroom crossed her mind.   Unless indeed
she had an image of him as the butcher appointed
by fate.   Poor Wilfred kept mopping his face, which
was excessively red and shiny.   When I said *almost*
everybody looked their best, I was thinking of him
as the exception.   He had cut himself shaving that
morning, and two absurd bits of cotton-wool stuck
out of his chin.   Even when the newly-wedded pair
were arm in arm and standing together, Laura
managed, by her expression alone, to detach herself
from Wilfred in the most extraordinary manner.
Though Laura is my friend and I can't help loving
her, I did yesterday feel a real loathing of her.   If
she hadn't pulled it off so perfectly, if she had

once, even for a moment, looked scared or sad or fluttered, it wouldn't have been so bad. But that beautiful resignation, with just a hint of tragedy . . . pah! Mrs. Sterling, of course, wept bucketfuls but looked extremely happy, and the girls were in tremendous spirits, each one handsomer than the other, though none with Laura's captivating aloofness. One felt they would all ' go off' now like hot cakes. I will admit to you, Ruby, that in spite of these my malicious observations I realised very strongly during the ceremony that it *is*, as a rule, a disgrace for a woman never to lose her virginity. Not a disgrace because of what people say, but for her own inmost self. I couldn't bear not to get married!

Feb. 25.——We are going down to Arrochar on Loch Long for Easter week, Aunt Harry and Ronald and I. Aunt Harry has had one cold on top of another, so needs a change. Ronald and I shall be glad to go. We both love Arrochar.

To-day was Aunt Harry's birthday, and before breakfast we gave her the fur coat. She was simply overwhelmed, pretending to be shocked at our extravagance, but all the while examining it closely at the seams and so on to see if it was as good as it appeared, and stroking the fur as if she loved the feel of it. I often think that if Aunt Harry's

Natural Man were to have full play she would be rather a dressy lady, or anyhow would always wrap herself in the most luxurious materials. She never can resist stroking any stuff that has a rich or smooth surface, and as she does so her whole face softens quite unconsciously. We chose a coat that was very plain outside—smoke-grey cloth without even a fur collar—as we thought she might find anything else too showy. But the fur lining is the best kind of grey squirrel, not that cheap kind that crackles and after a few weeks of wear tears like paper. She put it on as soon as she was dressed and looked at herself a long time in her wardrobe mirror. To our surprise, tears came into her eyes.

' Dear children,' she said, ' I seldom speak of it, as I think that would be wrong. God wishes us to be contented. But many a time I wish my Maker had seen fit to give me an ampler share of good looks.'

March 2.—Think of it! Don John came yesterday to my Room! His name is John Barnaby (so I did hit on his Christian name!), and once he was —but I must begin at the beginning.

Yesterday happened to be a mild and sunny day after a dreary fortnight of wind and rain, and the Library was intolerably stuffy. So I begged him to come out to my Room and he rode there with me

on the top of the car, I feeling very proud of my
distinguished visitor. For there is no doubt about
it, Don John is the most learned man I have ever
spoken to. And the great thing is you feel he
knows Life as well. This, indeed, is why he seems
so truly, deeply learned, because his knowledge of
books and history and things has never at any point
got detached from his everyday, human knowledge.
Such men, I feel, ought to be treated like kings.
They ought to roll about in the best carriages
dressed in simple but rich and dignified clothes, and
the common people ought to be made to bow down
to them. Instead of which . . .! Oh, it does
make me sick!

Well, while I was making tea at the Room and
wishing it was nectar and ambrosia to be worthy of
him, he sat down at the piano and began turning
over my music with the unmistakable *practised*
movements of one who understands what he is
handling. Presently he began striking chord after
chord, making peculiar progressions, very gently but
surely, and it dawned on me that what he was
playing was old Church music. I kept as still as a
mouse till he was finished, and then asked what it
was, and he told me it was out of a Mass by Per-
golesi. In the thrilling talk that followed I found
he knew all about early Church music—the old
scales and intervals and everything—and he named,

one after another, Italian composers of whom I had never even heard. I simply sat at his feet and drank it in. Afterwards I played some Purcell for him and the Paradiso Toccata, and *then* to my surprise and delight he began to sing, without accompaniment, strange traditional peasant songs, Italian and Spanish, to show me how much these had in common with the earliest Church music. It was after this he told that he had been educated for the priesthood, first at Bowmont, which is known as the Roman Catholic Eton, then at a college in Rome, and that he had later taught in a Jesuit College in Ireland.

'But you are not a priest now?' I asked, afraid of saying too much, yet dying to hear more. He looked at me as if considering something.

'I ceased long ago to believe, as the Church counts belief,' he said. And he spoke in such a quiet, grave voice that it was impossible for me to say anything further.

But, Ruby, how I thank my stars for sending me a friend of this sort! He uses no such words as 'sacrifice,' 'conscience,' or even 'truth' (such expressions can be left at this date to second-raters like Miss McRaith!), yet my whole soul bows before him in passionate respect.

March 5. — Such a fearful disappointment!

H

Ronald isn't coming with us for Easter. He is
going with Mungo instead to Paris! Of course I
want him to enjoy himself, and I know—as he has
us all the year round—that Aunt Harry and I can't
be very amusing company. Still, I think it was
rather mean of him first to say he would go, and
then to back out. I have done my very best not to
let him see how it hurts me, and I think I have
succeeded, simply because he is so free from vanity
that he would never realise of his own accord how
terribly I shall miss him. It's the same when he
talks of going to America as soon as he is through
with Mr. Murray's office here. And that will be
this summer! What a life for me with him gone!
It is very strange, this about brothers. Ronald and
I are both so full of our own 'ploys' that we really
do very few things together, and do not even talk
much. Half the time I don't know what he is
thinking, and I'm sure he never bothers about my
thoughts. Yet there it is. When he is not at
home the whole house seems empty to me, and I can
hardly settle down even to work.

March 17.—I have being doing up the Room!
Suddenly, in this lovely bright weather I couldn't
stand it any longer, and anyhow my fees from Miss
Sutherland will be coming in at Easter. It is
wonderful how little I have had to spend on the

whole thing.   But the fun I have had out of it!
With another visit from Don John all the while in
my mind's eye, I have stained the floor black, dis-
tempered the ceiling yellow (to give a cunning effect
of sunshine otherwise rarely to be felt in Harper
Street) and the walls plain white.   The two doors
(one is of a cupboard) and the wainscoting, I have
stained with Berlin black (how much easier and
cheaper than paint!) keeping a rather dull surface
and outlining the panels, which I only then realised
were rather nicely proportioned, with a quarter-
inch line of verdigris green!   It is most amusing
doing this.   You poise the fine paint brush, hold
your breath and, when the moment comes (not
before), sweep your line at one go, hit or miss!   I
must have a fairly steady hand, for I scarcely ever
made a bad break.   The lines do bulge a little here
and there, but this is hardly noticed in the general
effect, which Ronald admits is 'not half bad.'   This
is high praise from him where such matters are
concerned.   Every stick of furniture is now cleared
out except the piano, the chest of drawers (which I
need for papers and music) and the wash-stand desk,
for which I have made a fitted cover of green baize,
as the marble top gave me chilblains.   Miss Sprunt
has allowed me to paint the chest of drawers, as it
is just a deal one, the same as the doors—black with
a green outline.   The only thing I have had to buy,

apart from paints and brushes, is some chintz. How
happy I was to see the last of the yellow lace
curtains! And with the same chintz I've covered
the piano stool and several orange boxes for seats
(Miss Sprunt's chairs did not fit in with the new
scheme). A rug I shall not be able to afford for
ages, but what does it matter? Miss Sprunt, when
I displayed the result of my hard week's work, said,
'It'll be cosier like when it's finished.' And when
I told her it *was* finished, she swallowed and said,
'Oh, yes! Well, it'll be nice and cool for you in
the summer months if we have any warm weather!'

The worst of it is I'm so pleased with it that—
at any rate for the moment—I cannot do a stroke
of work there. I just sit smiling inanely at the
ceiling and doors, keep jumping up to see if the
curtains look nicer looped back or hanging straight,
and wish that I had the courage to write on my
walls as Balzac did—'Here hangs an Annunciation
by Ghirlandaio,' or 'Here stands a Venetian marriage
chest painted in red and green and gold.' But I
know if I did this Miss Sprunt would seriously think
me insane, and might refuse to let me have the room
any longer. Besides, but for Balzac I probably
should not have thought of doing any such thing,
and I'm not *quite* sure that I should like it after I
had done it. On the whole I'm glad I can't afford
any pictures, for in the long run I like walls better

without them.   I should like best to have one very
good but *small* (and by small I mean unheroic) piece
of sculpture.   Miss Hepburn among her photographs had one of a bronze turkey cock by Ben-
venuto Cellini.   That is a thing I should never
tire of.   I am going to put up one or two book-
shelves, and buy a small cupboard for my tea-things
which at present have to stand along the mantelpiece.   There is a gas ring, praise Heaven.   But I
have made a vow that I shall invite only certain
friends there.   I have drawn up a list of them in
two columns.   The first contains those who can be
trusted not to call again except when they are asked,
the second (a very short column) those I am glad to
see at any time whatever.   My only trouble is that
I don't know into which column to put Aunt Harry.
I suppose I 'll have to ask her, though she 's not one
that can be trusted not to come unasked.   If she
takes to dropping in, the whole thing becomes a
farce.   Yet if I beg her to stay away she will perhaps be hurt.   Can you advise me?   *Trials of
Tact*, see *The British Weekly*—' Miss C., a talented,
industrious young orphan lady who has been brought
up by a kind but trying aunt on the paternal side,
rents a studio at ten minutes' distance from her
aunt's house with a view to cultivating the liberal
arts.   Should she invite her aunt to the studio in
spite of the fact that . . . etc., etc.?   A copy of

Dr. Robertson Nicoll's new volume of sermons will be awarded to the competitor who sends in the best solution.'

March 20.—At tea this evening Ronald juggled with our dear old nursery mugs that Mother gave us, and broke mine. I was dreadfully sorry at first, but now I am quite glad that *he* did it, for after all, when I come to think it over, I loved it chiefly because it was connected with him and our old nursery teas in Blythswood Square, and now I shall always remember that he broke it juggling, whereas it might easily have been knocked quite meaninglessly against the pantry spout by Nelly. Nelly hardly ever washes up without breaking something against the spout. Then she will bring the thing in pieces to Aunt Harry and say (just as if she had discovered it so, and was virtuously wondering who could have done it), ' Look, Miss Carstairs, what's happened to your poor teapot ! ' Aunt Harry may think that for once she will be able to make Nelly feel bad about it. But not at all. ' Careless, is it ? ' Nelly will exclaim. ' It 's not carelessness, whatever it is. You surely don't think, Miss Carstairs, that I 'd go and do a thing like that *on purpose* ? '

Still, I can't help liking Nelly. She said to me the other day when she saw me in the fawn dress and hat (it really *has* been a success after all, Ruby),

'You are a perfect *mod'l*, Miss Ell'n ! You carry me away body and soul ! You do so !'

Sunday, March 24.—For three days it has rained coldly and steadily, and I have felt too depressed to do anything more than just scrape through with my lessons. On Friday night it is true I went to one of the Christies' 'evenings' (they have one every third Friday of the month), but did not much enjoy it. All the same I wish I could describe to you the strange atmosphere of that house ! Mrs. Christie gives you the feeling that she is a widow, but it is known that she has a husband somewhere and that he is a Glasgow man, though a very bad lot. He is also said to be brilliant, but I don't know in what line. His relations live in Langside and are quite dull and respectable.

You can certainly conceive of nothing less 'Glasgow' than Mrs. Christie and her two daughters (there are no boys). Though Mrs. Christie has quiet, even gentle manners, every one feels a little afraid of her. She has prematurely white hair, dark, burning eyes (one with a drooping lid) and the most exquisite nose I have ever seen—rather long but 'chiselled,' as the bad novelists say, and with 'quivering' nostrils. I'm sure she spends hardly anything on her clothes, as she is very poor, but she always looks more elegant than any one else in the room simply because of the expression of her face. Stella and Isabel must have got their height and broad shoulders from their father (Dr. Bruce once told me he was 'a mountain of a man'), for Mrs. Christie is very slight and small. The girls both adore her and are, I think, jealous of each other. When I am with the three of them together I get a most unhappy feeling. Somehow they make one think of fallen angels who are finding it not only difficult but distasteful to have to accommodate themselves to ordinary human beings. And they are angels that have fallen from pride, so they have something worse than human, something almost fiendish about them.

Their ' evening ' was not pleasant nor homely in the least. There were several young men from the University—clearly admirers of Stella. Also some dreadful specimens of female admirers—one wonders where she picks these up and how she tolerates them. Isabel had only one Art School friend there, a clever-looking girl with marvellous red hair who, I believe, paints very well. And I thought Isabel viewed Stella's crowd with a cool, secret scorn. It is the strangest sensation to close your eyes and listen for the voices of the two sisters. If either voice is perfectly toneless, you can tell for a certainty that one of them is addressing the other. If a curious, but somehow slightly false, *caressing* quality comes into the voice of either, she is speaking to the mother. But for friends and strangers alike there comes a pure, musical, but icily unconfiding streamlet of sound.

Except that I played once and Stella sang (badly but looking very fine), conversation on Friday evening was the only entertainment. And, I ask you, in such an atmosphere could the conversation be very rich? Stella, when she speaks to you, gives you the impression that she *could* converse wonderfully, but that you are not just worth it. Her actual talk with you is dull and rather stupid, but when she has left you and you see her speaking with some one else, you feel so sure she is saying interesting things that you strain every nerve to catch them. It was obvious that all Stella's guests were bored talking to or looking at any one but Stella. I could have knocked their heads together. Not so much because they wouldn't give me any attention when I tried to be pleasant—though of course that is always annoying—but because of the air of mystery and separateness they gave me, as if they were some exclusive brotherhood. I do hate a cult!

Sunday, March 31.—All this last week I have been writing steadily, and yesterday a most wonderful thing happened. I dared to show Don John my play and two short sketches, and he . . . no, Ruby, I can hardly believe it myself!

Let me tell you, though, perfectly calmly. I took some of my MSS. to his lodgings yesterday afternoon, he having asked me if I should like to see his books. He lives in one room in Endrick Street. But what does that mean to you, and how can I describe Endrick Street to any one who has never been in it. 'Ugly' is not the word that describes it. It is just one of those *desperate* streets which we have here and there in Glasgow and, so far as I have seen, you have not at all in London. It is long and black and melancholy as a stone chasm. All hope abandons you as you enter it. From morning till night there is the sound of worn carpets being beaten, and of stone steps being scrubbed by landladies in Hinde's curlers. The great windows are always left dirty, the broken black railings are never repaired, and there is a smell of soot as if a chimney had just been on fire. Nothing seems to thrive in the back greens but soot and cats. I have never once walked down it but there has been a half empty coal-cart on the roadway with a man standing up in it, his hand to his mouth, wailing the words 'Coal briquettes!' as if he were one of Dante's damned souls.

The house in which Don John lives is all let out in one-room lodgings, and there is a phrenologist with a brass plate on the ground floor. Don

John has a medium - sized room at the front on the top story. Every bit of his four walls not taken up by furniture (and he only has a camp bed, a table and a chair) is covered with his books. He has about three times as many as old Mr. Hepburn, and how much better I like his way of treating them ! Like Mr. Hepburn, he says he has long ago sold his first editions and rare copies, but he shows no sign of mourning them particularly. They are not his ' pets.' All that is in them has become, I feel, so much a part of his knowledge, rather of his *experience*, that it doesn't seem to matter at all whether they remain on his shelves or not.

But now about my play. Though I was shaking all over, I watched him very closely as he stood in his strange attitude (he always reads standing, even at the library, so that I can hardly think of him as sitting on a chair except that one time at my piano) reading page after page of my manuscript. He was very, very kind, but how I suffered !

To come to business, though. Of the play he said the conception was ' fresh and very interesting,' and ' *might quite well* ' (what agony in these three words !) be made dramatic. The dialogue, he thought, was ' lively.' The characters had not been deeply enough thought about and were too palpably inventions, not drawn from real observation and knowledge. It is like being skinned alive to hear such things, but I don't care if only I can learn anything from the process.

On the sketches I hardly expected him to make any comments at all, but to my surprise he was far more interested in them than in the play. 'Here,' he said, 'you are really getting at something individual. Here is your natural bent. You must learn to see that for yourself, as clearly you do not yet know it.' Then he talked to me a long time about writing. 'Write about what you know,' he kept saying. 'It is only fools that think it more imaginative for an artist to describe things he has never seen than things he has seen. The imagination, the *vision* of the true writer lies in the freshness with which he sees, and his power in the faithfulness with which he presents.'

Then, just as I was going home, he gave me the greatest and the loveliest surprise of my life. He said quite casually, as if it were an ordinary utterance— 'I think, if you would care to let me have it, I might be able to get that shorter sketch published in one of the London weeklies of which I used to know the editor.' 'If I would care . . . !' Even now, Ruby, I can hardly believe it can be true !

Good Friday, April 5. — *Arrochar.* What

violent but beautiful weather this Easter! Hail
and brilliant sunshine together . . . the hill-tops
covered with snow, the trees with young leaves.
How I love trees! Even better than flowers. At
least they move me more deeply. Aunt Harry and
I came down here yesterday, and this morning I
went a long walk by myself up Hell's Glen and
into the hills. I was so stirred by all my eyes
rested on that it was almost anguish. Lots of the
pine saplings were bowed archwise to the ground,
their tips held fast there by the sheer weight of
snow. Here and there a larch or a birch, sporting
new green, had been snapped right across the stem in
the night, the jagged stump sticking up out of the
snow like an accusation, and pale leaf buds scattered
broadcast. I saw several old yews with heavy
boughs torn off, and their sap, where the limb had
been so cruelly severed, showed bright red like
arterial blood. A hail rainbow! Did you ever
see one? It really seems this spring as if nature
was bent on an orgy of mixed seasons before bring-
ing the world to an end. The greater part of
March was very mild, so that everything is much
more forward than usual, and now blizzards again,
but blizzards followed almost immediately by the
sunshine of summer! To see the snow and the
blossom on a single branch is painful, but there is
no denying it is exquisite as well.

April 6.—Unfortunately Aunt Harry has been in a bad mood ever since we left Glasgow, and so far, if we have avoided mishap, it has been due to my self-control alone. She complains of the rooms being poky, of the food being cold, of the towels not being aired. To do her justice she is not generally difficult in these ways, and I think myself that this peculiar irritability has something to do with Ronald. He may even have said something definite to her about his going to America. He has not said a word to me on this famous old subject lately, but for this very reason the feeling has grown in me that his mind must be made up. Perhaps he means to go soon after he has finished at Mr. Murray's, that is to say, some time this summer. Whatever shall I do without him at home? I dare not think about it much. The only thing is, it does make me try harder to be patient with Aunt Harry at the moment. Not for the world would I do anything but help Ronald to get off if he wants to go, as of course he must. I shall never forget how decent he was about my going to Germany. But America—how far away it seems! And will he ever want to come back?

Later.—Your most interesting and exciting letter, Ruby, has just reached me, forwarded from Blandford Terrace. I say, what idiots we were not to

have seen it long ago! Why, *of course* caricature
is your line! Those very qualities you have always
thought drawbacks in your serious portraits will be
the making of you as a caricaturist. How well I
remember that day in Frankfort when we had to
wait interminably in the post office for our Christmas
parcels, and to pass the time you began doing little
drawings of the officials. I really thought we were
both going to be arrested when that fierce old one
with his 'Es ist erreicht, kolossal!' moustache came
up and in the name of the Fatherland confiscated
your note-book! Fancy my never once realising
what it was you ought to be at! Yet not one of
all your artist friends seems to have thought of it
either. Nor you yourself, till that blessed moment
last week. I suppose you had grown accustomed
to regard all such drawing as a mere relaxation.
How *very* interesting that all the while it was the
supposed serious work that was waste of time!
Now that you have found out, though, everything
you have learned will come in useful, and I feel
sure you will go straight ahead. That introduction
from Max Beerbohm should be a great help to you.
His praise and encouragement too. Congratulations!

April 7.—Since coming down here I have been
thinking a good deal about Ronald. He has sent

us several post-cards from Paris to say that he and Mungo are enjoying every moment of their stay, but so far we have had no letter. I expect he has no time to write. It is his first holiday abroad.

Do you remember that Sunday of the storm at the Forsthaus, when we saw the fireball, and so many people were hurt, some killed? And afterwards when the rain came down we took shelter in a hut, and I began rather wildly talking about my family, especially about Mother and how Ronald became a cripple? Often afterwards, in fairness to Mother, I meant to tell you more, for in that mood of emotional excitement I know I missed out many details that make a difference when one comes to judge of a person's behaviour. But somehow when we got talking again I always forgot.

Though it is true that Ronald was out alone with Mother when he got wet through that time as a child, and it was his sitting wet in a cold room for hours that did the mischief, still Mother *had* handed him over, as soon as they got in, to the landlady of the lodgings, asking her to see to him. I suppose Mother honestly thought that he would be all right. Of course she *should* have attended to him herself, but she had grown so accustomed in Constantinople to just handing us over to the servants. I mean it wasn't, was it, quite the kind of selfish forgetfulness it would have been if she had changed her own clothes while he was shivering forgotten downstairs? For she too sat down all sopping, just as she had come in, her brain, I suppose, on fire with the ideas that had come to her in the storm, and, without so much as taking her hat off, she went on writing till past midnight. The wonder was that she didn't die of it. But she did not even take cold. I admit it was unforgivably careless of her, when the woman came down and said that Ronald (I don't know if I told you he was only six at the time) couldn't sleep for 'growing pains,' to take it so easily as she did at first. But even then she didn't know he had been left so long wet, and anyhow he was in for it by that time, and how she took it would not have made any difference to him. Every one seems agreed that *once she knew* how ill he was she nursed him with 'the utmost devotion,' never sparing herself, and 'humanly speaking,' as they say, she saved his life. Also she blamed herself bitterly all the rest of her life, which, as it happened, was not long, for she died just six months after poor Ronald's 're-covery.'

There is no sense in saying it would have been better if Ronald had died. Of some people this might be true, but not of him. No one having the slightest acquaintance with him could think other-

I

wise. He is the happiest person I know, and has such a natural passion for his work (I mean he would have had this just the same if he had not been crippled) that fairly often I believe he is actually glad of the circumstances that cloister him, as it were, into a greater concentration and devotion than would otherwise be possible. Ronald is going to make his mark in the world. I'm so certain of this that when everything else, especially myself, seems hopeless, it keeps me from despairing. I know when Ronald was still at school he used to bear Mother some ill-will over the business, but I'm sure he doesn't now. So why should I? The only trace of the blame he once felt is his objection to women 'trying to write,' and his wish to see me married to some 'nice, sensible fellow who won't stand any nonsense.'

April 10.—Home again to the old routine! And I am as if quite suddenly weary of it. At last I have had a letter from Ronald. What a time they have had! They did not stay at an hotel, but shared a furnished room over a *crêmerie* in the Rue Boissy d'Anglas, which he says is very central. They paid three francs a day for bed and breakfast, went out all the forenoon, rested in their room after lunch, making tea from their tea-basket, and then went out again till bed-time, always having dinner at some restaurant. In this way they have been able to afford a lot more driving about for Ronald, and it seems to me there is nothing they have not seen in these eight days. They come back to-morrow night. To think I have never been to Paris! Shall I ever go anywhere again?

April 12.—This afternoon Aunt Harry's Tea-and-Prayer Gathering was addressed by a lady from Syria who showed us a crown of thorns. She had an exceedingly bright smile which seemed to say, 'Look at me. Am not I a bright Christian?' And when she was not smiling her face wore an important frown. She made me understand perfectly why Christians have so often been spat at by ordinary people.

I am off now to meet Ronald and Mungo at the station. It is a pouring windy night. In the morning one of the top windows was blown out.

Sunday, April 14.—Since Easter I have tried so hard to be nicer to Aunt Harry, but as soon as we have been together for half an hour without Ronald I begin to get nasty. I don't know what to do about it. There is no doubt writing makes me more irritable with her. To-day I have felt quite desperate whenever she came near me.

Now is this a sign that writing is wrong for me?

I am deeply worried these days about this old question. Is writing—serious writing—simply a mistake for a woman? Ronald, as you know, thinks it is. But Ronald, I do think, is influenced here by Mother's unfortunate example. The worst of it is I know so miserably well what people mean when they say it is 'a pity' that a woman should write. I can *feel* why it is so different from, for instance, a woman singing or acting. Because, however severe the technique of these arts may be, they are in their effect womanly. But writing! Except for a few nice little poems thrown off at intervals, or stories for children (and all the best children's stories are by men), or letters like Madame de Sévigné's, is there any womanly sphere in literature? There's the eternal trio of course—Jane Austen, the Brontës, and George Eliot (the last I don't really like, though I think she was a writer and had to write or be annulled as a human being). But I admit that for me, when I'm reading anything serious, to know that the author is a woman who sat in her petticoats and her hairpins, leaving life aside to put words on paper, puts me off like anything.

April 15.—To-day I went to the Library, saw Don John there, and—the London editor has returned my sketch! So that's that. I can speak quite calmly about it now, but I had to swallow my spittle pretty hard for some time after he told me.

He is more bitter over the whole business than I should have expected of a philosopher. His disappointment, I can see, is not wholly, perhaps not even mostly, on my account. He had, I think, taken it for granted that the editor could not refuse to do a thing of the sort for him, if only out of friendship and respect for his judgment. As for me, I kept telling him I am just as grateful to him as if it had been accepted, that his judgment weighs more with me than the rejection of a dozen editors, that anyhow I was not counting on its being taken. These things are all true, as I live. And yet . . . !

My one wish then was that he would keep off the subject, but it seemed as if he couldn't. He came over it again and again, so that once or twice, if the notion had not been too perfectly absurd, I could almost have imagined that he was drunk. After all, he and I are a pair of egoists.

Never mind! I continue to have faith in his judgment and in myself in spite of occasional lapses into the most sickening gloom and unbelief, particularly when I remember that *Mother's* faith in herself never wavered under any circumstances! What a blessed thing it would be if I could find one single page of Mother's that I thought was worth something! I imagined I had long ago given up all hope of making such a discovery. Yet this afternoon I began once more eagerly searching through her ' works ' (mostly in pamphlet form) with the idea that possibly the explanation of my failure hitherto might lie in myself. Had I up till now simply not developed sufficiently to perceive the nature and value of her ideas? This was always her own explanation when other people were disparaging. She did not blame them. She merely pitied them for their immaturity and blindness. Mother, Mother, what a legacy you have left me!

April 17.—Lovely weather again, very mild and bright with a silvery sunshine that seems as if it must come from some gentler planet than that which furnished the light for my Arrochar rainbows and brassy cloud-mountains. I, however, am sad and aimless, unable either to work or rest or enjoy myself. After playing this morning at Miss Sutherland's, I wandered about the Botanic Gardens and watched the rooks building their nests, flying from every side with bits of straw in their beaks. If only these unresting thoughts of mine were half as productive!

Now, having got through the day's work somehow, I am trying to console myself by unloading some of my complaints upon you. One comfort, or so I tell myself, is that it is no vague depression that I feel nowadays, but that real troubles confront me at every turn and become less and less easy to avoid. Aunt Harry is one. The unending conflict with her over things nearly all paltry in themselves, but vital when taken in the mass, saps far too much of my strength. Nor is this one of the troubles which ' by opposing ' can be ended. It and the opposition to it run on undeviatingly in parallel lines. I know I said I'd rather have her than your mother, because she forced me to find out what I wanted. But what about after having found that out? It seems to me you score heavily there, my girl! The one thing that keeps me on decent daily terms with her is—strange though it seems to me at this downcast moment of writing—my belief in my own powers, which has grown up in me slowly enough and is not now lightly to be banished. Yet after all what have I to show? And once more the nauseating question reiterates itself—is not this the same kind of belief Mother had in herself? There again, you see, Aunt Harry profits—by my doubts as well as by my belief. For I tell myself that if I am deluded as Mother was, at least I can take care to be punctilious and as little hurtful as possible in ordinary personal and family relations.

But how crippled and balked I feel nearly all the time! Even to Ronald I cannot speak of it.

I know it is cowardly to lay the blame on circumstances. I know things might be worse. I
know this cannot go on for ever. And these simple
pieces of knowledge should be enough to put me on
my mettle so that, instead of wasting my energy in
bemoaning things, I should spare no pains to wrest
all that is possible out of the present, which will
never repeat itself. Hereafter, upon looking back,
I daresay my life, as it is now, may seem rich in
opportunities. Even at this moment I realise there
are elements in it that I would not miss for a good
deal. It is not all waste. There is enough and
more than enough material for me to be always
working upon and learning my job. This thought
steadies me more than any other. Oh for more
time ! I waste lots, I know, but I need lots to
waste, for it seems I cannot work in any other than
the wasteful way.

Madge told me the other day that I was getting
' much too solemn and serious,' and asked what
on earth was the use of it. I 'm sure I don't
know. I 'd *like* not to be solemn. But in Glasgow
I don't see how a person like me can have very
much satisfaction otherwise. For any one with such
a keen relish for enjoyment as I feel I have, the
frivolities here seem unutterably tame and inadequate.
They do not seem to spring from anything deeper
than the need for distraction, and somehow for me

that isn't enough. Indeed I find it tedious. I do
long passionately for fun, gaiety, excitement,
pleasure, but I must have them coming from some
other source than the sheer necessity for diversion
from a daily life of essential dullness. So I grow
solemn, which also is hateful.

Thinking, I suppose, to set a good example of
cheerfulness before me, Madge insisted upon lending
me a book—a sort of autobiography by an aristo-
cratic lady called Mary Boyle. This person certainly seems to have led a very happy, light-hearted
life. I felt envious when I read about her. For
one thing I envied her her horses. Then there
were the lovely old English country houses where
she lived and visited, and all the joys of ' good
society,' which I am sure are not to be too lightly
sniffed at, and the kind of merriment for which
luxury is absolutely necessary. It might be fine to
live like that. But how can I tell ? And anyhow,
why should reading about it help to cheer me up
when I cannot possibly share it ? How queerly
Madge's mind does work ! One thing in the book
that does certainly help to reconcile me to what
Mrs. Lockhart calls ' our walk of life ' is the
wonderfully poor stuff that seems to pass for choice
wit among the peerage.

The more I come to think it over, the more I
feel that such a life as Mary Boyle's would not suit

me at all. I need so much leisure and being by
myself doing nothing in particular, and she seems
always to have done everything in company. I do
love meeting people, but a whole day with them nearly
kills me. Having to be socially polite for a couple
of hours at a stretch makes my face ache all over.

April 19.—Two nights ago I began writing a
sketch about a girl rather like Laura who marries
an ordinary—what Aunt Harry calls a ' fleshly '—
young man, and by her insistent gentleness and
'spirituality' puts a double share of wickedness upon
him, turning him eventually into something like a
devil, while she keeps all the public sympathy. I
wrote all through the night till five the next morning, and at intervals the next day, and to-day I
have typed it out and dropped it into Don John's
letter-box. I think it is the best thing I have done
up to now. Even after getting it off I could not
rest, but to-night (it is 2 A.M. now and I am in bed)
started rewriting the first act of my play ' Influence '
and reshaping the rest, changing practically everything except the theme. It may still be no good,
but anyway it has been a splendid exercise as it has
forced me to think clearly. Also I have realised
that Don John was right, and only too gentle in his
criticism. The thing as it stood was quite lifeless.
I will not show it to him again, however, for the

present.   When I have done all I can to it, I shall
put it aside for a whole year.

I do feel happier for having worked so hard these
last two days, but I am tired almost to madness.   I
don't feel now as if I should sleep.   I wonder what
Don John will think of the story !   'The Angel,' I
have called it.

April 20.—Last night I was too tired, and
perhaps also lacked the courage, to tell you of an
absurd thing I did on my way home from leaving
my MS. at Don John's lodging at about seven
o'clock.

It was rather a pleasant fresh evening with some
light still left in the sky, though the lamps were lit
in the streets and inside most of the houses.   And
I came home from the foot of Endrick Street on the
top of the car.   You know how, if one has to walk
or go by tram very often along the same route, one
gets interested in certain windows.   For a long time
past—since before I went to Germany—I have
never failed when travelling by this way to stare up
at a certain high corner window which the tram
passes about half-way on its journey from town.   It
had become an almost unconscious habit with me to
do so—indeed often, if I chanced to be passing in
the daylight, I had to recollect the reason with an
effort.   Once the lamps were lit, though, the reason

for my interest was self-evident. The curtains of
the room were rarely drawn, and even when they
were, one could almost always see the shadow of a
young man playing on a violin. Often enough I
have gone on the top of the car instead of inside, in
spite of bad weather, just to have a better look.
From what I could see on nights when the curtains
were not drawn, the room seemed ugly, bare, and
poor under the glare of an unshaded incandescent
light, but always there was this young man with his
back to the window practising away like mad.
How I longed to see his face ! In fact I wondered
a great deal about him, asked myself many fruitless questions, invented a hundred stories concerning
him. Was he a poor musician in lodgings there ?
Some foreigner, perhaps, struggling to make a living
in the terribly uncongenial surroundings of Glasgow,
after a distinguished studenthood, say, in Prague ?
Or was this his own home, and was he, even like
myself, working thus frantically to escape from it
and find himself in the great world outside ? Was
he handsome or a consumptive ? A gentleman or a
genius of low birth ? *Und so weiter !* Always
after seeing him I was filled with self-reproaches for
my own indolence, and I used to go home and start
practising with frantic diligence. Again and again
it came to me what a nice and proper thing it
would be—so simple and direct, don't you know—

to call and thank him for the constant inspiration and example he had been to me. But for some reason I had never carried this idea out into action.

Last night, however, on my way back in high spirits from Don John's, I looked up as usual, and there was the black shadow bowing away behind the yellow blind as vigorously as ever. I suppose I was in an exalted and reckless state of mind. Anyhow, without so much as debating the point within myself, I got off the car with all speed, entered the 'close' between two shops which I had often enough marked as the most probable entrance for the flats above, and ran quickly up flight after flight of stairs as if this were my hundredth instead of my first visit to the place. I rang the bell, and only then went suddenly weak in the knees. I would have given worlds to have got away now, but the deed was done. Almost at once the door was opened by a wheezy little old man in his shirt-sleeves wearing huge carpet slippers. Isn't it dreadful to think what hundreds of shuffling, odious old men and women, once sweet babes, are living in the world? This one had a thin beard, a large bald head, and a very red nose. But none of these things would have mattered if it hadn't been for the sound of the fiddle, which I now *heard* for the first time. Imagine 'The bonny, bonny banks o' Loch Lomond' being played on a bad violin, correctly but in a poor and very painful tone! Still, there it was. It was, after all, the diligence, not the tone nor the music chosen, that had so often inspired me, and I was going to go through with it.

ODIOUS OLD MAN (grinning and looking me up and down out of his red-rimmed eyes). What's your pleesure, Missy?

ELLEN (rather severely, trying not to bolt back into the street). I just wanted to convey my thanks to your son, or whoever is the gentleman that practises the violin. (Here my breath gave out.)

O. O. M. It's yin o' ma sons ye want? Step in, Missy! (Calling out) Edgar! Here's a fine young leddy come aifter yin o' yuz!

By now I was well into the smelly little lobby and the front door was closed. The sound of the fiddle mercifully ceased, and in a kind of stupor I followed the old man into the room of my dreams where his son was. It was certainly a surprising room. Almost no furniture in it, but upon the bare, unpainted boards every kind of known and unknown instrument was scattered. And, fiddle in hand before a metal music stand, with the garish light full in his blinking eyes, stood something like a white mouse in trousers.

'Come awa', mun, shake han's wi' the young leddy,' said the father, who seemed to be enjoying himself immensely from the way he kept rubbing his

hands together and grinning. 'She's ta'en a fancy
to ye. By the looks o' her she'll be the makin' o'
ye. If I wis twinty years younger masel' I'd be for
her like a fowerpenny rocket!' And he was about
to leave the room when we both simultaneously
stopped him.

What followed in actual speech I cannot remember. It was certainly nothing important nor
even amusing. My one idea was to get out of the
house as quickly as possible without being rude. I
could not help feeling sorry for the young man.
He was so perfectly at sea. (I suppose what
actually brought me there will remain a mystery to
him to the end of his days!) At the same time I
must admit I hated him, most unjustly, but none
the less violently, for being such a hideous disappointment. That pale hair, those white eyelashes,
those bent knees! He really looked a hopeless rag
of a creature. I suppose that was why my calling
amused the old father so highly.

I managed to tell them, though I'm certain
neither of them took it in, that I had been studying
music for some years, and had greatly admired the
diligence with which he always seemed to be practising every time one passed the house. Also that
I had come just to tell him so, as I thought it a
pity, when people felt grateful to one another, that
they should not say so. It sounded, I must say,

incredibly feeble, and even as I spoke I felt they
could not be expected to believe it. In fact I no
longer believed it myself.

Edgar never uttered a word. He just stood
blinking his (I really think they were pink) eyes,
and shuffling with his feet, very unattractively uncomfortable. But the old man told me they were a
family of freak musicians who were much in request
at grand concerts and *sa'rees* (soirées) in Glasgow
during the winter months, and in summer they
toured the country towns and villages with a concert
party. There were four sons, all fiddlers, so that at
different times it may have been any of the four, or
all in turn, that I had seen practising ! He begged
me to wait till the other three came in, when I could
' tak' ma choice.' (He spoke very broad Glasgow.)
They would soon be off on tour, he said, and as they
were short of ' a young lady,' he made the suggestion
that I should join them. If the others, he said,
' hadna mair spunk nor yon sumph '—meaning the
unhappy Edgar—why then, ' he wisna that auld
himsel', but . . .' and here he leered in the most
unspeakable manner and dug Edgar in the ribs. I
managed somehow to make my way out, the old
man begging me all the way to ' bear up,' ' no tae
lose heart,' and ' tae mind that the young fellows
nowadays required a heap o' coaxin'.'

Well, that is all. You will no doubt see clearly

enough how I deceived myself over the whole
business, and how *on the whole* the old man's motive
for my call came nearer the truth than my own
explanation.   Yet, will you believe me that it was
not until a good hour later that this really dawned
on my own mind? It was just after supper and I
happened to be talking to Ronald when it came upon
me in a most unpleasant flash.   Indeed, I turned so
red in the face all of a sudden that he asked me
what was wrong.   I did not tell him of course.   I
said one of the bones of my stays had run into me.

Sunday, April 21.—Madge's brother Duncan,
the doctor one she is always talking about, is coming
home from India on leave.   According to her he is
the most wonderful creature that ever lived—handsome, witty, brilliantly successful in his profession,
and extremely musical!   She declares that he sings
better than she does, but for that I'll wait till I
hear him, as we know Madge and her family!   This
Duncan is of course her full brother, not like Willie
who is only a half-brother.   But she thinks the
dreadful Willie such a marvel of cleverness and
virtue that I am taking Duncan with a pinch of
salt, anyhow till I see him.   He is seven years older
than Madge, that is thirty.   They are all surprised
that he is not married yet.   (Willie got engaged
just the other day.)   I need not say that Madge is

K

half crazy with excitement. Duncan does not reach home till the first week in May, but she has already arranged a party specially for me to meet him on the ninth! She says she's sure he and I will be 'congenial spirits.'

Sunday, April 28.—Nothing worth recording has happened all this week. The rain has hardly ceased for half an hour at a time, and I have gone dully about feeling as if a weight were pressing on the top of my head. I have not had a word from Don John about that story of mine, nor have I seen him in the Library. Perhaps he has got some coaching to do. But it often happens like this. He will be at the Library day after day, and then for a week at a time not a sign of him. I hope anyhow that his landlady delivered the envelope with my MS. I never liked the look of that woman. It may of course simply be that he thinks the story bad, and doesn't like to hurt my feelings by writing and saying so. But I should have thought he would at least have acknowledged it. Should not you?

I went this morning with Aunt Harry and Ronald to church, and to amuse myself began trying to look at everybody as if I had not seen one of them before. I made believe that I had entered for the first time the place of worship of some strange race,

and, as travellers do, closely observed the appearance
and habits of the aborigines.

I saw in this way a number of interesting things
which had never struck me before, but at the moment
I shall only describe one.

Our pew is in what is called 'the body of the
church,' that is to say, among the seats enclosed by
the side passages, and in one of the front pews at
the side, so placed that we have an excellent view
of all the occupants. There sit two sisters called
the Miss McFies. They are generally spoken of
together, but if they should have to be dealt with
separately, we speak of 'the pretty Miss McFie' and
'not the pretty Miss McFie.' And this though
really I don't think strangers would notice very
much difference between them. 'The pretty Miss
McFie' is a little less thin than the other, and has a
slight cleft in her chin which used to be a dimple.
At least Aunt Harry says it was. They dress the
same even to their hats and gloves, and have much
the same colour of hair. I cannot remember any
change in the appearance of either since I first went
to church when I was about six years old. Neither
can Ronald. People are always complimenting
them on never growing any older, and they smile,
showing their false teeth and blushing, but not somehow as girls blush. I never thought of them myself
as girls, and always thought it rather absurd when

Aunt Harry spoke of them so. It was not however till to-day in church, when I had a good fresh
look at them, that I realised with a shock that
they were quite, quite old ! There was only a kind
of crust of youth all over them. The real, *underneath* youth must have withered away a long time
ago without any one noticing, and nothing else had
taken its place. They made me think of pressed
flowers. It really was a horrible discovery. To
think that such a thing could happen to any one.
I remember Dr. Bruce saying that at one time
every one thought Dr. Sturrock was going to marry
the pretty Miss McFie. I am sure anyhow that
both she and the other are in love with him at this
moment. They take care to miss nothing in which
he ever takes part, and if he speaks kindly to them
their faces change and brighten marvellously. But
after what I saw in church to-day, it almost makes
me cry to think of them. *They* must know they
are old in spite of what kind people say. And the
worst thing of all is that they seem to have no more
right to a place among the middle-aged or the old than
they have to a place among the young. I suppose
they must cling to the end to their shell of youth,
never having acquired the experience and assurance
which would enable them to shed it in the natural
order. So there they move in a kind of limbo like
the unbaptised souls in Dante. What sort of human

contact can they possibly achieve? It is truly a hellish question to consider. For myself, I'd rather be a drunken old grey rat living in the basement, like Miss Sprunt's mother, than be like the Miss McFies.

April 29.—Behold what Heaven has sent me by this morning's post!

'101 ENDRICK STREET,
'*April* 27.

'MY DEAR ATHENE,—You are right. "The Angel" is undoubtedly, and by a long way, the best thing you have as yet written. Anyhow, it is the best thing you have let me see, and it confirms my belief in your literary vocation. It is fresh and vigorous, even in its faults entirely individual, and, if I may say so in a congratulatory sense, a markedly feminine piece of work. I must beg your pardon for not having acknowledged it earlier, but I was not well. I am now better, but it may be some time before you will come across me at the Library, as I am engaged upon a piece of work which for the present can more conveniently be done in my lodging. Directly I am myself informed, however, I shall let you know how "The Angel" fares on her trip to London. Risking a further rebuff from my friend the editor of *The Spokesman*, I have taken the liberty, without first consulting you, of sending her to him,—Your sincere friend and well-wisher,

'JOHN BARNABY.'

This time I really do not care two straws what the editor thinks of it. Don John's words are enough. I know he would never have written so, simply out of kindness. He must have thought it good. I wish I could see him, but you will notice he does not exactly give me an invitation! I do hope he is really better. It is wretched to think of him being ill without any one to look after him.

N.B.—I never told you that 'Athene' is Don John's name for me. One day, when I told him that from the first I had nicknamed him Don John, he replied, 'And you I always named "Athene."' And when I asked him why, he gave me one of his kindest smiles and said, 'Because you have grey eyes, wisdom is your quality, and there is just a hint of some grave goddess in your appearance.' I was of course deeply flattered, especially as he is not the kind of man that makes a habit of pretty speeches.

May 1.—This was such a lovely fresh morning. I went into town first thing with Ronald, and we ate rhubarb and whipped cream in a shop on the

way and made believe that summer was here. He
spoke with bright eyes about America. Coming
home in the car last night from one of the Tuesday
orchestral concerts, I sat opposite to a middle-aged
man—not specially good-looking or smart—whose
face I could have stared at for hours on end. How
I envied him! The observant smile in his eyes, the
grim lines round his mouth, showed quite clearly
that he was right *in* life, that he was finished for
good with that 'paddling near the shore' business
of youth. It is all very fine for people to say how
good it is to be young, but whatever this man
might tell you in words, I could see that he *enjoyed*
being experienced far more than I enjoy being
inexperienced. I am sure he did not envy me
nearly as much as I envied him. He may have
wished that he had more hair and fewer wrinkles,
though I gravely doubt even this. He certainly
did not wish himself back again on the brink of
things. Is it not truly frightful, Ruby, the constant
fear one has that one will never *oneself* have any
fullness of experience, that life is going to pass one
by as it has passed, for example, the Miss McFies?
Do middle-aged people forget that *onlooking* terror
of youth? I see the lovers in the Park, and I
wonder, 'Shall I ever have a lover?' I see the
mothers with perambulators, and ask, 'Shall I ever
have a baby of my own?' But that middle-aged

man in the car, looking at the lovers and the babies, would smile and say, ' Yes, I know all about that ! ' and he would hold his own unique experience between the palms of his hands, as it were, to marvel at and make the best of.   No one can take that from him.

I know, of course, that there are whole worlds of experience quite outside of love, marriage, and children, and I can very well understand how even a woman (to whom they must surely be supremely important by nature) for some special, passionately chosen reason might be willing to forgo them. But if there were no such reason ? If one were simply an ordinary mortal desiring one's own full share in the rich, normal life of humanity ?   Then, for either a man or a woman, what could there be in existence to make up for such an omission ? The poor Miss McFies—no wonder they simply *dare* not let themselves look old ! Think of having to stare night and day in the face of this fate—that you had missed life ! ' But,' I can hear you say, ' *do* your Miss McFies face it ? Could the pretty Miss McFie have that exasperating little giggle at the end of each sentence if she were really facing anything ?   Would not any one with the courage to face so grisly a thing with a simper have long ago plunged into life, even if it were only to have made a mess of it ? '   Perhaps.   I cannot tell.   It may be

that she only faces it now and again when it is
forced upon her—say when she has a sore throat
and can't sleep in the night.   Then, instead of the
thrilling and feverish thoughts that come to me at
such times in spite of the pain, so that fire seems
to run in my veins and my head is bursting with
splendid ideas, she may have to lie gazing into the
eyeless sockets of that spectre.   What a fearful
thought !

But I must say most middle-aged people do look
as if they had lived, and this makes them interesting and enviable, at least to me.   If only they
would tell us more about their living !   But either
they won't or they can't.   Even when you ask them
about something quite definite, as I have sometimes
asked Aunt Harry, they don't seem to know anything really essential or interesting about themselves.
Are they ashamed, or are they ignorant ?   One has
to go guessing from their faces, which isn't at all
easy.   It is too bad.   It almost seems as if it were
as rare for people to be able to tell you about their
actions *afterwards* as to tell you *beforehand*.   Will
Laura ever tell her children why she married their
father ?   Does she know herself ?   Or is it that she
would refuse to tell them ?   You cannot think how
I puzzle over such questions.   With Laura I do
think there is the—let us hope exceptional—
notion, held like a religious belief, that one must

never speak of anything really intimate. Her father's death—that is a 'disgrace,' a 'skeleton in the cupboard,' and must never be mentioned frankly and humanly. Her marriage—that is too 'sacred' or 'mysterious' or something to bear the light of common day. That is to say, *her* experience may not be used to help, interest, or enlighten others, but must die sealed up with her. She would be frantic if she guessed that I had drawn 'The Angel' from my knowledge of her. She would say I had no right to use any such knowledge as material for fiction, all such knowledge being 'sacred.' Oh, that word! Are not the uses of art more sacred than a million domesticities? How thankful I am for the reckless and indiscreet ones who have bared their own hearts and failures (and any one else's they could read aright) to the world, holding nothing sacred but life! Who cares to-day that Leigh Hunt was so much hurt by Dickens's Harold Skimpole? Laura would say that to prove my right to imagination I should write lies about people living in Borneo where I happen never to have been. As if there were anything more difficult and needing more imagination than for me to see *for myself* what is before my eyes in Glasgow and to set it down so that others may see it precisely from my peculiar angle! But no, the Lauras of the world will never see this if their own egoism happens to be involved. They will allow Dickens his Harold Skimpole because that is 'different.' They will not condemn Maupassant, although they may learn that he admitted never having 'invented' either a character or an incident for a single one of his stories. All that is already accomplished, recognised and removed into the light of fame, is 'different.' What is so curious is their complete failure to see that the more anything is talked of and examined, the more closely it holds its secret. I don't suppose Leigh Hunt ever made up his mind which vexed him more—Harold Skimpole's likeness to himself, or Harold Skimpole's unlikeness! In all their egoism the Lauras underrate their own wonderfulness.

May 3.—This morning at prayers we were reading about the sun being darkened at the ninth hour, when Aunt Harry stopped and, turning to the servants, said rather severely, 'I believe that this was a supernatural darkening of the sun and no *natural* eclipse which could be accounted for by those modern scientists. I was taught to believe this by people better than myself, and I shall continue to do so *until in another world I may be told that I was wrong.*' Not one of us smiled, but I took it down word for word on the fly-leaf of my Bible to make sure I had it right.

May 5. —That about Dobbin (I beg her pardon
—Dobinova now) and her first concert in London,
and all you tell me of her history between the time
we knew her and her *début*, is indeed interesting.
Best of all that her playing at eighteen even out-
does the promise she gave at fourteen. Not that it
is more than I expected, for if ever any one worked
hard those three years she did, and think what she
was to start with! Oh, Ruby, how I wish I had
been with you last week! My only comfort is your
assurance that she will before long actually give a
concert in Glasgow. And even that does not quite
make up for the fact that we are hearing her
separately.

The real surprise of your letter, though, is her
running away like that from Knopf. Her own
explanation *may* be the correct one, but somehow I
myself think that it could not have been so much the
mere fact of his making love to her (he must have
done that from the first) as his going on with it in
spite of his really serious affair with the Friedländer
and his divorce and everything all at the same time.
That, I suspect, offended her Yorkshire sense of
decency, and I don't wonder! But the spirit of the
child! For I'm sure she was more than a little in
love with Knopf herself, and certainly knew his
value as a teacher. And to think of her simply
packing her bag, spending the last mark of her

allowance on a ticket to Leipzig, and presenting
herself to Serbsky without any credentials except
her ten broad finger-tips! Well, she deserves
success.

As for Knopf and the Friedländer, I never thought
he would have done it. To be sure he was long
enough about it. But it just shows he must have
cared more than any of us knew, for as you say it has
meant his losing not only his post but the more than
probability of succeeding old Ellermann as Direktor.
He was fond of his children too. Do you remember
how sorry we used to feel for the Friedländer
because she always went about looking so sad and
untidy, as if she didn't care what became of her?
I wonder if she looks more cheerful now! But
what a couple, Knopf and the Friedländer! Won't
they just fight! How I should like to know all
about their married life! She, of course, is as
much of a genius as he, and by a long way the
better pianist, and in spite of her face being so
often spotty (perhaps it isn't now) there was something very attractive about her even when she
wasn't playing. When she *was* playing I 'd have
given her my heart to eat.

How I did laugh over your story of our fair girl
from Bristol. Wouldn't you have given *anything*
to have been there when Lilienthal tried to kiss her
and had his Stradivarius smashed to splinters on his

own bald head by way of remonstrance? All the
same, I think it was mean of her to report him as
well and get him the sack. Don't you? Surely his
hurt vanity and broken Strad. were enough punish-
ment. What a spiteful creature! I guess
Lilienthal will not be in a hurry to kiss a pupil
again! But if it had been Knopf, now, would our
friend have carried her revenge so far? It must
be allowed that poor Lilienthal is an ugly fat little
Jew, which makes for fierce virtue in fair girls from
Bristol!

I wonder if those Frankfort days seem to you as
far away as they do to me? I see them as a series
of pictures, fine and clear, but tiny, as if viewed
through the wrong end of a telescope. Will the
whole of my life appear to me so when I am old?
Is it so that people see their lives when they come
to die? If I am walking down a Glasgow street on
a sunny day when windows are open, and up in one
of the houses some one begins in a business-like
manner to play scales, I am on the instant trans-
ported with overwhelming emotion. The flavour,
the concentrated essence of three whole years seems
to lie on my tongue and to rise in my nostrils—for
with me the senses of taste and smell are always the
most immediately responsive to reminiscent emotion.
And this then is memory! This inexplicably
tender and despairing emotion over one's own past!

I understand what Tennyson meant when he called it 'some divine despair.'

Do you remember one evening we called by chance on that queer Mr. Hermann who was so fond of you, and he was practising organ-pedalling in his shirt-sleeves without any organ, and he gave us russet apples to eat and made you teach him to sing, 'She's my dainty love, She is my sweet, my honey dove'? Now why should I see that picture so clearly, and why should seeing it make me want to weep ineffable tears?

Then there was my Mr. Hunstable who always looked so terribly poor. (Why do people who look poor have such a deadly attraction for me?) I was more in love with him than I ever admitted to you. Often and often when I said I was just running out to post a letter at the corner box, I went only to lean against the railings and stare up at his lighted windows. But perhaps you guessed it.

All that behind me already! It makes me feel old. Yet even now I don't feel I know much about reality.

May 9.—Well, I have met the great Duncan (Madge Bruce's brother) and he is really nice, though not for me. He knows how to treat one, neither too gallant nor too brotherly, and he has none of Willie's commonness. At least I have not

seen any so far. Indeed no one would suspect any
relationship between the two. He would *never*, as
Willie does when he sees you home from their house,
say, upon reaching your door, 'And what am I to
have for seeing you home?' and *then* not seem to
mind when you ignore the question. (Do you not
agree that the vulgarity of asking a girl for a kiss
under such circumstances is more forgivable than
the casualness of not minding whether she gives it
or not?)

It is true that Duncan hasn't seen me home yet.
Nor have I heard him sing. You would never
guess that he was thirty. He is very clean looking
(not 'an egg-spoonful of dust' about him, I feel
sure), with fairish hair, laughing eyes—dark like
Madge's but not short-sighted—and a good forehead. He doesn't speak nearly so Glasgow as the
others, yet has not that horrible veneer on his
speech that so many Glasgow people acquire when
they have been long away, and which they fondly
think will be taken for an 'English' accent. In
fact, both in speech and manner he has just the
amount of polish that is pleasant. The right kind
of polish, to my mind, is that which allows the
grain of the wood to show through. With veneer,
you merely guess that there is unpolishable deal
underneath, *i.e.* only good woods will take on true
polish.

Madge, who ran in this evening in a state of excitement over things in general, says that my hair was looking 'extra nice' this afternoon. I had thought myself when I was doing it that it had happened to go rather better than usual, but in such things you never can be sure till some one else tells you without being asked. She told me, too, what Duncan said after I went away. 'She's all right,' were his words. And 'Let Glasgow flourish!'

It was certainly the jolliest afternoon I have spent for a good while, though I can't think of anything special in the way of incident that made it so. One small coincidence is perhaps worth recording here. Duncan was looking at an illustrated paper, and one of the pictures was a group of about twenty young men. He passed it to me, pointing to the group and saying, 'Choose the five faces you like best out of these,' and then he did the same to Madge, and when we came to compare our choices, my five were the very same as his, but only two of Madge's were the same. He was greatly impressed. I did not tell him that two out of my five were chosen from my instinct for his choice rather than from my own sheer preference. All the same, it was quite as interesting that way as the other.

May 11.—Poor old Mungo is no use as a mimic,

L

though he enjoys himself.   His secret ambition is
to be able to sing comic songs, and one of the joys
of our lives (Ronald's and mine) is to hear him try
' Two Fish Balls.'   He makes it sound like a dirge.
As he is very sensitive about the wrong kind of
laughter, Ronald and I have to control nearly all
ours and just let a little escape at the right times.
And we almost perish with the pain of it.   I am
lucky in being at the piano so that I can hide my
face.   Ronald screens his with one of his crutches.
Then at the end Mungo asks us very earnestly if we
think he is getting any funnier!   He is a great
admirer of Harry Lauder, but hardly laughs at all
when he goes to hear Lauder sing—he is always so
absorbed in ' trying to find out how that chap gets
his effects.'

Sunday, May 12.—I went twice to church to-
day.   It does nothing but rain this month and
to-day there is a cruel, biting wind as well.   When
I remember May in Frankfort . . . !

May 15.—The Lockharts have given a Musical
At Home.   I was invited in the ordinary way,
though I knew my presence was only wanted to
help provide the music—*desto besser!*

As they have no music in themselves and are too
stingy to pay professionals to come and play to

their friends, they simply get together a party.
Then, a few days beforehand, all those who are
supposed to sing or play at all are written to again
and asked to 'bring their music.' Can you imagine
anything more different from our musical evenings
at Zilcher's house or Knopf's, when d'Albert or
Lamond would be the honoured guest and play to
us for hours on end? And when even Zilcher
would not consider himself in practice enough to
take his place at the piano unless it happened to
be just after one of his concerts?

There we were, however, at the Lockharts' grand
house, all with our music carefully left upstairs
with our cloaks and hats. Madge had brought
some songs for herself and for Duncan, who swore
he had come only because Madge had said I was
sure to be playing. The meanest thing of all, I
thought, was that a Mr. Logan, who is an over-
worked organist and piano teacher, a real professional musician who happens to be good-natured and
sociable, had been bidden there quite under false
pretences. I mean he had *not* been asked to bring
his music—Mrs. Lockhart being aware that he
plays without—and he turned up thinking it was
just a few friends at afternoon tea, in which case,
as he told me afterwards, he wouldn't in the least
have minded playing to them for an hour on end.
But here he found himself well wedged into the

Lockharts' medieval drawing-room with close upon
a hundred other guests, and being sweetly called
upon to open the proceedings with a piano solo!
As Mrs. L. no doubt knew, he could not well refuse (though I will bet Zilcher, for all his good
nature, would have done so!) because there were so
many members there, including the minister, of the
church where he is organist, and his refusal would
have made an unpleasant impression. But my word,
he was sick! He played one short piece, none too
carefully, excused himself on the plea of ' a professional engagement,' and rushed from the house.
Quite right too! Don't you think it is shameful
that a woman like Mrs. Lockhart should think an
artist, in return for an invitation to her house and
a cup of tea there, should be falling over himself
to put his art at her service, and without being
asked beforehand?

However—enough of that. Madge sang, not
quite so well as usual, and Duncan sang — for
aught I know his best or his worst, but most
surprisingly well. He has the same lovely freshness as Madge, but more art and a much finer
taste in songs. It was a treat playing for him.
I got quite carried out of myself, and felt in
perfect harmony with him, and he said he had
never had so sympathetic an accompanist. We are
arranging to practise together twice a week, for in

spite of this chance success I badly want rubbing up in the matter of accompaniments. When I was not at the piano this afternoon I was mostly sitting in a corner with Duncan talking. I must say he gives one a nice *safe* feeling, as if all the problems of life were suddenly smoothed out and there was nothing left to worry about.

There was one notable moment towards the end of the At Home. Every one with any capacity whatever, and a good few with none, had sung or played, while the others had murmured, 'Thank you,' 'What a sweet thing that is!' '*What* is it called?' '*Of course*!' 'I always forget the *names* of the pieces, don't you?'—and after the decent interval of a few seconds had started chattering to their neighbours on ordinary topics with immense relief. Then just as the spring seemed to be running dry, *Laura*, of all people, said that if they liked she would play them a solo on a comb. A comb and some tissue paper were got for her, and with a very attractive mixture of mischief and nervousness she sat down before the piano and gave us 'Yankee Doodle'!

It was an amusing turn, of course, and all the more surprising that it came from Laura. She carried it off very well, playing the accompaniment with her left hand and holding the comb to her mouth with her right. I suspect she must have

practised it quite hard in secret. But the real revelation was the joyous response of the audience. What
unconcealed relief in every face! And the applause
—what a reflection upon any applause that had
gone before! Beethoven, Chopin, Schubert — for
the giving of sheer pleasure which of these could
compare with 'Yankee Doodle' sung, or rather
squeaked, through the teeth of a comb?

Just before I left with the Bruces Mrs. Lockhart
came up to me, and in a very mysterious fashion
whispered that she wanted me to call to see her
about 'something very special' at three o'clock next
Saturday afternoon. I wonder what can it be?
Perhaps she is not satisfied with the progress of
Rosemary and Fiona. If that is it, I shall tell her
straight out that in my opinion it is throwing
away time and money to go on with their piano
lessons. They are both in the highest degree unmusical.

May 18.—I felt a perfect fool this afternoon, and
an angry fool into the bargain. During the week
I have had several very fair mornings of writing at
my Room, but those pupils of mine cut up my day
deplorably. This morning I was happily free, and,
after some shopping for Aunt Harry, was able for
once to settle down in the comfortable knowledge
that I might safely allow myself to get absorbed in

what I was at. I looked at my watch once and saw
that it was already twelve o'clock. 'That's an
hour more till lunch,' I told myself. Then in
what seemed about ten minutes I thought I'd look
again, just to make sure that I had seen aright and
to find how my hour was wearing. And it was
past two !

If it hadn't been for my promise to Mrs. Lockhart I could have gone on writing all the afternoon. As it was, I went on till about three
o'clock and grudged very much having to stop
then.

I found my lady reclining, nicely arranged, upon
a couch in the drawing-room, and wearing a tea-
gown which on almost any one else would have
looked something more than merely expensive. Already some time ago she had told me that she was
'taking care of herself,' but as I never knew her to
do anything else, I give you my word the phrase
had conveyed absolutely nothing to me but a slight
sense of bewilderment that she should be at the
trouble of telling me anything so obvious. Only
when I saw her this afternoon did it dawn on me
that she was expecting another baby. But what on
earth could it have to do with me ? Or with the
grand piano in its carved oak case (of which I'll
tell you more in a minute), which stood suggestively
open near the couch ?

Can you guess what she wanted ? She wanted me to play for an hour before tea, not to *her*, as she is incapable of listening for so long with any degree of attention or enjoyment to classical music (and this, she said, must be classical), but to the unborn child, so that he—she was very sure about its sex, the other three being girls—might have a better chance than the others of being musical ! Now that I come to write it down it looks as if the whole incident might have been rather sweet and pathetic. In fact it was neither. Her heavy solemnity, the expensive, unbecoming tea-gown, the calm assumption that I should be only too delighted to play in this way, without any question of a fee, ' every day or every second day for the next few months,' *while she took her afternoon siesta*—these things, quite apart from the embarrassment of the situation, made a most offensive impression on me.

As I had come, I sat down and executed two Bach Preludes and Fugues, choosing the very severest of those I know by heart. *Executed* is just about the right word ! I played them with such vigour that sleep was out of the question for her, and I scarcely paused between the end of one and the beginning of another. Strangely enough, I don't think I ever played them better. I was in a devil of a temper to start with, but the piano is a fine one *as regards sound*, and with the last chord I

emerged in the highest spirits.   Mrs. Lockhart tried
rather wanly to thank me suitably, but it was clear
that she had expected Chopin at his gentlest or
Schumann at his most yearning, not this performance
'rather like exercises.' When she had said her say
I shook hands, told her I couldn't stay to tea, and
departed.   Nothing was said about a second performance.   I shall simply not go again, and I am
confident that she will nevermore mention the
matter.

About that piano of hers, I feel there is something so characteristic here that I must put it down
for you.   I have already told you that the Lockharts
are wealthy people, and they think a lot of themselves and are a lot thought of for that reason alone.
At least it is difficult to discover any other reason
for such a good opinion as is held of them, but in
Glasgow this one reason amply suffices.   Their fine
large house is furnished in the style that makes
other Glasgow people dining there look round a
room and tot up in their minds the price of the
curtains, carpets, chandeliers, pictures, inlaid cabinets,
etc., etc., so that when they speak of it outside
they say with a solemn, almost religious expression
on their faces, ' Mind you, the things in yon drawing-
room alone cannot have cost much under £5000 !'
Are things really as blatant as this in London?
They are as bad, I daresay.   But surely the London

vulgarity takes a subtler form ? The other night at
the Bruces' house Dr. Bruce was telling us he had
been spending a week with Sir Andrew Crossmyloof,
who has bought a little estate in Ayrshire. 'And
is it a nice house?' I asked. Would you believe
it, Dr. Bruce stopped eating (we were at dinner),
and stared at me with perfectly round horrified eyes
(so like Madge's on such occasions) as if I had said
something sacrilegious.

'A nice *house*!' he repeated my words; 'Glen
Grozet is not a *house*.   It is a gentleman's mansion,
a *residence*!'   Just then my eyes met Duncan's, and
he very solemnly winked at me. Thank goodness
for that!

But to return to the piano. The Lockharts
have furnished their drawing-room with elaborately
carved oak. The windows are stained and leaded
like church windows, the chairs upholstered with the
richest Lyons brocaded velvet, the walls hung with
expensive reproductions of medieval tapestries. The
whole effect is very rich and solid, but not in the
least suitable to the house or to modern Glasgow.

It will at once jump to your mind that in this
room the piano must have presented a real problem.
A piano there must be. Neither Mr. nor Mrs.
Lockhart plays a note, and it would be a good
thing if their children had not begun to learn.
Further, no one in the house enjoys any kind of

music half so honestly as they enjoy the music of a barrel-organ. But rich people of their kind *dare* not say frankly, ' We are not musical,' and have done with it. They dare not have a house without a piano, and it must be a grand piano, and by one of the best makers. But how to fit in a Steinway grand with all that carved oak and tapestry? That was the question, and I imagine Mrs. Lockhart, when she was furnishing as a bride, must have spent some sleepless nights over this difficulty. On one side her musical, on the other her artistic taste was threatened.

Well, she had a bright idea. She had the guts taken out of the new Steinway, scrapped the case, and had another receptacle made purposely of carved oak. Not counting the instrument and the expense of the instrument's removal from one case to another, it cost only £500! The beauty of it is that, until you actually open the keyboard, you would never suspect there was a piano in the room. It might easily be some queer kind of bureau. But of course every one who has ever called at the house has been told about it, so that long ago it became the talk of Glasgow. There is nothing in the Lockharts' house that Dr. Bruce admires more.

May 21.—You say you are always shocking

people and on the whole enjoy it. I think I am getting over *setting out* to shock, but I am discovering that none of that intentional shocking is to be compared in its effect with the unintentional kind which seems to happen more and more frequently with me. Instead of saying something deliberately outrageous, as I used to do, just so that I might amuse myself with the look of horror on their faces, I find myself uttering something that has become almost a platitude in my own mind, and to my astonishment I create a really painful sensation compared with which the former business was child's play.

Only to-day something of the kind happened in the teachers' room at Miss Sutherland's. As a rule I spend no time there, merely dashing in to leave some music or to put on my hat and coat. But to-day I was lazy and sociable, and stayed drinking milk and eating biscuits with the others. There were perhaps six of us in the room together—Isabel Christie, Mona Black (a very sentimental girl who teaches English), Miss Barclay (a little, pale, clever person who is said to be a swell at mathematics), Miss Sutherland, of whom we are all rather shy, as one is of a person who is both brilliant and morbidly timid, and a sewing mistress whose name I forget. We were all talking away about nothing in particular when Miss Barclay began telling us about her Cambridge days. It seems there was a tutor at Newnham for whom every one ' schwärmed ' like mad. Among other things, Miss Barclay said that the girls used to wait outside their bedroom doors at night, sitting on the floor in their dressing-gowns, hoping that in passing on her way along the corridor the beloved one might by chance brush against them with her skirt !

ELLEN (breaking into the meditative, uncritical silence). How old were these girls ?

MISS BARCLAY. Oh, about nineteen, twenty—up to twenty-two.

ELLEN (severely). Grown women ! How perfectly shameful ! At that age they should have been falling in love with men !

What a sensation ! You would really have thought I had uttered a most improper sentiment. Mona was drowned in shame, Miss Sutherland vexed and disapproving, the sewing mistress frankly scandalised. The extraordinary thing is that not one of them had thought the Newnham story any-thing but quite pleasant and as it should be. Mona, of course, in spite of all she says about marriage being the ideal for a woman—' a home of her own and little ones '—is a born Schwärmer, and Miss Sutherland a born centre of Schwärmerei. Still I should have thought some one would have protested. No one even smiled at my outburst,

and the only one that came to my rescue at all was
Isabel Christie, who had not been listening particularly to the conversation. Isabel is so often like
that, lost in puzzled, not very happy dreams. She
said she quite agreed with me, and that ended the
episode, as of course, when they came to think it
over, the others could not exactly take up the
cudgels against us. They simply maintained a
shocked appearance and began talking of other
things. Isabel and I left together immediately
afterwards, but parted at the street door, as we go
different ways. I like her very much, though she
makes you feel that she is miles away from you all
the time. I wonder if she is in love? There was
some talk of her being engaged to a boy in Ronald's
office, but she wears no ring, so I daresay there was
nothing in it.

May 24.—How am I to tell you what happened
this afternoon at the Library? I can hear you say,
as you have so often done when I have come with a
tale to pour into your ears, ' Begin at the beginning !'
Well, I shall do so, refraining from comment as far
as I can. You must judge for yourself of the sadness or the shamefulness of my discovery.

I think I told you once before how, when one
o'clock comes—an hour when I am very seldom at
the Library—Don John, if he is there, will munch

some dry bread as he stands reading, and later in
the afternoon will go out for a cup of tea.   To-day,
as it happened, I went in at three o'clock wishing to
get an hour's reading in before I met Madge and
Duncan for tea in town at half-past four.   Don
John was at the Library, and as I had not seen him
once to speak to since he had written about ' The
Angel,' I was overjoyed at the prospect of a talk.
For the first time, however, since our acquaintance
began, he seemed in a taciturn mood, seeing which I
made myself scarce and took my book to a chair at
some distance from him.   I do not mean that he
was not as perfectly courteous as usual.   It was
simply that he did not smile at me, and from the
compression of his lips and the drawn look about his
jaw and cheek-bones I feared he was still ill, but in
such a way as forbade inquiries and sympathy as
intolerable.   I know myself just how it feels to
dread companionship.   How it was that I did not
take the simple course of leaving the place at once
and so relieving him completely of my presence I
can't explain.   I can only say that, though I felt
unhappy and in the way and found it almost impossible to fix my attention on what I was reading,
something kept me from going.

What was my surprise when at about half-past
three he came across to me and asked in a peculiarly
off-hand voice if I would ' be so kind ' as to lend

him sixpence. At his request I looked up, involuntarily met his eyes, and in that instant knew *that he was starving*! It was the most dreadful experience of my life. For what could I do? The expression on his face made it impossible for me to initiate any remark or action. I was compelled to sit there helpless while I heard him say that he had stupidly come away from his rooms that morning without his purse, that his tea never came to more than fourpence, that he only wanted sixpence and would bring me the change directly. His actual words at the time made no impression whatever upon me. I simply understood that for some reason, inexpressibly painful to me, but vital to him at the moment, he was begging me to behave as if nothing unusual had happened.

As I handed him my purse I was praying hard that my memory did not play me false when I calculated that there were hardly any coppers in it and no silver piece smaller than half-a-crown. He hesitated a moment when he saw this—I urging him carelessly to take all he wanted. Then he picked out one of the half-crowns, thanked me, and moved off. I did not offer to go with him, as he made it so clear that he preferred to be alone. It was a bright sort of day, but with a biting wind for the time of year, and I begged him in the tone of an elderly aunt to make a good tea, as he looked chilled and tired. At this he thanked me again and asked me to wait till he should come back with the change. I protested against that, for my idea wàs to cut and run, comforting myself with the thought that anyhow he would have the half-crown. But, as he was so insistent on it, I agreed to wait where I was.

He was away nearly three-quarters of an hour, during the whole of which time I kept turning over plans by which I might help him, without, however, coming to any definite conclusion. Then, just as I was beginning to wonder how I could keep my word to him without failing Madge and Duncan, but determined to fail them if it came to a choice, the door I had been watching for so long opened, and he came in. He made straight across the room to me with a curious skating movement and a fixed smile on his face, and sitting down beside me he said something in Latin which I did not understand. Several times over he repeated the same thing as if he enjoyed the sound of the words, but also as if he was unaware that he had already uttered them with precisely the same intonation. And then I realised that it was not tea he had been drinking.

I was not the first to see it either. Every one in the place was staring at us, some reprovingly, others with the kind of smiling sympathy you always find, in Glasgow anyhow, when a man gets drunk. And

M

presently one of the attendants began coming toward us.

Luckily I noticed that the man had a kind, sensible face, and when I told him that my friend had been ill he did all he could to help. By this time Don John had laid his head on his arms on the table we were sitting at, and so did not interfere when I asked the man to call a cab. When the cab came, the man and I each took one of his arms and between us coaxed him out of the place. It was hard work, as we practically had to carry him all the way. If he had been a heavy man we could not have managed it, but though he is tallish, he is, as I realised when we were on the steps, practically skin and bone. Also fortunately I am very strong in the way of lifting.

In the cab he sat silent and morose with his head on his hands, and I felt that he had become more or less alive to the situation, but he did not say a word and neither did I. I stared out of my window, only turning once for a moment to look at him. In that moment, though, I received the most vivid impression of his face that I have yet had. It was as if across his sharp temples, sunken cheeks, and burning, deep-set eyes, I saw written the terrible admission of failure. I knew then that long before I first met him he must have failed irretrievably, must long ago have sat in judgment on himself

and accepted his own verdict.   But I also knew that
somehow, though all the incidents of his life were
hidden from me, he had failed for truth's sake, so
that my pity for him was quite swept away by an
even stronger feeling of reverence.   I saw nothing
but his indestructible dignity, and acting on a sudden
impulse, as surprising as it was uncontrollable, I took
one of his hands and kissed it.   Had I been a pious
Catholic, I might just so have kissed the hand of the
Pope.   But he drew it away at once and shrank yet
farther back in his corner.

When we reached his lodgings I paid the cabman,
Don John standing silent by, and I went in and
upstairs with him as far as the door of his room,
where I left him.   He seemed by this time able to
look after himself and fully aware of everything.
When I begged him very seriously and with all my
might to take the loan of some money, he pushed
my purse away with a stern and unhappy gesture,
but still he did not say a word.   It was a great
relief to separate.

May 26.—-This morning he sent me a postal
order for five shillings (the cab and the half-crown)
with this letter :—

'*May* 25.

' DEAR MISS CARSTAIRS,—I am more than sorry for
what happened yesterday through my fault, more

than grateful to you for your humanity. In this
world a man has to be stronger than I to give up
the drug of religion without being forced into the
use of some other narcotic. It may be that for
most men religion is still a necessary drug. But I
do not regret. At least as a drunkard I harm no
one but myself. I try to console myself for yesterday by remembering that the quality of mercy
blesseth not merely " him that takes."

' I am still waiting to hear from London about
your story, but it may well be that the editor will
write direct to you as I gave him your address.
The long delay may be, and I sincerely trust is,
a favourable omen.—Your sincere and grateful
friend,   JOHN BARNABY.'

You will notice he does not call me Athene, and
I somehow have the feeling that I shall not see him
for a long time.

May 28.—You remember my telling you a week
ago about a conversation on the subject of *Schwär-*
merei in the teachers' room at Miss Sutherland's?
To-day Janet Binnie, a teacher who was *not* there
on that occasion, came up to me with a quizzical expression on her face (I have always liked J. B., though
she is a bit of a cynic) and said, ' What 's this Mona
tells me about your preaching immorality to the

Staff, Ellen?' And when I asked what on earth she meant, she continued, 'Mona says you are an advocate of every woman entering into immoral relations with any man at all as soon as ever she comes of age'!

So you see from this how reputations are made and lost in Hillhead! When I recounted the true story, J. B. was highly delighted.

June 2.—Do you know anything of a London painter called Pender? I met him at the Lovatts' house the other day (he must, I think, be fairly famous or Mrs. Lovatt would not speak of him as 'my friend Pender'), and thought him very attractive. Joanna Bannerman (no one ever calls her by her married name) was there and another girl from the School of Art whom I had met before, and a dark youth whose name I didn't catch. I had not seen Joanna since the 'Social' at school. She was quite friendly and nice, but there was one queer moment. Annie Murdoch (the other girl), who is said to be very good at black and white, asked me to come up to her studio and sit to her. The Pender man stared hard at me, nodded, and said *most emphatically*, 'Quite right. I envy you your model.' Our friend Joanna gave me one look and got as red as a turkey-cock, but she turned at once and began an animated conversation with the dark youth.

I should think the dark youth is sweet on her. How entertaining people are!

Later.—That Pender has certainly the gift of looking at a woman boldly, yet without offence (except to the *other* woman). Poor wife, if he has one! And poor Joanna Bannerman! Though of course, I don't know if there is anything in this. It was a bad habit, Ruby, that you and I acquired in Frankfort of always coupling up in an intrigue whatever man and woman we saw together and obviously interested in one another. In Frankfort I admit that (with the famous exception of 'the innocents,' Ruby Marcus and Ellen Carstairs) any such conclusions were generally correct. But in Glasgow one *might* just make a mistake. As Mrs. Lockhart said to me one day when everybody had been talking of a love-tragedy in the newspapers, 'Such things do not occur in *our* walk of life!' Could you but have seen her air of conscious, slightly regretful virtue, as if she had missed heaps of lovers by not being in another walk of life! It was on the tip of my tongue to retort, 'Not in *your* walk, perhaps!' She is a most unattractive-looking woman, and would probably not even have got a husband if her father had not been a very rich man indeed.

June 5.—I was sitting in my bedroom at the open window trimming a hat, and I could hear Aunt Harry on the doorstep (my room is in front) sending Nelly to the beadle of our church for her umbrella, which she left in the church hall at the Wednesday night Prayer Meeting.

AUNT HARRY. I have noticed, Nelly, that in our beadle's nature Grace has not yet triumphed over the Natural Man.

NELLY. No 'm.

AUNT HARRY. So when you ask for the umbrella you must be careful not to irritate him, but ask very politely.

NELLY. Yes 'm.

AUNT HARRY. Don't forget now. You are so apt to forget, Nelly.

ELLEN (putting her head out of the window just above them). But where Grace abounds, Nelly, you can be as rude as you like ! Remember that !

AUNT HARRY (looking up severely). I won't have profane speaking in my house . . . etc., etc.

I know it was impudent of me to shout like that out of the window, but I could not help laughing at their two faces looking up to hear the oracle, from Heaven as it were, and the whole incident cheered me up wonderfully. I sat trying on my hat afterwards and grinned at myself for about five minutes.

Last night Aunt Harry went to a meeting about Jesuits and the 'Romeward tendency,' and came home terribly cut up about my not being there. The speaker was 'a man who has *written a book*,' she said, and *yet* I did not bestir myself to go and hear him. This might not be to my 'utter and final casting away,' but it would certainly be to my 'eternal loss' that I had missed such a man. Cold good-nights were exchanged. I do wish Dr. Sturrock had not recommended Christians, instead of using violence or strong language, to 'imitate the look that Jesus gave to Peter when the cock crowed.' Ever since that sermon Aunt Harry has tried it on me. Preachers should really be more careful and should study human nature a little.

June 8.—I have just come home from meeting Mr. Gustavus Thom, a man I was madly in love with the year after I left school. You may remember my telling you of him. At the time I was convinced that he was the love of my life. He was a lecturer in History at Queen Margaret College, where I went to some classes the year I left school. All that year I lived for his class, and the poems I wrote to him (long since destroyed) would have filled a volume. Best of all—for he was by way of being a poet himself—I took my effusions to him for his criticisms. Very likely he guessed they

were addressed to him, for he used to look exceedingly
embarrassed.   I believe in my heart I wanted him
to guess.   For quite a fortnight (having read what
an impression Cleopatra had made upon Antony by
starving herself) I cut down my breakfast to one
piece of thin dry toast, and I used to hope he would
notice how thin I was growing, though I never could
see much difference myself.   I certainly got dark
under my eyes with sitting up writing these poems,
and the way in which I used to sprint after a tram-
car and leap on if I saw him sitting on the top
ought to have reduced my weight more than the dry
toast.   Not that I was so very fat to begin with,
but at seventeen there's a plumpness.   At least with
me there was, and I hated it.   But how hungry I
used to be by midday !   Will you credit it, I used
to lie in wait for the green tram-cars about the
hour he was likely to go into town, and if I saw his
cadaverous face and black hair—I could spot him
miles away without seeming to look—I would start
running before the car came level with me, increase
my pace as it reached me, and then leaving the pavement hurl myself quite recklessly on to it.   I would
then climb the stair and, gazing obliviously into
space, pass his seat and sit down as nearly in front of
him as I could get.   This is an interesting point.
I invariably wanted *him* to see *me*.   Whereas when
I was in love with Mr. Hunstable in Frankfort and

used to look out everywhere for him and gaze up at
his windows at night, I only wanted to catch sight
of him without being discovered. I think there
must have been more real feeling there than in the
other. Yet what is even Mr. Hunstable to me now?
As I write his name a tender feeling comes over me,
and I think affectionately of his shabby coat and his
delightful playing of Scarlatti. *Weiter nichts!* I
believe he now teaches music in Huddersfield or
some such place, is married and has twins. Good
luck to him!

Which brings me back to my History lecturer,
who is also married now. I think his marriage was
the death-blow to my passion for him, though at the
time I vowed I would continue to love him, wedded
or single, for the rest of my life. But he chose such
a dull-looking person, the very mature daughter of
the Principal of another University, which fact gave
him an undoubted lift in his academic career. People
of course said the obvious thing, and though I
always refused to admit it, they may have been
right.

But to continue — or rather to begin again.
Yesterday Mrs. Lovatt called (great honour) to ask
me if I could go with them to-night to see Compton
in 'The Rivals.' Luckily I was at home and Aunt
Harry in bed with a cold, and I accepted at once.
No sooner had Mrs. Lovatt left than Aunt Harry,

who had heard us at the front door, called me into her bedroom, and I had to tell her about it. She wept and I went away to a lesson. How absurd it is, as if I were a child! Later in the day she sent Eliza for me, and told me she had been 'praying about it,' and was going to write to Mrs. Lovatt. She said it was 'the thin end of the wedge,' that Germany had 'seared' my conscience, and finally that she was thankful Father had been 'spared from seeing his daughter on the downward course.' When it came, as it has so often done lately, to her condemning my doings for no other reason than that I am my father's daughter, my patience suddenly went, and I said all the horrid things I could think of in one long breath, which was a very fair number, for my wind on such occasions is excellent. Surely Father was a missionary because he wanted to be, not because of anything *his* father was! Yet because Father chose to be a missionary Ronald and I must not even want to see a play by a classical writer like Sheridan! That is to say *I* mustn't. Ronald, because he is lame, may do what he likes. That is one blessing. All the same, of course, I went with the Lovatts.

And I *did* enjoy myself! Compton as Bob Acres is all one can wish—I suppose you have often seen him? The women were rather disappointing I thought. Also I found the Lydia and Falkland incident a blot on the play. They should both be more lovable characters and with a real cause of jealousy to be cleared up at the end. I am sure Sheridan did not mean people to laugh at some of the bits they do laugh at, and it must surely be a fault that a comedy of the sort should arouse so many tedious and disagreeable sensations.

What I really wanted to tell you, though, was that Gustavus Thom was in the Lovatts' party. It was years since I had seen him, as he no longer lives in Glasgow. When I first realised who it was, I was just the least bit flustered, though I don't think I showed it. He certainly looked doubtful and taken aback, and actually glanced at Mrs. Lovatt as if to say, ' What people you do invite to your house ! ' And then he gave me the tip of a cold, flabby hand, half holding it back as if he was afraid I might kiss it ! It was the first time I had ever touched his hand, and it completely cured me of any lingering sentiment I may have had for him. How I despised him !

All evening I was coldly polite to him, and I could not help feeling that in my rose-coloured bridesmaid's dress I showed up rather well sitting next to his wife. She is a poor, crushed-looking creature with a lace collar and a pink, shiny nose as if she cried a lot. Most of the evening I talked to a Mr. Brown, an English assistant at the University,

and we got on very well.   We sat in the stalls, and
Madge and Duncan Bruce were in the front row of
the dress circle at the side, just above us.   In the
interval they came down to speak to me, and Duncan
said it was a shame I wasn't sitting beside them.
He looks very handsome in evening dress.   I found
it pleasant being between him and Mr. Brown and
feeling that they both wanted to talk to me.   Such
things do not come about so very often in the life I
lead here.   Yet, just as I was realising how enjoyable it was, for no reason at all the thought of Don
John came into my mind, and I felt suddenly then
that the whole theatre and everybody in it were as
nothing to me compared with—no, not with Don
John himself, but with something I cannot express,
which from the first he has *stood for* in my mind,
and which has not been destroyed but rather strength-
ened by the discovery of the other day.   How very
strange and frightening this was I cannot express
to you.

On the way home Mrs. Lovatt made us all come
in for a while to her house—all, that is, except the
Thoms, who said they couldn't.   And Madge and
Duncan came too, as they live quite near in Wood-
side Crescent and we had come out by the same
tram.   It was great fun.   We had a kind of picnic
supper with things fetched out of the pantry, as
nothing had been laid for us and the servants were

in bed. Duncan and I made a wonderful kind of
fruit salad out of odds and ends, and got our fingers
very sticky taking out date stones and putting in
almonds instead. We washed them together afterwards, and he told me, so very nicely that it was not
like an ordinary compliment, that he had never seen
a woman with hands that were at once so pretty and
so 'strong and capable' as mine. I may say he has
very nice hands himself, real surgeon's hands, that
look as if they could be trusted to cut you up with
perfect safety. I said I was sure I was not the first
woman who had told him that, whereupon he
laughed just a little self-consciously and said,
'Young woman, you know too much.' But he
declared he could lay his hand on his heart and
swear that he had never made the same remark to
any other woman about *her* hands. Which, for
some reason, I quite believed.

At supper the talk turned on the different
lecturers who had been at Queen Margaret College,
and at length Gustavus Thom came under review.
Mrs. Lovatt, who seems to have known him pretty
well when he was in Glasgow, made a lot of uncomplimentary remarks about him. She was fairly
witty, but I thought it horrid bad manners for a
hostess to talk so of a guest who had just left,
especially when we were not her intimate friends
and there was another lecturer present. In the

middle of it she ran to the bookcase, pulled out a
volume of his poems (once kept by me nightly
beneath my pillow), and bade us all listen to the
' ridiculous dedication,' which she begged would be a
warning to Mr. Brown if he ever brought out a book
of poems.   Now I practically knew this dedication
by heart.   Once I had thought it most lovely and
touching, but that was nearly four years ago, and
certainly as she read it aloud it sounded silly enough.
She asked us if we had ever heard ' such stuff,' and
the others apparently had not.   Duncan seemed
particularly amused by it.

Will you believe it, I had to make a *very great*
effort to stand out, and I only just did it and no
more !   What a coward I am !   Here was a man I
had at one time at least *thought* I was in love with,
and he had given me many a thrilling moment.
Besides, I 'm sure some of his poems are fairly good.
I managed, thank goodness, to pull myself together
before it was too late.   I said I didn't find the
dedication specially funny, and taking the book from
her I read out the first sentence as it was intended
to be read.   ' Perhaps a little youthful,' I said, ' but
don't you think it 's easy to forgive that when several
of the poems show such a sense of beauty as that
one about the tiger-lilies ? '   I know this must have
sounded awfully stilted, and I saw Duncan looking
at me with uncomplimentary surprise, but I felt

better after it in spite of that, and in spite too of
Mrs. Lovatt's clear annoyance.

I did not have another chance of talking to
Duncan as he had to take Madge home, and their
house lies in the opposite direction from ours.
Mr. Brown came away with me. I did envy Miss
Gillespie, a professor's daughter, who was one of the
party. When she had said good-night she came
running back to say, ' Oh, Mr. Brown, mind you
come round to our house one evening soon. Father
will be delighted to see you.' 'Ah,' thought I,
' shouldn't I like to be able to say that ! But what
about Aunt Harry ? ' Isn't it damnable ?

On the way home I talked to Mr. Brown just a
little about Aunt Harry, and he seemed to understand beautifully. His father, he said, had been a
very strong Evangelical, so that he had been through
' that particular mill.' Certainly his remarks were
so intelligent that they could have been made only
by one who knows exactly what it is to live in such
an atmosphere. I found myself thinking it was a
pity he was married. He has the kind of face I
like, long and rather sad, a bit lantern-jawed, with
searching, but good-humoured eyes. He told me a
story about Herbert Spencer visiting a household
where there was family worship every morning before
breakfast. Spencer had lived so much alone that all
family life was novel to him, so he asked his hostess

if he might come to prayers. She said she would be delighted to see him there, and next morning he came. While they were reading the Bible he sat listening attentively, but when they all turned suddenly and plumped down on their knees he took his stand on the hearth-rug, his back to the fire and a coat-tail under either arm, and watched them with the greatest interest until the prayer was done.

Though this is rather an amusing picture, I couldn't help thinking there would have been more in the story if Aunt Harry had been the mistress of that house !

Sunday, June 9.—Which reminds me of Aunt Harry's parting shot when she saw me starting, dressed in my rose dress, for the Lovatts' house— ' Well, my child, I shall know how to pray for you ' !

She has made me promise not to repeat our conversation in the bedroom to Ronald. Poor Aunt Harry, I always love her best when I am disobeying her ! To make up for the things I said to her when I lost patience that time, I have been sewing a white coat edged with red for a black man in Livingstonia. It has taken the greater part of a day, and I have used a good deal of audible bad language over it, but Aunt Harry does not seem to mind that. She only smiles, says, ' Hush, child ! '

N

and declares that the garment is 'Ellen's contribution
to the Great Work.' She is no hand at sewing herself,
and always thinks my achievements in that line very
wonderful. I will say this for myself, I do know
how to use a needle. I think my black man will be
pleased with his coat, as it is both gay and strong.

June 13.—To-day I sat for the third time to
Annie Murdoch, the artist girl I met at the Lovatts'.
The first sitting was sheer waste of time, as she
spent most of the hour in making tea and talking,
and when at last she did begin a drawing she tore it
up without letting me see it. At the second sitting
everything went swimmingly, and she nearly finished
a head of me which I thought very flattering—
turning a little sideways and looking down. To-day
she put the finishing touches to this one, and did
some rough sketches in other positions. As we were
drinking tea afterwards, Professor Nilsson, who
teaches design at the School of Art, came in, and
she showed him the finished head. He looked at it,
then at me, then at it again, screwed up his face as
if he was sucking a lemon, and laughed. Annie,
looking dreadfully vexed, asked him what was wrong
with it. 'Nothing wrong,' he said quite kindly.
'It is all right. Quite a nice drawing. They would
hang it in the Royal Academy. But '—and he
glanced, as if for the first time, at me—' though a

man *might* possibly see Miss Carstairs as a Madonna, no *man* would ever see her as *this* kind of Madonna. A man would know she had no meekness in her composition.' As he said this, smiling right into her face, Annie was holding the drawing in her two hands. And without taking her eyes off him, her lower lip trembling all the time like anything, she began to tear it across and across. And he did not stop her.

Feeling that I was in the way, I put on my hat with all speed, and sure enough, when I held out my hand to Annie I found she had forgotten all about me. She was quite nice, though, and made me promise to come again. I cannot quite decide whether she is in love with Professor Nilsson or simply fearfully keen on her art and sensitive to his criticism—probably both. I'm sure I could very easily be in love with him. He has something of the same attraction as Knopf, only gentler and less immoral.

Sunday, June 16.—I am always finding exquisite things in unexpected places. On Sunday nights I sometimes have to wash up the supper things. I get out of it if possible, for, in spite of her fault-finding, I consider that Aunt Harry spoils the servants ridiculously, but to-night I had to set to. Our washing-up basin is the ordinary white enamel kind with a dark blue rim, and as I was filling it to-night with hot water I noticed that all round the curved part close by the rim the enamel had gone into thousands of curving cracks as fine as looped hairs. When I came to look into them more closely, the beauty of these lines and the design they had brought about made me hold my breath. Not the finest graving instrument held by the most skilful of human hands could have swept so delicately and with such inspired precision, yet there was no monotony. Each line was different, but the scheme was a perfectly harmonious arrangement, perfectly obedient to some hidden series of nature's laws. The very colour of the lines was an added charm. They were a pale seaweedy brown deepening to black on the white ground, and the band of strong blue at the top held the whole marvellous circle of fringe together. Something of the spider's web was in the pattern, but, taken simply as a pattern, it was far more complex and interesting than any web I ever saw. The whole fringe was not more than an inch and a quarter in depth. Had it been executed in jeweller's enamel instead of upon kitchen-ware, and had the line of blue been made of sapphires of no finer a shade, but set there in a row, it would have been regarded as a priceless treasure. But it was in our scullery, and by the merest chance had been seen at all. In a few weeks' time I suppose it will be gone for ever. The enamel will peel off and the iron below will show through in mere formless blackness. I am glad I saw it.

June 18.——Why is it that I so seldom do the things I talk about beforehand? Is it that I talk *because* in my heart I know I shall never carry out that particular action? Or is it that in the mere speaking of it so much of the energy necessary to the action is dissipated? This interests me very much. Watching myself, I find that if I long greatly to talk of a thing—say to Ronald—and yield to that longing, after having talked I go off with a feeling of accomplishment and elation, and my determination to carry the thing through is by so much the weaker. Then, even if I get the length of approaching the action, I feel a sickly coming short in myself, and as likely as not I sheer off for good. If, on the other hand, I am afraid to let a word out, and allow that fear or diffidence to govern any more communicative feelings, then I am fairly sure of performing the action by the mere ripening of my thought and desire. The question is, why do I talk of some things and not of others? And do I talk in fact only of the ones I am not vitally interested in? Or is it just chance and mood? I watch other people and remark that, without any question of hypocrisy, they hardly ever do as they say they will, or if they do, at least they drop the saying a good while before the action comes about. When Ronald was always talking of going to America I did not feel half so sure that he would go as I do now that he never mentions the word. Then Laura used always to say how wicked it was for a girl to marry from any motive but love, and look at her now! Madge, on the other hand, has declared ever since she was at school that she was determined to have a rich husband at all costs, yet only a few weeks ago I know that a very wealthy middle-aged man proposed to her, and she never for one moment regarded the idea as a possibility. Of course talk is fun and all that, but it is what people *do* without a word said (or with every word said in contradiction) that is so desperately interesting. There may be some few people in the world who speak and act in perfect harmony, but I have not met any of these yet in Glasgow or in Frankfort.

June 19.—I stayed away from home all afternoon so as to go and see 'Twelfth Night' without having to tell Aunt Harry beforehand. I had to borrow a shilling, and Madge, though she had been the night before, came with me to the pit. My word, how Shakespeare makes you love everybody— vain men, fools, drunkards, and knaves, so long as they are at all human in their failings! Especially

when he makes them start singing the tears simply
pour down my face—tears of joyous emotion at
having been born into a world where such a poet
was not only possible but true in his presentment of
life. There were things in this production that
offended you if you loved the play as well as I do.
The farce was overdone in places, so that quite
suddenly you could not laugh any longer, and the
scenery was too gorgeous except in the garden
scenes. The young actress—not long out—who
played Viola was good enough. She has a particularly pretty and happy smile. The trouble was
that for one who is supposed to be letting ' con-
cealment like a worm, etc.,' she smiled far too light-
heartedly and too often. I wonder if any of the
dramatic critics will have noticed that ? Ruby, to
be a dramatic critic ! Could any existence be more
perfectly enjoyable ?

Sunday, June 23.—Madge Bruce is engaged.
Everything is just as it should be except that the
man is not particularly well off. But I 'm sure, and
so is every one else, that before long he will be.
For he is very clever and all his professors in turn
have prophesied a distinguished career for him. He
is a gynæcologist and has been only a few years in
practice, but with most encouraging results. He is
popular, handsome, and good-natured, the kind of

young man who everywhere inspires confidence. Madge adores him and goes about with a perfectly beaming face. Every one is pleased——his people, her people, and all their friends. And there is no reason why they should not get married without delay, as Dr. Bruce can well afford, and is only too delighted to help them in setting up house. How splendid ! It really seems as if Madge were one of those people for whom life holds no problems. Yes, I envy her. And yet would I change with her ? No, I suppose not, though I cannot quite explain why.

Later.——Yes I can, though ! My story, ' The Angel,' has been accepted and is at present *in print* ! By the last post to-night, direct from *The Spokesman* office in London, I got the proof to correct. Ruby, my first proof ! Can I bear to part with it ? I wrote off on the instant to Don John to tell him the news and to beg him either to come to my Room or to let me come to him as I miss him so much. Besides I want his practical advice about some small changes in the proof. Whom else have I to talk to that really knows about writing ? But since that day at the · Library I have neither seen him nor heard anything from him. I wrote a long letter to him in reply to his when he sent me my money back, but he did not answer it. Several times I have walked down Endrick Street, and one day I thought I caught a glimpse of him at his window. If it was he, however, he moved away quickly, and I did not like to ring the bell and ask for him in case he simply did not wish me to. Now surely he will let me see him and talk.

June 25.—But no, he will not, and what am I to do ? Here is his letter in reply to mine of two days ago—thank goodness he calls me Athene again, anyhow !

' MY DEAR ATHENE,—Indeed I congratulate you most heartily. May this be the beginning of a happy and successful career. I feel sure, however, that you are well able to make the necessary corrections in your proofs without help from me. If you take my advice you will alter nothing more than any printer's errors there may be. It would be the greatest mistake in this particular sketch to start tinkering about with it. I send you my blessings for what they are worth. Perhaps the following lines best express my feelings toward you—

> " A shipwrecked sailor buried on this coast
>   Bids you set sail.
> Full many a gallant bark, when we were lost,
>   Weathered the gale."

Your friend,   JOHN BARNABY.'

June 26.—On the top of the car this afternoon whom should I meet but Miss Rory, my old music teacher, with her husband. She was just through from Edinburgh, where she lives now, for the day, and looked very elegant and interesting all in black. She spoke to me in the old, sweetly playful way as if I were fourteen again, and though I have long since got over that infatuation, and indeed, as you know, owe her a grudge at times for so having over-praised my talent and sent me to Germany with such high hopes, I must, I suppose, have slipped back for the moment in a sort of mechanical way into the old subjugation. Anyhow, when I left them I remembered that I had not addressed a word all the time to her husband, whom I then met for the first time. I did nothing but talk to and look at her, so that I daresay she has the idea that she still holds sway over me. This would be an annoying thought if there were more substance in it. Even as things are, it is curious to notice for what a long time after an influence has ceased to exist its former force will appear in small but living actions. I remember so well the day Miss Rory told me she was engaged to be married to an Edinburgh architect. She laughed like anything at my look of blankness followed by acute but controlled distress. And how I cried as soon as I got away from my lesson! I honestly hated the sacrilegious brute of a man who was to marry her.

Not long after this meeting to-day I was kidnapped in Buchanan Street by Mrs. Bruce, who insisted on my walking her way while she talked with the greatest emphasis and solemn relish about Madge's engagement. She kept saying, ' Now I can say this to *you*, Ellen,' as if she regarded me as a specially reliable, discreet sort of person, or almost as if I were one of the family. It gave me a queer, not wholly pleasant sensation. It is true I have been a great deal at their house lately, and I am *very* fond of Madge, and very happy about her. That must be it.

June 27.—The schools are all breaking up this week, but as yet we have not decided anything about holidays. The only thing that seems to be fixed irrevocably is that Ronald will go to New York in September.

Later.—Lately I have been thinking a great deal about you, Ruby. Though you do not say much in your letters I feel that things are difficult again just now and that you hardly know which way to turn. How I wish we could meet and talk. Ronald and I had a talk about holidays to-night. He wants to spend July yachting with Mungo in the West

Highlands, and then to go somewhere with Aunt Harry and me for August. Now I think with a little persuasion from me Aunt Harry would go off by herself for the greater part of July to her beloved Keswick Convention, which is a combination of Evangelical meetings and coaching in the Lake District. In that case could you not come north, and you and I should stay in rooms together at some place where Mungo and Ronald could visit us between their cruises? Wouldn't that be splendid? I do hope you will be able to come. The Bruces have asked me to spend the month with them at Aberfoyle, but I don't think I want to go. Let me hear from you soon.

Later.—Just as I was going to post this batch of journal off, your letter arrived. Fancy my forgetting that you have no holidays till August—what a wretched English custom! But it is still worse to think that all August you are compelled to be in such a crowded seaside place with your family. About my spending July in London with you—that is indeed a suggestion fraught with glorious possibilities, as they say. How to work Aunt Harry round to it is the only difficulty. But I shall see what can be done, you may be sure of that; and I'm sure Ronald will help me.

I am thrilled by your idea of leaving home in the

autumn and living in rooms of your own. You ask
could I possibly join you.   Ah, if I could !

July 1.—Ruby, I am coming to you for almost
the whole of July ! It is all arranged. I can start
on Wednesday. By then I shall have seen the
others off and put things straight at home. It was
Ronald that managed it, bless him ! Madge Bruce
is sulking because I am not going to Aberfoyle, but
in her present state of radiance I really don't see
that she need be considered. Duncan says I am
quite right to choose London when I have the
chance, and he thinks he may take a run up while I
am there. In that case you will meet him. I don't
think you will be able to help liking him. I have
written to Don John and to Miss Hepburn telling
them that I am going, and asking them both to
supper to-morrow night, when I shall be alone. But
I don't suppose either of them will come.

July 2.—I saw Ronald off this morning and
Aunt Harry in the afternoon. To-night was a wild
fiasco. I cannot even *begin* to tell you about it till
I see you. To my great surprise Don John turned
up and so did Miss Hepburn, *and so did Miss
McRaith* ! I don't know when I spent a more dis-
tracted and miserable evening. Each of my guests
was highly suspicious of the other. Don John had

the good sense to leave early, and the only satisfactory moments of the evening were those I spent saying good-night to him on the doorstep. He has given me two literary introductions in London, and says I ought also to call on the editor of *The Spokesman*. I shall do all he tells me. When I went back to the drawing-room I found Miss Hepburn and Miss McRaith having a really venomous argument about the Holy Ghost. It took me all my time to separate them and persuade Miss Hepburn to go home as I had all my packing still to do.

July 3.——Miss McRaith left early, thank heaven, and now everything is ready. I do hope the weather will be fine in London, for I have a new white dress that I am dying to wear. Here it is pouring with rain. How free and happy I feel at this moment! I only pray that I shall not meet any one I know in the train. For then I might have to talk instead of sitting and thinking by myself all the time. Do you know that desperate longing just to be alone and to think? Especially when I start on a journey among strangers I always feel deeply and quietly thrilled as if I were carrying some hidden treasure in my breast. Slowly, carefully, with a calm face, I draw it from its hiding-place and hold it, as it were, between my hands and upon my knees, not letting my eyes rest upon it at first, just wondering what it will appear like this time, what strange and wonderful changes I shall find in it when I come to examine it after so long of never looking at it. Then I give one glance at it and look away again, then another glance, then I turn my eyes full on it and gaze and gaze. What is this. treasure? Is it my soul? my experience? life? I don't know. I only know it is a treasure, and in being alone with it I am reconciled to the whole world, which is the highest form of happiness I know.

I have just time to say good-bye to Eliza (Nelly has gone home for a holiday) before the cab comes. No more journal to Ruby now for a month at least!

I forgot to say I have had a cheque for *three guineas* from *The Spokesman*! We shall spend it together in London.

THE JOURNAL

III

FANTASIA ON AN OLD THEME

III

FANTASIA ON AN OLD THEME

25 Blandford Terrace,
Glasgow, *August* 3.

My dearest Ruby,—Duncan and I had a very happy journey and got safe home three nights ago. I should have written at once, but since our arrival at the station, where, to our perfect surprise, we were met and treated to a regular reception by about a dozen friends, I have been in a state of mental and emotional distraction which is really painful. Somehow I never realised there would be this aspect to our engagement. In London there were only the two of us, so cosily lost among all those millions of people to whom our feelings and doings were no concern. There was no one but your dear self to bother about us, and you were so full of understanding and every true sort of kindness (all the more appreciated by me for the knowledge that you were yourself struggling against hard circumstances and depression) that it was always a joy to both of us to be with you. Any constraint between you and Duncan would have been a grief to me. But you do truly like him,

don't you, Ruby? I mean, you were not, were you,
being so nice to him *merely* out of friendship toward me? I know anyhow that Duncan likes and
admires you very much indeed—as well he may,
being a man of sense.

I cannot write more now. Again and again I
thank you for all you did for me in London, for
the wonderful time you made of it for me. I only
wish Duncan and I were still there and need not
have come back to Glasgow till we were married.—
Ever with love,   ELLEN.

Later. Sunday, Aug. 4.—Shall I ever be able
to write any more in my journal to you? I don't
think so. Now that Duncan and I are engaged,
the poor thing's back is broken for good. Now that
my thoughts are centred round him, I cannot set
down a record of them for any one else to read,
not even my dearest friend. Yet the impulse to
write in my journal has not left me. Far from it.
I never felt the need of it more than at this
moment, at the end of this whirling month of
silence, crowded impressions, and sensations. After
all, why should my getting engaged make me less
interested in the things around and within me, or
less anxious to get my thoughts clear by setting
them down? For me there is no clearness of
thought apart from writing. I doubt if there is

even full observation without writing. Because I hardly ever observe consciously at the time. I feel at the time. But it is not until I come to describe an incident on paper that the significant detail is made manifest to me. It is as if I only observed in retrospect and when the mists of emotion have cleared off. Perhaps it will be different when I am married. Very likely it will be. I feel that strongly. For one thing marriage must surely be of itself a clarifying and a liberating process. With such a channel for one's emotions one must be left beautifully free for detached observation, and with such an incomparable intimacy in one's life what need can there be for the intimacy of a journal? In a married life of even reasonable happiness I should imagine that such a thing would be an impertinence if not a sheer impossibility.

But I am not yet married. Nor shall I be, according to Duncan's inscrutable plans, till Christmas. And if I were to conclude that observation and clearness were dangers to my happiness, would you not say there was something wrong with my engagement? Mind, I am not certain about this last. I am simply asking the question—to myself as much as to you. Possibly at such a time a rightly constituted woman would either not want to think at all or would not feel the desirability for clear thinking. But even a rightly constituted woman could not, I think, assert that an engagement is of itself a clarifying experience.

I do, however, want to be clear within myself. Also I will confess that there is a second and perhaps even stronger, certainly a more passionate, motive in me which has grown to full consciousness since that Sunday evening three weeks ago at your house when you gave me all my entries of the past year to read over. How much I had already forgotten! How interesting I found it to be reminded! As I read I realised that twenty or forty years hence all our burning present will be no more, unless in some way we manage to preserve it. If we do record it, no matter with what intimacy and daring at the moment, it will then seem to us as remote as some Greek classic. As remote, but also as fresh, and possibly far more interesting to ourselves.

For think a moment! It is all very well to say that nothing dies, that every word, action, experience of a person's early life is stored up indestructibly in some kind of an essence which is given out long after in the shape of *character*, that is to say in a new, unrecognisable set of words, gestures, actions, and so forth. But is not this very transmutation a sort of death? I cannot understand the comfort that people like your mother find in the idea of transmigration of souls. If you are unable to remember your former life, and will not in your next life re-

member this, where is the difference between such
a process and common death? It is satisfactory,
of course, to know, as we all do without any exercise
either of faith or of fantasy, that our bodies, when
they rot, will go toward the living growth of
plants, and thence will help to nourish living men
and beasts. But where in all this is there any
survival of the personality? And to the individual
does anything else count *as survival*? If when I
reach fifty I have never borne a child, never even
had my youthful portrait painted, never, above all,
created, or had created for me, something definitely
individual, something unmistakably in my image
yet separate from myself—that is to say, some
personal record or some impersonal work of art
which shall yet enshrine my unique personality—
what is there left of my youth but a few incom-
municable and fading memories? Dare any one,
looking at the face of a very old and recordless
man, deny that his youth is almost completely
dead? His bright and glancing eyes, the gloss
upon his hair, his sweet ways as a child, where are
they now? His mother, who might at least have
told you of them, is dead these many years, and
stare into his own countenance as earnestly and as
long as you please, you will not catch a glimpse of
them there. He himself has forgotten them. Ask
him and see.

Ruby, how I love and treasure every kind of human record; no matter whether it be sad or gay, full of imagination or barren of invention, so long only as it bears the marks of truth and of the individual, I am grateful for it to the bottom of my heart. Just fancy, if no one were to cast such human bread upon the awful waters of life, how insupportable would be existence! And as I myself am neither more nor less than a human being, why should I not take heart and add my crumb to the rest?

P.S.—After all we are staying in Glasgow for August. With Ronald going early in September there are lots of things to be seen to in town for him. The Bruces are still at Aberfoyle, but their town house is open, as Dr. B. can only leave for week-ends. I expect Duncan and I shall do some coming and going.—Your friend,

E. C.

JOURNAL.

Sunday, Aug. 4.—Two whole weeks since I promised to marry Duncan! How lovely our first ten days were! London—no problems or ordered thoughts, not a single consideration outside our precious selves and our happiness. But these last four days in Glasgow have been full of questions, distractions, quite irrelevant excitements. I must adjust my altered life to fit the old framework. I resent this frightfully. That I should have to do so, and for so long, fills me with rebellious thoughts.

Only this morning Duncan and I nearly quarrelled over it. At least he would not guess that we nearly quarrelled, because he was unconscious of the sudden, terrifying seethe of anger against him that rose in me. I loved him all the more for it afterwards when he took me in his arms and we lost count of time, kissing and talking together. But there it was, and he never for one moment suspected it. How horribly easy it is to deceive a man ! One thing anyhow is clear to me from our talk. Duncan, deeply in love with me as I believe he is, really enjoys being engaged, even in Glasgow. He does not find it harrowing and upsetting, as I do, or he would *never* suggest our waiting till Christmas to be married. Why should he ? He is not the man to have asked me unless his own mind was fully made up. As for me, in the very moment I said *Yes* I shed my old life like a snake's skin and was ready to go forward into the new life with him as soon as he said the word. Yet it seems he thinks we must both go on marking time in our old surroundings for nearly five months ! Why ? It is not as if he were too poor to marry at once. He will be no better off by Christmas—much worse off

indeed, judging by the lavish way he is spending his
money at present, mainly on me. Is it for the sake
of other people—so that, as he said this morning,
‘ they may have time to get used to the idea’? I
should have thought, seeing no one up to now has
uttered a word except in congratulation, that this
was a case where we had only ourselves to consider.
But suppose it is, for some reason I can't fathom,
advisable. Then should I not be better to go on
with my teaching as before for the coming term?
For one thing I shall want to help Aunt Harry all
I can with the money for my trousseau. For
another, with Ronald gone on the first of September,
and existence a series of rapturous meetings with
Duncan and sickening partings from him, would not
at least a certain amount of compulsory work help
to steady me? I know I shall not be able to write.
That must be laid aside for the present, perhaps for
a long time—possibly for always. But teaching is
different. Teaching would, I feel, act as a sedative
and keep my nerves from going to pieces. Yet
Duncan wants me to give up my pupils and Miss
Sutherland's school all at once. When I objected
he said, ‘ Am I not enough for you then?’ As if
the trouble were not that he was far too much for
me !

Aug. 7.—Called at Endrick Street to try and

see Don John, but he wasn't there nor at the
Mitchell. Hope this means that he is busy with
coaching, but didn't like to ask his landlady. She
always peers suspiciously at me with little squinting
black eyes. D. J. does not know yet about Duncan
and me. Came straight home and wrote a short
note telling him the bare facts. Asked him to
come and meet Duncan at my Room. Duncan is
quite keen to meet him, but does not, I think, quite
realise him. ' Must be a queer old cove,' he says.
I have not told him about D. J. being drunk.

ABERFOYLE.

Sunday, Aug. 11.—Duncan is wonderful. He
say he *wants* me to write. He merely does not
want me to fall into ' the usual feminine mistake of
overdoing things.' The trouble is, I 'm afraid it is
my nature so to overdo !

We came down (he and I) yesterday to spend
Sunday with his family here. It is the first time I
have seen Mrs. Bruce or Madge since getting back.
Madge, besides being so happy about her own
affairs, is bubbling with joy over Duncan and me.
She says that for years it has been the dearest wish
of her life, and I feel she is speaking the truth.
Dear old Madge ! His parents are less demon-
strably pleased—Mrs. B. just a little fluttery and
anxious lest I should fail the least bit to appreciate

all her boy's wondrous qualities and the honour
done to me. Honestly I don't think I do fail. I
can't, it is true, lift my hands in admiration of
qualities he *hasn't* got, even to please her—*e.g.* I
cannot agree that his water-colours of Indian native
life are artistic masterpieces, and though Duncan
says I am right there, I can see he is just the least
bit vexed that I don't see them as better than they
are. On the other hand, I see lovely things in him
to which I think his mother is blind—*e.g.* his
adorable, terrifically masculine simplicity, and the
strength that goes with it, making hay of all my
subtleties and twists. A humiliating confession,
though—this tremendous, always superlative admiration of his home circle does continue to arouse
a definite hostility in me even now that we are
engaged. I thought this would go, but I still find
myself looking at him now and then with alien eyes.
When I see him as one of his family, a little wave
comes over me of an old, dreadfully familiar longing
—to give them all the slip, to fly away far and
alone. Then Duncan and I go for a walk and are
so pleased with one another that we hardly know
what to do with ourselves.

Aug. 12.—I lay awake for hours last night,
and little bright, as it were jewelled, pictures were
imprinted, each only for a few instants, on the

insides of my closed eyelids. It is a queer, exciting
game this. I discovered it when I was about fifteen,
and at one time used so to indulge myself in it that
I would lie sleepless for nights on end, and go about
by day with dark rings round my eyes. It is not
myself — consciously at least — that chooses or
summons the pictures. I merely will that the game
shall begin, after which I take the place of an eager
spectator. Once started, the scenes keep swimming
up as if by the decision of some hidden showman.
Each is a perfect surprise to me, not only in subject
but in the arrangement of figures and objects, yet
each is so clear and shining and so full of faithful
detail that I marvel at its fidelity. They are true
to life as art is true, but like the best art they
are purged of all irrelevances, and the primary
colours stand out purely. If I make any *conscious*
effort of memory all is spoiled at once. As it is, I
have scarcely time to examine one picture closely
before it vanishes, leaving but a few whirling lines
and stars until the next appears. None can be
exactly repeated. One of the most vivid last night
was of that evening in London when Duncan and I
got engaged. After the hot day, the hot summer
night with short heavy rain showers . . . the big
raindrops coming straight down through the darkness like splinters of crystal . . . after the shower
the smell of water, of watered dust, of thirsty trees

in the Bloomsbury square . . . to me for ever the smell of London. How I longed, as the trees for the rain, for Duncan to kiss me and tell me he loved me! And when he did, I felt so very happy, as if I had never really been unhappy in my life before and never would again, as if happiness was the basis and whole fabric of existence. There can be nothing so surprising and strange in a woman's life (except perhaps the birth of her first child) as the first kiss of a lover. Nothing in one's earlier life prepares one for that. My father, Ronald, various boy cousins had kissed me often enough. But I could never have foreseen this absolutely new, terrifyingly lovely experience . . . the energy, the flame, the savage force in a man. . . .

GLASGOW.

Aug. 13.—We came back together early yesterday morning. It was calm and misty—autumnal. I loved the drive to the station, though we had not much to say to one another. I felt neither happy nor unhappy, almost in a kind of coma. Duncan looked sleepy and very handsome. I wondered vaguely what he was thinking of . . . he certainly has that look of experience which I so much admire, especially in a man. I love the deep lines round his mouth. Yet when I ask him what he is thinking about, unless it is of me it is of nothing

very special.   And even of me he seems to think
'just generally,' as he calls it.   Except when he is
actually caressing me, I have hardly any inkling of
his feeling or thoughts.   Is it always so with men
and women ?

In the train we had a carriage to ourselves, and
something in the papers started us off on a stupid
discussion about suicide.   From that we got on to
the subject of foreigners, whom D. seems to dislike
almost as much as Madge does.   I listen with
deference to him as, unlike her, he *has* lived abroad
and has met all kinds and nationalities of men.
But I get unhappy and cross when he divides them
all into Dagoes, Dutchmen, and Niggers.   Boris
Fabian he would have called a Dutchman !   When I
said I *liked* foreigners and felt at home with them, he
simply laughed at me.   Then I grew hot and said I
felt him and his family more foreign to me—more
difficult to understand and be myself with—than a
person like Boris.   But he only laughed still more.
He refuses to take such things seriously.   Is he right ?
I am getting to know the peculiar, very physical joy
of giving way to his compulsion in certain matters.
This I distrust, as it leaves me feeling a little sick
afterwards, sick with him and with myself.   Yet I cannot be too sure that he is wrong.   He has an enormous
advantage over me in experience, and I should be a
fool if I were to run counter to that from merely

sentimental feelings. Besides, I want him to be right.

Aug. 16. — Joanna Bannerman's mother persuaded Aunt H. to let a Mr. Abramovitch address our Friday Meeting to-day. His subject was 'Jerusalem To-day,' and his face shone as if with oil, perhaps the authentic oil of joy . . . quite a youngish man. He spent the evening with us and talked to Ronald about Paris. He had only been there once on his way from Palestine, but enjoyed himself famously. He asked Aunt H. if she had ever been at the *Opéra Comique*, or at a *café chantant*! When she said she had *not*, he rubbed his hands and exclaimed, 'Ah, bud you od to make a point to go, Mees Carstairs! You are just wud of dose dat would amuse wudself *kolossal*!' He then began praising the excellence of the brandy they gave him with his black coffee in Paris, smacking his lips and asking if Ronald did not agree with him. Aunt H.—with an eye on Eliza who was clearing the things—loudly extolled the famous excellence of French coffee. But Mr. A. would not be headed off. 'Bud it vas de *brandy—eau de vie*—dey gif you *wid* de caffee,' he insisted. 'It vas of *dat* I am spikking. Do you nod agree, heh?' Impossible to discover whether he was pulling Aunt H.'s leg, or was quite simple. Ronald and I both

thought the latter.   When he went Aunt H. was
very angry with Mrs. Bannerman and said she would
never devote another of her meetings to Jerusalem.
She does not believe Jews ever 'get properly converted'!

Sunday, Aug. 18.—Am I a tiny bit hurt in my
vanity by the immediate and enthusiastic approval
of both Aunt H. and Ronald?   I'm glad, of course,
and should hate it otherwise.   Yet I thought they
would show just a little more distress at losing me.

Later.—R. and D. get on splendidly.   They are
so different; perhaps that's why they admire each
other so much.   Yet they are in some things alike.
D. thinks R. 'a very brilliant chap.'   R. says of D.
that he could hardly have chosen better for me himself.
R. is in great spirits these days, looking forward to
New York, pleased and relieved about me!   It is
curious to see how *relieved* every one seems about me!
The note is clearly discernible in their voices when
they congratulate me.   What did they think?
That I would be an old maid, or that I'd go wrong?
R. keeps saying that I am a lucky girl and that,
though it is no more than I deserve, still few in this
world get their deserts.   A good many other people,
including the Bruces, make no bones about it, and
our friend Miss McRaith especially tries to rub it in

that I am getting something much more like *her*
deserts than my own.   Up to now the only person
in Glasgow (flatterers like Dr. Sturrock aside) who
has suggested that Duncan is lucky to get me is
poor little Nelly.   She told Duncan the other day
that he was ' a braw man an' a',' but that if he
were ' three times as braw an' had twice the siller '
he 'd be ' no more than a match for our Miss Ellen ' !
Duncan was delighted with this.   So, I confess, was I.

When Ronald, Duncan and I are all together (fairly
often as Ronald is going so soon) R. likes to tease
me by begging D. not to fail in ' knocking the
nonsense out of me.'   To which D. replies that he
will do his best.   I feel like an unintelligent, unin-
telligible piece of goods that is being handed over
with nods, becks, and wreathëd smiles by one intelligent owner to another.   This is somehow not wholly
unpleasant.   I suppose all men are like this.   My
two dearest are, anyhow, so I may as well reckon
on it.

Aunt H. says—' As you feel no call to the Great
Work from which your father never turned back, not
even to that degree of choosing your husband from
among the Workers, the next best thing that could
befall your father's daughter is surely to be mated
with a good man usefully employed, and above all
employed in one of those distant climes where there
is great *natural* beauty, but of spiritual beauty none

whatsoever save that shed by the bearers of our
glorious Gospel overseas.' (I notice that for some
days after the Tea-and-Prayer Meeting Aunt H.'s
utterances are apt to be of this periodic nature, and
she takes great pleasure in rounding them off in the
true platform style.) The plain fact, of course, is that
she is heartily glad that I am to be handed over to so
steady, presentable, and successful a man as Duncan.
This is something of an eye-opener, for I had often
wondered how I should ever be able to leave her,
now that R. is going, without feeling her on my
conscience. She will miss me in certain ways, I
know, but not so much as she will miss R., and her
health and energy are such that our both going will
leave her free to throw herself more completely into
' the Great Work here at home.' I can imagine the
perfect orgy of meetings she will indulge in! It is
a comfort to know that in all material ways she will
be well looked after by the devoted Eliza. Already
she is planning a visit to us in India, and D. is
perfectly sweet, telling her all about the missions
and missionaries in our neighbourhood. He warned
me privately afterwards that I shall do well if I let
' these same good people ' see my ' very chilliest side,'
as they are mostly ' Dutchmen ' and social climbers
to boot, and should be steadily discouraged. Though
I have no great love of missionaries I found this a
bit hateful, and said so; but D. said I 'd soon realise

the wisdom of his advice when I saw the people and the situation for myself. Perhaps they are all like Miss McRaith, in which case I should certainly agree with him.

Aug. 24.—Have Don John and Miss Hepburn given me up for good? Are they the only ones who don't approve of me now? D. J. has not answered my letter written a fortnight ago. I have been three times to Miss H.'s house, always at different but likely times of day, and twice at least I could have sworn she was in, but I rang the bell in vain. The last time (three days ago) I thought I saw her peep at me between the slats of the drawn-down venetian blinds of the dining-room, and if this was so, then her refusal to see me is deliberate. I shoved a note into the letter-box telling her my news, just in case she may have heard it elsewhere and is offended because of my not letting her know myself. But she has not acknowledged my note. She is not ill, because Madge and Laura saw her in Sauchiehall Street yesterday. But though they passed her quite close and were nearly stopping to speak to her, she cut them dead. Madge says she looked 'a bit in the air.'

At nine this morning went to Endrick Street but did not call. Walked the length of the street slowly. My idea was that I might catch D. J. on his way to a pupil or to the Mitchell, where I have not been for an age. But he never appeared. Nothing but the dreary sounds of carpets being beaten and stone stairs scoured for Sunday.

ABERFOYLE.

At 10 A.M. met Duncan at Charing Cross, took train to Balloch, and spent the day on Loch Lomond. The little steamers are nice, like toys. Everything looked lovely and placid . . . a very still, warm day again with the leaves just beginning to fall round the water's edge. I wore my white dress and a sort of coat I made out of an old Paisley shawl of Mother's, which people stared at rather too much. We had a picnic on the shore near Luss and were caught in a heavy thunder shower, but crept under such a low, dense thicket of trees and bushes that we hardly got wet at all. The afternoon was fine and we went by boat to the head of the Loch and walked over to Aberfoyle. Duncan told me a lot of interesting things about his schooldays. He is a darling. It was perhaps silly wearing the white dress, and it got very draggled before the end, but it was this one, with the same yellow sash, that I wore the night we got engaged. We got here just in time for supper. R. and Aunt H. had gone earlier.

Sunday, Aug. 25.—Ronald's second last Sunday, so we are here all together—a joint family party. What is wrong with me? Am I fundamentally unwomanly, or what is it? This afternoon every one was chatty and full of Christian lovingkindness (Aunt H. and Mrs. B. don't really get on well under the surface), but I alone felt out of it . . . critical, hostile, rather miserable. A sickness comes over me. A voice cries in my ear, 'This is not your world! Get out of this! Find your own place!' But where, what is my world? I don't know. I only know I felt nearer to it—less hopelessly cut off—when Ruby and I were students in Frankfort. Why should Mrs. B., when she gives me solemn advice about bed-linen, or shows me the crochet she is doing for Madge's toilet covers, either bore me savagely or make me want to shriek with laughter? Are not these the people I have grown up among? Why should their thoughts be so unfamiliar, even grotesque, to me?

At night when I was going to bed, almost dropping with fatigue, Duncan whistled outside, and I threw on my clothes again and ran down to him in the garden for a few minutes. This made up for all that had gone before. In the moonlight he suddenly looked very young, like a boy god with ardent eyes, and he made me feel lovely too, and full of gifts

which were all for him alone.   But why are we
engaged?   I feel as if there were nothing but
crochet toilet mats keeping us from being married!
How, if all D. says is true, can he tolerate the
situation?

Aug. 27.—Very busy finishing things up for
Ronald, and while Aunt H. and I are in the shops
we keep getting things for me too.   R. has given
me a most beautiful little old silver teapot and
cream jug.   Aunt H. and I between us are getting
him a dressing-case with the plainest possible
fittings, but all of the best.   I think he will like it,
but he can never love it as I love his cream jug and
teapot.

Heard to-day that Archie Moncrieff, the doctor
cousin in Aberdeen, has married again (just seven
months after the beloved Peggy's death!), and what's
more, the woman he is marrying has two young
children that *are said to be his*!   'A most *lamentable*
business!' says Aunt H.   It just shows what his
famous devotion to Peggy was worth.   I expect she
herself put the devotion story about to save her
pride.   But perhaps she was too stuck on herself
even to suspect it.

Aug. 29.—Dobbin's concert in the Burgh Hall
to-morrow night!

Aug. 30.—Just come home from Dobinova's piano recital. I don't know which is the greater, my delight at her playing or my shame at the behaviour of her audience. A pianist of the first rank, but young and unknown, a heaven-sent genius with fire and honey in her finger-tips—and because she cuts her hair short and wears a black velvet jacket like a boy's, one can hardly hear her softer passages for the titters of Hillhead! She sits down at the piano, quite unaffectedly pushes a lock of hair over her ear, and—the imbeciles burst out laughing! She plays a Chopin study magnificently, and there is some applause at the end, but the whole way through, at the slightest, most natural move-ment of shoulders or hands in a staccato passage, people dig each other in the ribs and giggle audibly. Once, to their delight, she looks at them over her shoulder with a furious frown. With what satisfaction could I have murdered them all! She was ill-advised enough to play several pieces by an unknown composer—interesting but difficult music—and this gave her audience the greater opportunity to be facetious over her mannerisms, or what they considered her mannerisms, for to none but crassly provincial and ignorant minds could there have seemed anything here not consistent with the simple, youthful ardour of a highly expressive person. Dobbin in no way obtrudes herself between her music and any decent listener. It is simply that a striking personality and the effort made *by some one obscure as yet* to simplify her costume and coiffure strikes the Burgh Hall as intensely comic. In the Queen's Rooms or St. Andrew's Hall she might have been all right—protected. But her fool of an agent had exposed her to this! And in spite of it all she continued to play magnificently.

At the end I went to thank and congratulate her, and she was absurdly delighted. Her greatest success up till now has been in Munich, where she at once made good. Munich, and then this! I felt it impossible to apologise for Glasgow, but partly, I suppose, because of this, I had the overwhelming desire to see her heaped with honours and luxuries. But I had not money on me even for a cab. She had been travelling all that day and all the night before, giving a concert first at Leeds, then at Manchester, and arriving only just in time for her Glasgow recital. She had had nothing to eat since breakfast but a pork pie in the train. I went with her in the tram-car as far as her hotel, where I thought it kindest not to go in as she was almost beside herself with fatigue. I gave her my cairngorm brooch as a keepsake. It was the only thing of any value I had on me. Luckily it was the nicest piece of jewellery (not counting my engagement ring) I ever possessed. As she leaves early to-morrow morning and I have a lesson at the hour of her train, I shall not see her again. Good luck to her !

Aug. 31.—A day of small worries and constant demands on me which I should not mind so much if they served any special purpose. But I resent them because they are mostly *invented* demands. A bit disgusted with clothes and things. It is overdone . . . those consultations . . . this unending shopping, sometimes with Mrs. Bruce, sometimes with Aunt H. The two differ fundamentally on the trousseau subject. On the whole I prefer Aunt H. (though trying) in that line as in most others.

It is strange being engaged . . . all the familiar landmarks gone and my mind filled with restless, rather fearful visions of what the new ones are to be. They have not appeared yet.

It is like one of the changes wrought by magic in the fairy tales. A few weeks ago D. was only Madge's nice, attractive brother, the shape of whose back always gave me a queer thrill down my own spine. Now he is my present, my future . . . his shoulders blot out all the rest of the world. Yet till we are husband and wife I cannot really know very much about him nor he about me. When I try specially to be frank about myself he seems to *prefer* being left in the dark. As for me, I have no time, no peace to come to any decision or clear up the turmoil in my mind. I can hardly think. Between the two excitements — the novelty of showing myself off and being re-examined by every one as a woman betrothed, and the swamping hours of love-making, when my life is left like a shore strewn with wreckage—I have lost my old considering ways. I no longer live. I *palpitate* in a monotony of emotions. I can neither examine nor control anything. I merely react. Here is one clear observation that emerges. When I am with D., in spite of the deliciousness of being wooed and of feeling myself swept each time off my feet into ardent response, I am conscious of a deep and constant longing to get away from him, to be quite alone, to examine this new treasure of love without fever or elation. Yet no sooner am I alone than my mind begins to wheel in circles and I can examine nothing, nor feel anything but a longing to be once more in his arms and unconscious of a mind at all. There is something wearisome—frightening, too—in this pendulum existence. I often feel as if a touch from the outside might suddenly crystallise things for me and give me what now I wholly lack— some clear satisfaction and sense of direction. This, I think, is partly why I long so hungrily to hear what Don John has to say, or, if he would not speak, to read in his eyes what he in his wise remoteness

thinks of the whole thing. Once or twice I have
tried to tell Duncan something of my trouble, and
each time he has explained it logically enough, yet
not, I think, completely. He says it is quite natural.
This is a transition stage. Once we are married
and away by our two selves in India everything will
straighten out. But I can see that *he does not share*
my present distress. He could not so prolong our
engagement if he did. He thinks I have grown
'just a wee bit morbid,' being too much alone with
my thoughts, which is 'bad for women.' He believes
the life in India, with its tennis and riding, jolly,
rather superficial chatter, and *determined suppression
of serious talk*, will be the best possible antidote for
me. How I hope and try to believe that he is
right! He says I 'm sure to be a tremendous success
out there—that of course would be enjoyable—and
that I 'll have any amount of human nature to study
(*vide* Kipling, whose work unfortunately has never
meant much to me). But he warns me to beware
of one thing as of the devil. I must not speak of
anything abstract or 'superior,' or of 'high-brow
works of art,' unless I am content to be regarded as
a bore and a blue-stocking. I am to keep all my
real thoughts for him, and to 'let others be dazzled
by the small change of my wit.' He says life will
be all the more thrilling this way. For it will be
our delicious secret that he has married 'such a

serious little woman.'   It sounds all right, even very
flattering when he says it, but after a while I have
a paralysing vision of myself glum and silent on a
veranda among all the jolly Anglo-Indians, unable to
utter a single word *in case* I may blurt out something serious and so disappoint Duncan and make
an ineradicably bad impression in the station.   I
have told D. this, but he only laughs.   He laughs
at almost everything I say.   Perhaps it is the best
plan !   We were very happy this evening sitting in his
father's study till after midnight in the empty house,
for Dr. Bruce had gone to Aberfoyle for the week-end.

The date of our wedding is fixed for December 3.
We are going to the south of France for a Christmas
honeymoon, and sailing for India early in the New
Year.   It sounds very ' grand,' as Madge says.   All
very well, but Madge herself is to be married in
ten days.   And December . . . and this is still only
August !   It seems a bit silly to me.

Sunday, Sept. 1.—Ronald's last Sunday.   Nothing
of any significance was said or done, except that
we all went to church together at night—a custom
long since disused with us—and Dr. Sturrock seemed
to take account of us in his sermon, which was from
Revelations, about there being no more sea.   I cried
a good deal, though quite secretly, during the
service.   During the day I tried not to hang round

Ronald too much, and never even began to say any of the things my heart was bursting with. R. is very Scotch in those ways and prefers to take things as said, but he knew well enough what I was feeling. He was very gentle with Aunt H. and with me. But oh, how deeply glad he is to be off! And how I sympathise with him!

Sept. 2.—R. left this morning. He said he would rather say good-bye in Glasgow, so neither of us went to Liverpool with him. I woke before six, heard him moving in his room, and went in for about half an hour. We talked of nothing special. Only one thing . . . ' *whatever* happens at any time, Peg,' he said (he very seldom calls me Peg), 'remember there's always me.' And I said I'd remember. In the afternoon Aunt H. prayed a long time alone in her bedroom and was very sweet to me all evening. I had a good cry at night. I never felt the end of childhood till now.

Sept. 3.—The doctor taking Duncan's place in the district has turned ill. This may mean that D.'s leave will be cut short. I'm glad now that he made me give up my pupils. Everything is so far forward that I could be ready for us to be married in a week's time.

Sept. 4.—What a lovely autumn! To-day is colder. I had to wear a coat. But it is still beautiful, quiet weather with a very slight fog in the mornings. I like to see the melons in the fruiterers' windows. I miss Ronald fearfully.

Sept. 5.—Had a horrible dream about Duncan last night. He was coming toward me to kiss me, and all his face was mouth—one huge voracious mouth. In my terror at being devoured I woke up. Did not sleep again for a long time.

Sept. 6.—Our first real quarrel. Simply don't know what to do. Several cables have arrived from Duncan's *locum* to say he is worse. D. will have to go out within a fortnight. He is disgusted, but we both see the clear necessity. The question is our marriage. As this has happened, I ask why we should not be married at once. I can be ready, and should love, more than any Riviera honeymoon, the voyage together and the necessity of helping him in his work at once when we arrive in what is to be our home. But no! D. says September is *not the right time* for a bride to go to India . . . that we should have to separate at once, I to go to the hills for the rainy season . . . that even so, I might suffer from the heat . . . that he's sure I will want more time to get my trousseau together (oh,

that damned trousseau !) and so on. I have dug
out of him that in his district the climate is really
not considered bad in the rains, certainly not danger-
ous . . . only a little trying, but not so much so as
to have kept one of the German missionaries from
taking his bride there from Europe last August and
keeping her there . . . that 's to say, she has not even
needed to go to the hills yet. It must either be,
then, I tell him, that he regards me as a fragile
flower which must under no circumstances be allowed
to take the faintest avoidable risk, even for love's sake,
or that he dislikes the idea of what people may
say of him for not doing the absolutely conventional
thing. If the first is the reason, then he must
in his heart of hearts hold me inferior to
the missionary's wife and our love as less fervent
than evangelistic zeal. If the second is the reason,
he must consider himself superior to the German
missionary in fineness or breeding, or something else
that is ' undefinable but unmistakable,' as he once
said was the superiority of Englishmen to the rest
of human creation. In neither case can I see that the
point is arguable. With another woman it might
be, but I am not flattered by this particular kind of
solicitude. It isn't even as if the missionary's wife
has suffered from the heat, for the last thing Duncan
did before coming home on leave was to attend her
for her first baby, and if there had been any ill

effects, he would, I feel sure, have made use of them as unanswerable arguments. Three times now we have discussed the matter, and each time I have asked him to give me some good reason—good as between him and me—for the delay a sort of *wooden* look has come into his face, and he has told me that if he were to fail in 'perfect consideration' his love for me would not be 'the kind of love a man should have for his wife.' Then he actually told me with perfect solemnity—reminding me dreadfully of his mother—that the missionary's baby, though a full-time child, was born within seven months of its parents' wedding! 'And that's the sort of woman,' his expression said, 'that you are asking me to put you on a level with!' At this I completely lost my head, exclaimed that he could take all the credit for that himself, as personally I should be not only willing but delighted to be in the same case myself . . . that I thought it 'a long sight more decent' than what seemed the ordinary course of an engagement between two young and warm-blooded people like ourselves . . . that I didn't want 'the kind of love a man *should have* for his wife,' or anything that any one *should have* . . . that I only wanted his—Duncan's—love for me—Ellen. At first I thought he was going to be angry, but instead, a look I have never seen before came into his eyes and he kissed me almost brutally. He called me 'a jewel of a girl,' said that other men would envy him fearfully if only they guessed what I was like, and swore we were going to have a glorious existence together. But though I could not help responding in a way, I never before felt so mentally cool and observant in his arms. He too must have been less carried away than he seemed, for afterwards, when I asked the same question again, ' Shall we be married at once then ? ' he simply laughed, took his arms away, and shook his head in as perfect an obstinacy as ever. ' You thought you 'd get round me that way, you little villain ! ' he said. ' But I mean to do the right thing in spite of all your sorceries ! ' I didn't know whether to slay him for his lack of understanding or to adore him for his sheer masculine fatuity. Anyhow I have made up my mind not to have another argument on the subject. If *for any reason* he prefers to wait till the New Year for me, I 'll not be the one to thwart him.

Sept. 7.—Cooler to-day, within and without ! There may after all be something in what D. says, that getting married out there will be much jollier than it would be in Glasgow. Both he and I dislike the dismal middle-class feeling of a Glasgow wedding, especially when the ceremony takes place in the drawing-room, as Aunt H. would wish it. In India we can have everything arranged just as we choose without considering any one but ourselves. Also, he says that he will take me to Kashmir for our honeymoon in January and we shall live in a house-boat. That of course will be splendid. He leaves on the fifteenth. I don't realise it yet.

Sept. 8.—Two Anglo-Indian friends from D.'s district — a Deputy Commissioner and his wife (English)—have been seeing the Trosachs, and D. has invited them to lunch to-morrow at the N.B. Station Hotel, so that I may be introduced. I had thought of wearing my white dress if it was a fine day, but D. says this is an occasion in which such 'sweet-seventeenishness' might make the D.C.'s. wife rather patronising. 'They think a lot of themselves, those I.C.'s,' he says, and 'this is a case for smartness above all. . . . I want to watch the condescension fade out of Mrs. B.'s eagle eye when she sees the little Glasgow girl who is marrying me . . . what about that black silk frock with the ruchings that make the skirt swing ? '

So the black it shall be. I mean to do my very best to please D. and impress his friends.

Sept. 9.—What a day ! I did my best, but I failed.

First thing after breakfast I went and had my hair washed at Brumby's, and got the man (such a clever German) to dress it in the new way, rather close to the head and in a roll at the back which becomes me surprisingly well, though I think it makes me look a bit older, especially with the black taffeta, which is a French model and one of my best trousseau things. I wore my black patent shoes, which pinch me a bit, and black silk stockings, and white gloves—no colour at all except for my little rose-coloured bridesmaid's hat. When D. called for me he said I looked ' so bewitchingly smart ' that he was half afraid to kiss me. But he did kiss me, so much indeed that we almost made ourselves late, for I had to go and put on my hat again and practically re-do my hair. Just as I was going to tidy myself D. pulled quite an ordinary looking little crushed paper packet out of his pocket and rather shyly handed it to me saying, ' You might try these on at the same time and wear them if you like them well enough.' ' These ' were pearls ! Real ones—a most lovely string, neither too big nor too small, and the most beautiful colour ! Oh, Duncan ! When I came back with them on I almost scolded him, but he knew by the tears in my eyes how I loved them, coming from him. He said they were not half good enough for me. He just spoiled things a wee bit by adding, ' Mrs. B. will be green with envy, I'm thinking!'

When I saw Mrs. B. I marvelled that Duncan could think it worth while taking any trouble whatsoever to impress her. There are people below the average in every apparent way—in looks, in taste, in charm, in manners, in brains, and in feeling— who yet go about declaring, as it were, with every accent and gesture that *for some reason,* unknown and undiscoverable by others, they are *special* sort of people deserving, without themselves making any effort, to have special treatment on their way through life. Mrs. B., I think, is one of these. If the waiter was a bit slow, if the window was not at the right angle to her seat, if the soup was cold, it was not simply a nuisance, as it would be with most people ; it was a thing that *ought* not to happen where she was concerned, or probably where any of her family was concerned. This attitude to life is so interesting to watch that once or twice I quite lost myself in observation, thinking what a good character such a woman would make in a play. Aunt H. has a friend like that—an ugly oldish woman who wears horrible clothes and has a moustache and straggly hairs on her chin. She does not even keep her ears clean, is not rich nor clever, is no more a saint than she is a sinner. Yet with each word she utters she proclaims that she is an important and remarkable woman. And many people in Glasgow take her at her own valuation, perhaps because it happens that her father was a remarkable and eloquent Free Church minister.

Mrs. B., to do her justice, was not so bad as
that. She was just commonplace and thought herself a lot more. She was touched up, though not
dashingly so—the kind that doesn't *dye* her hair,
only 'uses a hairwash'; doesn't rouge, only rubs a
little lip-salve on her cheeks. And with half-hearted
results. Her husband had a thin, withered-up face
—rather nice—and wore spectacles. All went fairly
well at first. After a few polite remarks to me
about the Trosachs—something as if it was a
private garden of mine and as if I were responsible
for the bad weather they said they had had there
—they plunged with D. into an extremely animated,
gossipy conversation about people in the District.
The talk *in itself* was not very exciting, as they
did not seem concerned with the people they talked
of *as people*, but only in so far as their doings affected
life in the District. Naturally I could not join in
much, and once or twice I found myself wanting
to yawn. Yet I was interested of course. Those
were Duncan's friends they were speaking of, the
people I am going to live among, and it was quite
amusing trying to piece together characters in the
District from the remarks and stories I was listening
to. But what interested me far more deeply was
the liveliness of the talkers. D.'s vivacity simply
amazed me. Though a cheerful soul, he is usually
rather silent. But here he was, chattering and

laughing without pause, and with perfect spon-
taneity. I could hardly take my eyes off him. He
became aware of this, and began to parade himself
very subtly before me. Once, as I was watching,
at the same time smiling and fingering my pearls,
our eyes happened to meet and I felt myself go
hot all over under my clothes. He and I knew,
but I don't think any one else could have guessed
anything from my face.

When we came to the ices there was a lull, and
it seemed as if they felt, all three at the same time,
that I ought to be included more in the conversation. Mr. B. had already half apologised once or
twice, but I had each time begged them to go on,
saying it was very interesting to me. Now, however, they felt it was time some remarks ought to
be addressed directly to me, and Mrs. B. pulled
herself together. For a few instants she cast about
for a subject, staring all the while at my pearls
as if she was wondering if they were real. Then
she asked me if I was ' fond of reading.'

I daresay it is silly and socially unskilful in me,
but this question, ' Are you fond of reading ? ' always
has something of the same effect on me as the
question Aunt H.'s missionary friends used to ask
me in my teens if I was unlucky enough to be left
alone with one of them for a minute—' Ellen, do
you love Jesus ? ' As I don't like to be rude and

laugh, I feel myself getting red, and I wildly question within myself whether I should answer ' Yes,' or ' No,' or ' It depends on what you mean,' or ' At times,' and what the immediate effect of each answer would be. In this case, to make things pleasant I replied fairly quickly and in a cheerful tone, ' Yes, I 'm very fond of reading . . .' and then something compelled me to add, ' some books.'

Mrs. B. smiled, though in rather astonished agreement. ' *Some books!* ' she echoed. ' How true that is ! There 's such a lot of trash, isn't there ? Now, myself, I have a perfect *passion* for reading, but I can't stand trash. Who are your favourite authors ? '

The conversation that followed was frightful in its sheer hopelessness. I honestly struggled not to be ' superior,' but perhaps the look in D.'s anxious but unhelpful eye drove me on to say things I should not otherwise have thought of. I had not read a single one of the novels she enthusiastically praised for their ' quaintness,' ' daring point of view,' etc. And when I was driven back on to the standard novelists (when she asked me what *had* I read ?) it became too obvious that she was lying when she pretended to know more about them than their names. I saw a quick, *summing-up* glance pass between husband and wife, and D. saw

it too, for a little frown of displeasure came between
his brows. By this time I didn't care if he *was*
vexed, for I thought it mean of him not to have
come to my rescue in some way. Again and again
I longed to say, ' Let's change this painful and
futile conversation.' But that would have been impolite, so it had to peter out drearily.

By good luck we got next on to clothes, and I
asked Mrs. B.'s advice about having my habits
made for side-saddle or riding astride (I have been
having lessons in both ways). But then unfortunately Mr. B.—meaning I am sure no harm—asked
if I played bridge. When I said I didn't, and was
not fond of card games, another glance was exchanged. It was as if I had told strict Church of
England people that I was ' Chapel.' Mr. B. tried
to rally. ' That's bad,' he said, only half jocularly.
' You'll have to put that right ! '

' Why the devil . . . ! ' I nearly shouted out . . .
' I hate cards. They bore me. And I don't mean
to learn to please you or the whole of India ! ' But
for D.'s sake I refrained. I merely said, ' Don't you
think it might be stupid of me to learn a game that
doesn't attract me, and for which I have no apti-
tude ? I should only spoil it for the good players
like Duncan. I shall be quite content to sweep up
his winnings.' This last remark, as it turned out,
was singularly unfortunate, for, as D. has now told

me, he is not merely a good but a lucky player, and off and on Mr. B. has lost a good deal of money to him !

When it was over I felt all anyhow, and very nearly cried walking down Buchanan Street with D. And then he really was sweet. He damned the B.'s and everybody, said what did it matter if I played no bridge or was a regular blue-stocking. I was worth all the treasure of the Indies, and I was not to bother my head with such trifles. It was only three o'clock, but he took me to Brassey's, and we drank tea and sat there talking fairly happily till after five. Once I asked him——*Suppose*, after we were married, that instead of playing tennis and things I wanted to sit dully at home writing 'high-brow' stories, would that be painful to him ?

At this he looked a little troubled, but he took it seriously, as I had prayed he would, and very reasonably said he would never like to stand in my way, but he thought I was ' so much a woman' that what I suggested was unlikely to happen. 'Life,' he said, ' is a bigger affair than books, and life is pre-eminently your business. Wait till your hands are full of life, and I doubt if you will have the time or the wish to add to the mass of feminine writings already in the world.' This, I must say, deeply impressed me.

When I asked—didn't it seem unfair that men-

writers could write, and yet not be stinted of life?
—he agreed that perhaps it was unfair, but that
things were like that, and had to be faced.

I feel that he is right, and yet that *somewhere*
there is an untruth in his argument. It is true that
if I had to choose between writing and life I should
choose life. But then I couldn't do otherwise, for
without living myself I *know* I couldn't write : I am
not imaginative enough. And is any one? Besides,
I feel that even if I had ten children D. would still
want me to play tennis and ride with him. And
how are tennis, dancing, riding *more* ' life ' than
writing?

While we were in Brassey's Mungo came in. He
was by himself, quite clearly not meeting any one,
and was just making for the only vacant table with
his queer stooping walk when he caught sight of us.
He then immediately made an elaborate pretence,
not only that he had not seen us, but that he was
looking for some one he expected to be there, passing
his eye over each of the other tables except the
vacant one, and finally retreating with a vaguely
disappointed air from the shop. Dear old Mungo !
I suppose that is his way of showing delicacy ! I
wanted to rush out, seize him by the arm, and make
him join us, but I know he really doesn't much like
Duncan. Duncan swears he is in love with me, but
this is nonsense. He is just a bit vexed that his

beloved Ronald's sister is engaged to a man he doesn't take to. I had forgotten Mungo when I said that Nelly was the only person not falling over herself with congratulations.

Sept. 10.—Madge's wedding to-day. She looked ever so sweet and happy, and all was well, but somehow the ceremony depressed me, or rather struck me as vulgar. There was a little dance afterwards, but by eleven I felt so weary that I slipped off home without saying a word to any one. Aunt H. had gone to bed. I threw myself into the big arm-chair in the dining-room, almost too tired to undress. I could hardly bear the sight of a pile of my unanswered letters (all duty ones—congratulations and presents) on the writing-table. Deep sunk in meditation when D. turned up, having missed me and followed me home. We had one of those strange talks in which I keep trying to be clear and honest with him, but in which he seems as if he would prefer me to be otherwise. Then I gave it up, sat on his knee, and we ended as usual. I was almost fainting with exhaustion when he left at 2 A.M.

Sept. 11.—A queer, dark, foggy, oppressive day.

Is this indeed a part of love—this strain and effort to be what the loved one wants, or at any rate

not to appear different from his ideal? It is a
kind of discipline, and so may have some good in it.
All the same there is something wrong somewhere,
I'm sure, if it makes itself too much felt.

Last night in bed (in spite of being so tired) I
thought of a wonderful idea for a short story. I'm
convinced it is the best I have had yet, and I lay
awake, first thinking out the detail, then sleepless
with sheer dread that I might die before getting it
written. I heard the University clock strike every
hour till the five-minutes bell began clanging for
the eight o'clock classes.

Sept. 12.—What would D. say if I would only
marry him at New Year on condition that we should
be lovers in the full sense of the word before he
goes? I can see his face—a mixture of wooden-
ness and horror—at the mad question, which of
course will never be asked! Yet my Puritanism
does revolt against what seems the ordinary course
of an engagement. I should feel it far less dis-
orderly, both morally and mentally, for us to be
living together without any last reserves. It is
these last reserves that are the devil! How is it
that he doesn't see it? I certainly feel quite as much
bound to him as if we had discarded everything.

But have I 'the love a wife ought to have for her
husband'? Does he in his heart want me to give

myself—my real, natural self—to him? Can I give him what he wants of me, even if I am willing to maim and bind myself and cut off half of myself to please him? Have I the right to go on trying to alter myself just because he attracts me, and because he asks it of me? Will it not somehow in the end hurt *him* more than me if I persist?

Later.—To be simply honest, simply decent— what courage that takes at times!

Later.—D. says a husband makes his wife's world . . . that she gets to like his friends better than her own. This may be true. But I don't *want* to like people like Mrs. B. He says she is 'very decent when you have to live with her'! But fancy *choosing* to live with her! (He has admitted she is fairly typical of the station.) He says one does not choose such things in life. But why not? Surely some people do. Of course one may *choose not to choose*, as men do when they go into the army, the navy, the priesthood . . . as women do when they marry men whose minds are made up. . . .

Sept. 13.—D. goes to-morrow. I can hardly bear it. To-day he hired a car and I got together a picnic and he drove me down to Loch Lomond— just our two selves, not even a chauffeur. It was a glorious hot day, and we camped by the edge of the water where it was half grass and half gravel, with a little copse of silver birches running right to the loch's edge. We both paddled out up to our knees, and afterwards lay in the sun and dried ourselves. He looks his best in the country and when he is sunburnt. I love all the photographs he has shown me of himself in India. He looks such a *jolly*, hearty sort of man. There under the trees with his bare legs, eating sandwiches and gazing lovingly at me, he was beautifully manly and so simple that I adored him and felt at peace. Only when he began talking of how dreadfully long the time was going to seem to him, all my blood rose in my throat as if to choke me. I felt such furious anger against him that I had to cram nearly a whole hard-boiled egg into my mouth at once to prevent myself from crying out, 'Isn't it your own doing?' and so opening up the vain discussion. I turned my head away so that he shouldn't see how unbecomingly full my mouth was, but one tear after another began running down my face, and as his hand was in my lap one tear fell on the back of it, and he looked and saw I was crying. How could he know they were tears of pure anger? When he hugged me I just let him think it was sorrow. Perhaps it was cowardly, but I couldn't bear to spoil our last day.

It was late when we packed up to go home.

There was a greenish sky, like some fabulous liquor that, if you could drink a great draught of it, would make you live for ever, and the long curving clouds, enclosing it into many lakes, were dark dove colour, and little silver stars began swimming in swift, straight routes across the lakes of lucent green. From one dove-coloured shore to another they passed intent, like homing bees that had stayed too late away from their hives and feared the overtaking of the darkness. Up there, there must have been a wind, but in our copse it was perfectly still. We did not speak at all, but sat locked in each other's arms, and gradually every thought died out of me till I was empty as a shell, but like a shell vibrating to the faint and marvellous humming of the living universe. It is only now I come to write of it that I know what were the colours of the sky, and that the stars seemed like bees in their straight, unerring flight. If I were capable at one and the same moment of conscious, observing sight and of the emotion aroused by such a spectacle as the sky at sunset, I do not think I should go on living. It would be too intense a condition for the frame of my flesh to endure. There have been moments—rare and soon over—when my emotions and my reasoning faculties have both been wide awake at once. But at such times I have been nearly shattered by the fullness of existence.

The drive home in the dark was heavenly. D. kept his left arm round me as long as we were in the country, and I felt I didn't care if we ran over a precipice and were smashed into smithereens. Even that would have seemed bliss in that exalted moment. All the same I knew well enough that D. was perfectly sure of his driving or he would not have risked using only one hand. It was just a lovable little bit of showing off to impress me; which it did. When we got among the traffic again he took his arm away.

Later.—D. says the B.'s were 'greatly impressed' with me! They spoke about me to some one who mentioned it in a letter to D. I can see that D. is gratified. The absurd thing is that so am I.

Sept. 14.—I could cry and cry. Duncan went this morning.

Later.—We only had a hurried, scrappy good-bye (not even 'distasted with the salt of broken tears'— how marvellous that use of the adjective 'broken'! How it betrays not only Shakespeare's genius, but his own experience of love!), and were by ourselves scarcely more than five minutes. Just as well perhaps. Everything that could be said (how little!) was said yesterday, so however long it had lasted, we could only have dragged out the misery of parting. D. was still quite sunburnt from yesterday. And my forearms have each a bright scarlet patch, quite painful when he kissed them again and again, saying he would never forget last night by the edge of the loch. I am to write to him and he to me every day.

Everything at home seems echoing and empty. I can't read or anything and almost wish I had to give a lesson to keep my thoughts from turning round and round in the same fruitless circle. I hate a waste of energy and emotion. If it could not be helped, I should at least not feel such resentment. But it is so *stupid* that I am left here behind . . . such a sin against nature and common sense. I could cry and cry. I did cry a good deal in the afternoon, but ended by being angry again. Bother everything!

Sunday, Sept. 15.—Very tired, sleepy, and nervous after a bad night. Refused to go to church, and while Aunt H. was there took down the crystal chandelier, washed all the dangles and put them back. A long and tiring job, especially having to hold one's arms up for such a time. But had to do something. Aunt H., who came back before I was finished, was angry at first, but suddenly after a look at my face became quite mild.

Sept. 16.—Felt gloomy and wretched. It was a positive relief when Aunt H. came and asked me to type a lot of post-cards for the Prayer Meeting next Friday. So passed the morning. In the afternoon the day turned very dark, and then it rained. I tidied all my drawers and wardrobe.

Sunday, Sept. 22.—A dreary week. How on earth am I to pass the time between now and January, with Ronald gone and all? It's very fine for Duncan with his work, but he has taken mine away from me! I shall look up Miss Hepburn and Don John. If no one answers the door I'll get in by a window.

Sept. 24.—Since D. left, I have written as I promised, a letter every day. I don't find much to say, though, and the question is always cropping up —why have I to write at all to him? Why are we separated? Perhaps when I hear of his arrival it will be easier. He will have lots to tell me about, even on the voyage. Oh, how I envy him being on the sea just now, seeing new people and everything!

Sept. 25.—D.'s first letter this morning from Marseilles. Naturally nothing much in it. He has bought me a pink embroidered kimono which should arrive soon. Pearls, kimonos . . . all these things instead of taking me with him !

Sept. 27.—Aunt H.'s Tea-and-Prayer Meeting. We had limelight views (something very special, not at home but in the Burgh Hall) of missionary work in Patagonia. What a place to live in ! The missionary himself was so enthusiastic about the climate and the people and everything that it was impossible to understand the need for any one to go trying to alter the ways of life out there.

Pink kimono arrived. Very pretty and suits me.

Oct. 5.—First letter about voyage from Duncan, posted at Port Said. He tells me less of himself in it than of the people on the boat, and I don't find them interesting as I should if I were with him. His descriptions—' very decent fellow,' ' pleasant girls,' ' amusing chap '—don't give me much to go upon. He says no one has succeeded once in driving me out of his thoughts for even a moment. I hope not ! Yet when he tells me of a very pretty girl on board who shows a ' friendly disposition ' toward him, I feel he does it to see if he cannot make me feel a little jealous. Perhaps he has succeeded. I 'm not sure. I wish his way of writing did not make me so critical of him.

Sunday, Oct. 13.—An unforgettable day.

Will any one ever be able to explain why on some days, though one may feel quite cheerful and even happy, one sees a world without any magic in its outlines and colours? With me, when such days have followed one another in a fairly long succession —say for a week on end—I begin to wonder if this may not be the true and normal vision of life. It isn't so bad . . . not deplorable at all, and I am almost prepared to accept it and to condemn any other vision as highly coloured, sentimental, or false. Then one morning I wake, and opening my eyes I see the light coming through the blind and falling quietly on the bed, or I notice a bubble of light quivering on the ceiling, and it is as if at that moment I saw light for the first time. I feel as if I had been allowed to sit beside God while He uttered the words ' Let there be light,' and I am overwhelmed by the majesty and mystery of everything. After lying still a while, adjusting myself with joyous caution to the pressure of emotion that threatens my very identity, I get out of bed and pull up the blind. Again the walls of my being are almost shattered by whatever first meets my sight. It may be something admittedly beautiful, like budding trees, or grass, or the blue sky and sunshine. But it may just as well be a dull sky and a grimy back garden wall; the marvel of life strikes no less powerfully at me. It isn't that I think the grimy wall as beautiful as a budding tree, but at the moment it conveys the mystery equally well, so that my being is flooded with worship. I suppose it would be the same on such mornings if I were to wake in a cell out of which I could not see at all. The clamorous voice would reach me through the very stones and plaster, the floor and ceiling, each held in its place by the force of gravitation and a hundred other marvellous laws. Sometimes I wonder could I endure it if a scene of tremendous and famous beauty—say the Bay of Naples—were at such a moment to lie stretched before me! Would not my being then fly upward like a tiny smoke-wreath from some altar fire?

And such days do not come only when there is physical well-being. I have known them come when I felt tired and neuralgic, quite as surely as when I stretched myself in perfection of bodily health. They may of course have physical causes, but are not these causes as mysterious as the result? Sometimes in the middle of a day it will come upon me suddenly. I cannot understand or explain it. I can only say that when it comes it simplifies everything, and I *know* that I am then nearer to reality, more normal, less apt to be misled and carried away into mistakes, than during the days when there is no magic.

To-day has been magical from the moment I woke. As I dressed I felt an exquisite fire running in my veins, and during breakfast I had to hold myself carefully and quietly in case I should fly to pieces from the sheer extremity of my aliveness to everything. The bread and butter and bacon were beautiful in themselves and were symbols of a greater beauty—of all the corn and oil and wine of human life, the salt, the herds of beasts used by mankind in the world through the ages. The tea poured into Ronald's old nursery mug showed me all his childhood and mine as if in a single bright drop of crystal water, and I saw that he and I had our places and our histories in the world along with all the other men and women that had ever lived. Tears rushed like a fountain from my heart, but none to my wondering eyes, as that would have broken and dissolved the vision.

After breakfast I could settle to nothing, could only wander about gazing at everything and touching things here and there as if I had never seen them before, till I began to feel a little light-headed. So I put on my hat and went round to see if I could not get hold of Miss Hepburn, which after all I had not done since Duncan left. It is necessary at such times, I find, to tether myself by doing some definite, and if possible useful, action such as tidying up all my drawers. When I got to the house the blinds in front were down as usual, but I rang only once before the door was opened by old Mr. Hepburn, who at once asked me to come in, and then in the little dark entrance hall, before I could ask a question, he said in a perfectly quiet voice, 'She's gone.'

I answered with equal quietness, 'Gone, Mr. Hepburn! Is she dead?' To which he replied, 'No, she's pit awa'. They've ta'en her tae Woodilee.'

'To Woodilee?' I asked. For the moment I did not grasp the significance of the name.

'Ay, tae the asylum. . . . It's better so. I've nivver had any comfort. Ill tae live wi', she was, puir buddy. It was aye the same. . . . Her mother—I'd a heap o' trouble wi' her. A heartbreaking time . . . the change o' life, ye understand—I'd no peace till they pit her awa'—but I shouldna talk—ye're a young woman. Ye'll excuse me.'

He went on to tell me how, ever since that supper party she had given for me and for him, she had thought they should neither eat nor drink any more, as eating or drinking more would be a desecration of that occasion. She did not allow him, he said, to eat what remained of the feast, but three times she made soup of the chicken bones, using every scrap off the plates. This, she declared, was, as it

were, a rinsing of the holy chalice with water, as
they do in the Church of Rome, drinking the three
rinsing waters so that not one tiniest drop of the
sacramental wine should be thrown away. But of
course the last boiling was hardly soup at all, and
after that any food he brought in she burned on
the fire as an oblation, so he had got nothing but
what he ate outside or in the office, while she sat at
home smiling happily but growing every day thinner
and weaker.

It was impossible to offer him sympathy, as he
seemed quite happy and relieved about the turn
things had taken, now and then pulling out his
little green bottle of smelling-salts and sniffing at
them with his small, sharp, waxy nose. So after
talking a few minutes longer and saying I would
visit his daughter at Woodilee any time he thought
wise, I shook hands and went away.

Out in the street I wondered what I should do
next, and began vaguely walking westward along the
ridge of the grey, stony hill with high black houses
on either side. Here again I seemed to see the
stones and houses and lamp-posts for the first time
—no, rather as if I had been long dead in the
grave, had come to life again, and these stones,
houses, and lamp-posts, full of passionate memories,
were the first things to meet my restored sight.
There was at once a freshness and a familiarity in

merely looking at them which was deeply moving and exciting. 'Am I too going mad?' I asked myself. But not in any real anxiety. For I knew that I was perfectly sane, and that it was only the rarity of such naked glimpses of reality that made me feel strange.

Glasgow is a curious place. Sometimes for weeks at a time you seem never to see more than a strip of unimportant sky between the high dark buildings. Then one day you find yourself on the summit of a hill like Cathedral Street, and there you are, suddenly aloft as on a stone cairn with nothing round you but leagues and leagues of grey sky. When I had been walking a few minutes I found myself so to-day. Then, just as I was standing looking round me and drawing a deep breath, there was Don John on the opposite pavement. He was not looking at the sky but on the ground, pacing along slowly like a monk in a cloister, and did not see me till I ran across and took hold of his coat. We walked on together till we came to a seat where we sat down and talked for more than an hour. I told him all about Duncan, and he spoke both prudently and well about my engagement and about many things. D. J. may have given up all that makes life sweet and easy and successful, but he has got the seeing eye in exchange.

MEMO. OF SOME OF THE THINGS D. J. SAID TO-DAY.— Importance of being able to differentiate *in time* between circumstances which will right themselves and so may be let alone and may easily be endured, and circumstances which one must oneself take in hand and change without delay, with violence if necessary. . . . Equal importance of remembering, and never missing out of one's reckonings, the circumstances which cannot and never will be altered during one's lifetime . . . most disastrous mistake of all to flatter oneself into thinking that *because* the alteration of such circumstances would be highly convenient and pleasant to oneself, *somehow* there will come the desired alteration. Such a belief may give courage, but it is apt to be a momentary courage only, and even if it should endure, being a courage founded on a lie it will somewhere do an injury, the worse for being unconscious. (I suppose he means that circumstances of the unalterable kind are chiefly temperamental, temperament being more utterly fatal—*i.e.* not subject to free will—than the more external circumstances which mere courage and faith may shatter. 'Faith,' says D. J., 'will certainly remove some mountains. But there are other mountains that are irremovable by faith, and it is a great thing to distinguish one kind from the other.'

He never once talked *at* me, but since I left him

I have been applying all he said to myself and Duncan.

Oct. 26.—To be a perfectly womanly woman—how I should like that! I 'm not *quite* sure what a womanly woman is, but I know at least some of the things that make one unwomanly. Some are quite simple, such as lack of attention to one's person and appearance, a too intense interest in intellectual matters, a too critical attitude, a lack of domestic gifts, a desire to fight for oneself, or to be regarded —at times anyhow—not essentially as a woman but as a human being. But these are all things that can be held in check simply by making an effort. I want to go much farther than that—farther, I suspect, than modern middle-class life will let me. I should like to be the chosen love of some great warrior or statesman or artist of genius who would know how to give a woman her place in his life and how to keep her in that place. Then I should use all the brains and energy I had in making myself beautiful and for ever interesting and desirable in his sight. I could sit for hours on end brushing and braiding my hair, scenting and arraying myself, never reading in a human book, but gazing at the sunlight and the trees and waters, and weaving my own thoughts into tales for my beloved which he would say confounded the wisdom of sages in their depth and simplicity. Yet as well I should learn of the wisdom of the sages from my master, whispered between his kisses, and through him alone I should know of the world of men, just as he through me would know of the earth, stars, and flowers. Of the love between men and women there would be nothing I should not know. Also I should be skilled in charms for sleeplessness and all anxieties and illness. Joyfully I would bear and suckle many children, growing fat and comely as I became older, a mother and comforter to all the men that came my way, one to whom they would run like children with their troubles asking me for counsel gained direct from life and the quiet untaught thoughts of my own heart. Then when I was very old— a shrunken little clove of a woman or a lumbering ancient female, wise as a serpent, I'd sit over the fire, smoking an old pipe, reading the hearts of my grandchildren, and dreaming of my own rich life.

But for such an existence not merely the women but the men are needed and a revolution of the whole social framework. If we would passionately insist—not merely fretfully exclaim—that women should be 'kept in their place'; if all men were individually male and creative, it could be done. But the men as much as the women want to eat their cake and have it. The woman must remain womanly, yet she must also be this and that and the other, all incompatible with the essence of womanliness which is surely leisure. Like the girl in Meredith's poem—

> 'She must flourish staff and pen
> And touch with thrilling fingers,
> She must talk the talk of men
> And deal a wound that lingers'

—which sounds very jolly, but is really rot—that is to say, nature doesn't work that way, so will be sure to revenge herself on the woman that tries it. Can't I see the poor girl, goaded on by Meredith, trying to live up to this and getting thin and stringy about the neck with the effort to keep going? And can't I hear the sighs of relief with which, when she left the smoking-room, the men would lie back sucking at their pipes and begin to talk ' the talk of men ' at its most Rabelaisian?

We are all tarred with the same brush to-day. What, for instance, does Duncan want of me as his wife? He wants me to be womanly, but not to go too far even in that direction . . . likes me to be what he calls *au fait* with books and questions of the day, but always to skim the surface lightly . . . hopes I shall be a good housewife and mother but without being too much taken up with domestic details, as this ' makes many married women such frightful bores.' Somehow one feels one is being made into a kind of shop-window that the admiring world may be shown what a modern woman can be like, until in time what one really is, is quite lost sight of, even by oneself.

Oct. 29.—Aunt H. took me to call on Mungo's mother, and both his sisters (older than he) were at home. They are very quiet, modest, gentle people who profess to admire every one else tremendously, and perhaps they really do, though not, I think, *quite* so much as they profess, the truth being that they have very little life in themselves and seem to gain for the moment some of the vitality of those they praise, besides attracting the praised person to come about them. Still, even this shows they must have rather sweet natures, for so many others lacking life grow bitter-tongued. Aunt H. does not like paying calls as a rule, but she enjoys visiting the Flemings. On our way home she said, ' I don't know how it is, Ellen, but somehow these people draw me out and make me talk.' And talk she certainly did ! So did I, I may say. They seemed so desperately anxious to hear about every detail of the trousseau and the wedding and everything connected with me, and they made any kind of doubt or dissatisfaction seem so impossible, that I rose to the occasion, and for the moment really felt like the nice uncritical girl they imagined me.

While we were there, Dr. Sturrock and his wife came in, and the subject turned on 'speaking out.' How far can one justifiably go in withholding one's opinion in company without becoming a hypocrite? Some funny things were said, especially by the younger and more timid Miss Fleming, who seemed so overwhelmed by this intellectual conversation with Dr. Sturrock taking place in her own drawing-room that she tried to agree with every one at the same time. Dr. S. does not approve of running against people's prejudices if you can avoid it; for once you do that, he says, they are in arms against you, and you will talk in vain afterwards, even about quite different matters. That's to say, you lose your influence, which he thinks is a pity. Here, to my great surprise, his wife, whom I have always thought a dull little woman, chipped in rather timidly, saying that she on the contrary thought the people with it in them ought, in duty bound, to come out strong with their opinions 'for the sake of the little people' like herself. For, she argued, her face turning red and her eyes quite dancing suddenly, there are so many people who disagree in their hearts with what is being said, but never dare —or perhaps it never occurs to them—to express their disagreement, because they think they are alone against the great world. But when some accredited person says out the very thing they are secretly feeling, they give a tremendous cheer and are braver ever afterwards and less alone. I see I have misjudged Mrs. S. completely up till now. I squeezed her hand very hard when we said good-bye.

Nov. 2.—To-day I went to see Laura, found her alone, and had—for us two nowadays—quite a long talk. Most of the other times I have gone her husband has been there, and though I don't mind Wilfred, there is something in the atmosphere between him and Laura that paralyses me. She almost never addresses him but with an endearment —'dear,' 'dearest' 'darling,'—and he the same with her, but I can't help seeing that it is when she is most vexed in her soul with him that she uses the superlative ' darling ! ' She is very polite to him and even affectionate, but in all she says and does there 's a terrible suppressed reproach. She is conscious of every movement he makes, every expression that crosses his face. When he is depressed (as he often seems to me now) she gets hatefully cheerful, watching him all the while out of the corners of her eyes, and when he forgets himself for a moment, and begins to laugh and chat in his natural rather fatuous but good-natured way, her face freezes under her smiling. They say hate is akin to love. Perhaps this emotion he clearly inspires in her is a kind of love or will turn at length into love. It

s

certainly makes a third person want to escape from them.

To-day she was sitting sewing for the baby, which is expected in February. All the strain which has spoiled our talks for so long seemed to have gone. She was at ease and ready to laugh. It was almost as if we were back at school again. We talked about Madge and her marriage, and a little, though not so much, about Duncan and me. It is queer to think that by next year all three of us will be married women! Madge has confided in Laura that she hopes to have a baby just as soon as she possibly can after the wedding. Laura herself was fearfully disappointed when the first month or two passed with her and there was no sign of anything. She thought she was going to be childless! And yet the newspapers are always saying that the young people of to-day do not want to have children! Certainly Laura looked happier this afternoon than she has done for years. Very beautiful, too. Everything seems to bring out a new beauty in her. Though she is *huge*, she looks like something to worship, and moves with a lovely swaying, generous movement from side to side as she walks . . . as though her body could hardly hide the pride of its condition. She is the first expectant mother I ever saw that made me feel there was truth in Lord Nelson's description—'the two most beautiful things on earth—a ship in full sail, and a woman with child.' I suppose Lady Hamilton must have looked like Laura.

When we had drunk tea and I got up to go, Laura threw her arms round my neck and kissed me with tears in her eyes. She said, ' My best wish for you, Ellen, is that you will love your husband as dearly as I love mine !' And she stared right into my eyes through her tears to see how I was taking this her first declaration to me of any feeling for Wilfred. I stared back at her, I do hope kindly and believingly . . . but fearing that she must see surprise and questioning and nothing else. Does she after all love him ? Have I been quite wrong ? If I was wrong, why such misery in being with them ? I can't make it out. Perhaps it is the baby. She talked — for her—a great deal about it. She said she hoped very much that it would be a girl, because then it would always be ' such a companion ' for her. I have been thinking this over, and find that I should want mine to be a boy, perhaps just for that same reason. I have so many ' ploys ' of my own that I shouldn't want children for companionship (I 'm not sure that I shouldn't find the companionship of a husband almost too much for me !). I 'd rather my children had their own ' ploys ' and would let mine alone, which I think boys more than girls likely to do. Besides, fancy for *any* reason wanting girls rather than boys if one could choose !

Sunday, Nov. 3.—It seems years since those weeks in London. Lay miserably awake last night asking myself why D. and I had got engaged. Was there anything more in it than in ninety-nine out of a hundred engagements ? Need there be more ? Lovely sunshine, flowers, the excitement of a familiar face in unfamiliar surroundings, the feeling of attraction growing stronger and stronger every moment, betraying itself in every look and movement till at last the moment comes when holding out any longer becomes impossible, and without a word the two fall into each other's arms. Sweet . . . inevitable ? . . . anyhow perfectly natural. Isn't it enough ? Why then this tortured questioning now ? For alas, it is true ! Hardly a day or a night passes but I am full of doubt. Did Laura endure this ? Yet she is radiant now at the prospect of having a child. She even says she loves Wilfred, though she was certainly not in love with him during the engagement. And Duncan and I are surely in love. Madge, I suppose, has no such troubles. I wish I were like Madge.

I do love Duncan. I miss him terribly . . . have only to call up his face and voice to feel the old response rise in me. But his letters rouse nothing but criticism, and in return I can't write more than a few lines without a sense of falseness. Does he feel the same? I have asked him, but he seems not to understand the question. He simply repeats what is, of course, true, that letters are bound to be unsatisfactory things. Then why did he not marry me? If he *knew* that letters were unsatisfactory why did he take such a risk? *I* didn't know they would be unsatisfactory, yet I fought not to let him go.

I suppose that is the trouble. *So far* we followed nature blindly, but Duncan will not have us follow her to the end. He calls a halt. To start with, he says he loves me for my naturalness. Then he begins to rule lines across the way toward which every natural impulse points. And what about after we are married? Where will the lines be ruled then if I am to please him? In how much am I to be myself, in how much assume a rôle laid down by him? Could I submit to his ruling even for love of him? Do I love him at all to ask such questions? If I did love him, should I not want at all costs to be his and take the rest on trust, ready to do my best, risking any failure gaily? Does he ever question himself, or is he secure as a rock? Does he feel any fear at all that my love is less stable than his? Or is it just that, knowing me so well as he does, he knows that I shall keep faith with him whether I have doubts or not. I expect if I could see him now he would in an instant laugh my fears away and wrap me up in his own security. How I wish I could run to him and hide in his love as in a cloak! I am like a shivering, naked creature with no faith in myself or in my ability to love.

Nov. 5.—Since Keswick Aunt H. has been unflagging in her missionary zeal. She lays a regular siege, and is always planning to take me to some meeting or other, especially if there is anything going about India. Sometimes I go just to please her, but increasingly often because in a meeting I can sit and think without any one wanting to talk to me. I have long been an adept at not listening.

This dark, cold, drizzling weather is depressing.

Nov. 7.—*Did* I so simply follow nature when I yielded to Duncan's attraction, went into his arms, and said I would marry him? Was I not partly obeying the convention which bids us do such things at such times? I think there were the two things driving us both on. For me there was my growing need of marriage and the attractiveness of Duncan, but there was also the desire to do what is held to be the right thing, and so to become a part with the great world which till then had always seemed to thrust me out from its common experience.

My thoughts wheel round and round and I get no peace. Will Duncan be happy with me when he finds out what I am really like? He himself seems so beautifully simple that I long most lovingly for him. Yet again isn't there something wrong about the kind of simplicity that just shuts its eyes to what it doesn't want to see?

I don't know. I know nothing. There will be a letter from him to-morrow, his first since actually starting work. Perhaps he will say something quite unconsciously that will help and settle me. It is always the unconscious things that help most . . . hurt most too, perhaps.

Am drawing up a scheme of work and activities to fill up my days till Christmas . . . must keep from futile thinking . . . better not think at all than think uselessly in circles as I have been doing.

Nov. 8.—Nothing special in D.'s letter, yet it cheered me a bit. He seems so perfectly happy. Perhaps he is right about my being morbid. . . .

Started writing a short story this morning, and got on fairly well. Wrote a longer letter than usual to Duncan. Paid calls with Aunt H.

Nov. 12.—Crossing Renfield Street to-day was as nearly as possible knocked down by a taxi. The mud-guard did actually strike against me, and

the driver dismounted to ask if I was hurt. Had
been so deep in my thoughts that for the moment
I had quite forgotten where I was. Only laughed
at first, but after five minutes felt suddenly so very
shaky that I had to go and sit down in a shop.
Incident would not be worth recording if it had not,
while I was sitting collecting myself, recalled very
vividly a thought I had utterly forgotten—indeed
not noticed much at the time. It was in London
. . . the morning of the day Duncan and I got
engaged . . . had walked by myself all the way into
town from West Hampstead, going through Hyde
Park . . . had been up late the night before, and
by the time I reached Marble Arch began to feel
tired. The traffic made me nervous, so that twice
over I started to cross and had to run back, though
other people got to the other side almost without
hurrying. Then there came such a close-packed
stream of traffic that I had to wait some minutes for
any chance at all. I watched the people driving
past in cabs and carriages, cars and buses . . . they
all looked so safe, so delivered from my painful
anxiety, being borne along like that through everything. It didn't matter to them how dense the
traffic was. They trusted perfectly to their drivers.
One woman's face I specially noticed. She was in a
brougham, leaning back comfortably, playing with a
pet dog. She looked at the crowds on the pavement

with pleased indifference. Perhaps it was because she had something of Madge in her face—the same short nose and upper lip . . . anyhow it came to me suddenly that never to be married would be like coping on foot all your life with the world's traffic, not once getting a lift, not once being able to lean back in security watching the stream of life with interest, always having to gaze anxiously at it with the fear of turning tired or giddy, and so of getting submerged. Marriage seemed like some divinely appointed wheeled chariot into which a woman could climb and be carried along the great high roads.

Now that I come to write it down, this thought, which at the time took but an instant to pass through my mind, seems both complicated and exaggerated. At the moment it seemed no more important than a dozen other thoughts that came before and after it. But—and this is my reason for trying to set it down here—remembering it to-day, when the taxi had touched me, I was compelled to remember also what I had as completely forgotten— that when Duncan kissed me on the evening of that day the thought of the morning flashed again in me. Did it make me readier to listen and respond? Am I partly marrying Duncan to get a lift? So long as I care for him do such things matter? But suppose the chariot of marriage sweeps me far, far in the opposite direction from the road I naturally

wish to walk along? Does that matter either?
Do I really know what I most want?

Nov. 13.—Fogs have started early this year.
For two days now we have had dense yellow fog.
It has even got into the house. If one opens a
door or window it breathes horribly in one's face
like some huge monster. I sat all morning at home
to-day trying at intervals to practise, but each time
ended by leaning my head on my hands. My whole
body ached. Madge ran in to see me. She looked
all the prettier for the weather. The frost had
reddened her cheeks and brightened her eyes, and
the fog had drawn black lines under them as if she
had been made up. When I said I was feeling very
low, she laughed. Madge is always philosophical
where other people's troubles are concerned. I
don't think she really believes in them unless the
other person can show at least a broken bone. She
simply laughs and says, ' Never you mind ! '

In the afternoon went to my poor old Room and
sat for some hours trying to write till my hands
were nearly frozen . . . had to give the fire up
after one or two attempts, but even so, it seemed
better than sitting at home with Aunt H. coming
in every few minutes. Then began looking through
old work and tore up heaps, including the play
' Influence.' Why keep them ? The sight of them

would only make me fret if I did cart them away
with me to India. Besides, surely if there is anything worth while in them it will come again to me
later on and perhaps in some better form? Not
that I am positive about this. For the present,
though, must give up all idea of writing . . . shall
only go on with this journal till my marriage day.

Nov. 14.——Third day of fog.

Nov. 15.——Still fog-bound and wretched. As
if the air will never be clear again. Everything,
even inside the house, is black to the touch; the
chimneys have taken to smoking at home as well as
in my Room, the water is tepid in the boiler.
Could anything I should have had to put up with in
India be as bad as this? Started a sore throat last
night and this morning have a raging cold. All
the same went into town to have a linen riding-
habit fitted. Shivered the whole time. On getting
home found a long letter from Duncan, which I
seized upon eagerly. He writes chiefly of tennis
parties and dances which does not help much, but I
take what comfort I can from the words of love at
the end.

Later.——Got to bed after a mustard and soda
bath. Fairly sure I shall not be out of bed again

for some days, so took care to write first to Don John saying I was ill and begging him to write. Refrained from asking him to come to see me as I thought it would be no use, but feel sure a quiet talk with him would help me to get into a better frame of mind. Wrote to Duncan too, but had to make a fearful effort (which I always seem driven to do with him) to seem cheerful when I'm the opposite. Posted both letters myself, running out in the fog while my bath was filling. Raw air and filthy underfoot . . . but I think it is going to thaw . . . that's one mercy.

Nov. 16.—Thaw sure enough. Fog quite gone . . . clear and mild and sunshiny . . . only the mud looks disagreeable. Not up yet, anyhow. Had temperature of 102 in the morning, so Aunt H. sent for the doctor, who says it is influenza. Aching all over, especially my loins. Lay dozing and miserable, yet the day passed quickly. I do hope Don John will write.

Sunday, Nov. 17.—In spite of dozing through the day, lay wide enough awake all night till five A.M. All my thoughts tended toward an intense dislike of my own character, circumstances, everything connected with myself. If only I could shed my temperament without losing my sense of identity!

I don't want to die, but how differently I should like to live !

Yet when at length I asked myself with what person known to me I would completely change natures I could not truthfully think of any one. I felt I could not be *sure* that any one of those others I envied ever feels so intensely, almost excruciatingly happy as I do at times for no apparent cause. And I could not risk losing these moments in exchange for anything else. The other day, for instance, when I was walking over the hill and met Don John . . . the whole of life—pain as well as pleasure, evil as well as good—appeared to me as a harmony which could not be heard but with extreme ecstasy.

Nov. 18.—In the morning my temperature was below normal. The doctor made me stay in bed, but I read and slept and felt better. All my feelings and perceptions blunted again. Things that yesterday appeared crucial have receded. Nothing seems to matter much. The doctor came again at night and said I was going on well . . . praised my constitution for ' functioning admirably.' In the afternoon I wrote very affectionately to Duncan.

Nov. 19.—After good night's sleep felt all right. Got up and tried to practise, but then felt so weak and giddy that I had to give up in a few minutes. Went back to bed and lay without any thoughts, good or bad. Aunt H. very sweet. D. J. hasn't written.

Nov. 20.—It snowed in the night and was lovely this morning with blue sky and sunshine. Got up for breakfast and thought of going to Endrick Street, but by about eleven the sky grew dark and another fog descended, so I stayed indoors and wrote to Duncan, after reading over all the letters I have had from him. How I wish I knew what he feels for me apart from all this business of marrying a wife! His letters do not tell me. He never seems to wonder what I feel for him. So long as I've said I'll marry him, that's all he cares to know. Perhaps all men are like this. One knows very little of men and their thoughts and feelings. Fog or no fog, I'll go to-morrow to Endrick Street.

Nov. 21.—Don John is dead. He died yester-day of pneumonia. I went to Endrick Street to-day and he was lying dead in his room. Spent a long time there morning and afternoon.

Nov. 22.—Went to-night to St. Ignatius's R.C. church and saw D. J. for the last time. His brother from Newcastle is looking after things. The body was in the coffin before the altar clothed in priestly vestments. Funeral to-morrow, but I shall not go.

Nov. 23.—Very shaky when I rose. Took almost an hour to dress, with pauses for weakness. Train to Loch Lomond. Went to the place where Duncan and I had sat that last evening. Saw everything about myself and him with perfect clearness, the kind of clearness that has to be acted upon. Walked back to Helensburgh. Very cold but no wind . . . the sky covered with ribbed cloud like miles and miles of sand when the tide is out. Had to wait an hour for a train and reached home chilled to the bone. Did not sleep, though my mind was made up.

Sunday, Nov. 24.—Wrote to Duncan breaking off our engagement. Made it quite final. Told Aunt Harry. Called and told Dr. Bruce, also Madge and Laura, who both happened to be there. Have done for myself now. Wrote to Ronald. Wrote short note to Ruby. At six o'clock felt pretty ill. Wrote up diary of last two days. This ends, I think, the journal of my old life. Now I shall either die or start the new life. Don't want to die.

End of Ellen's Journal.

'ALSO, VORWÄRTS!'

T

'ALSO, VORWÄRTS!'

25 Blandford Terrace, Glasgow,
Sunday, December 8.

My dearest Ruby,—I have just reread your last letter written ten days ago in answer to my note about Duncan and me. At the time I blessed my stars for it, feeling it to be full of friendliness and understanding. Arriving in the midst of my disgrace with everybody here, it certainly seemed so. After the non-comprehension and distress of Aunt Harry, the chill condemnation of Laura, the furious disapproval (mixed with indubitable relief) of Dr. and Mrs. Bruce, and the complete removal of Madge's friendship, I drank up your few and careful words like drops of water in a desert.

And yet, my dear friend, though I cling to the hope that this may be due to my generally flayed condition at the moment, on rereading those same words this morning I feel all unsure again. I have the sad idea that from mere dislike of wounding me you were trying as you wrote to hide certain puzzled and reproachful thoughts.

I agree with you that 'jilt' is an ugly word. Quite right too, for it is an ugly, indeed an unfor-

givable action. I have always thought so and do
still. But surely you, of all people, will agree with
me that no number of fine, pretty, or commendable
actions can ever turn a false position into a true one.
And once I knew clearly that the position was false
I could see no alternative but to act in this ugly
manner and so end it. At the time I only managed to
scrawl that single line to you. For one thing I was
ill. For another it is the simple truth that my life
was cut in two by Don John's death as by lightning,
and at such times one cannot sit down and write at
length. This reminds me that *if* I am right in my new
reading of your letter, the cause may lie with me for
having told you the mere fact so baldly and without
explanations. In that desperate moment I counted
on your taking everything on trust. But if you
couldn't, well, you couldn't, and the sooner one
knows that one has to stand quite alone in the
world, the better.

To you, though, above all, indeed only to you,
Ruby, do I now want to plead my own cause as far
as it can be pleaded. I am out of bed to-day for
the first time this fortnight, and for the first time I
feel I must put before you as clearly and soberly as
possible what the facts were that made me change,
or rather what it was that directed me with such terrible clearness that I had no choice but to obey. Not
that I shall ever be able to explain *why* the sight of

Don John's. dead face should have made all this difference when no living word or action of his could have had such power. I see him now much as I always saw him, as a poor scholar with whom I never became very intimate, and as a lover of truth whom I admired because he had chosen failure rather than bolster up his weakness by accepting what to him was a lie, also because he never once complained of the result even while he admitted it. To Duncan I have not so much as named him in connection with breaking our engagement. To have done so would only have been an irritation besides confusing the issue between us. For there is nothing in me now that was not there before. It was merely that Don John's death crystallised what before was confused and obscure. If Duncan would have me I'd go at once and live with him. I'd go with joy. With joy I'd keep the real essence of my pledge with him. It is only that I cannot marry him. He and I were never meant to be husband and wife. But where would be the use of offering him anything but what he has made up his mind that he wants? So I had to tell him simply that I would not be his wife and that nothing now could alter my decision.

Let me try now to tell you how things came to this point with me.

On November 21, after having been in bed a

few days with a bad cold, I called at Don John's
lodging and asked the landlady if he was in. It
was the first time I had ever done this uninvited,
but something drove me to it. She said he had died
the day before, and at once, with an air half injured,
half elated, began to tell me how devotedly she had
nursed him—'jist as if he'd been yin o' ma ain,' as
she put it, and that she hoped I would come and
speak for her to Don John's brother, who was
arriving from Newcastle that evening to make
arrangements for the funeral. It was easy enough,
without listening to her explanations about the
illness, to guess what had happened—a bad chill
which Don John would neglect and no one else
notice . . . that threadbare overcoat of his . . .
those four terrible days of fog. . . . She took me
to his room, whining and sniffing all the way, and
though I hated her and was fairly sure she had done
no more than she had to for Don John (which with
her would not be much), I felt a bit sorry for her
too, and promised I'd see the brother next day.
At Don John's door I managed to shake her off.

I had never seen a dead person before. I waited
till I heard the landlady go away, then crossed to
the bed and with shrinking curiosity turned back
the sheet that was over his face. I had heard that
there was majesty, even beauty, in death. I saw
none here—that is, not at first. At first I simply

could not believe that that long, yellow, tallowy
face, tied up with a large, folded handkerchief and
with a penny on each eyelid, could have any connection with my friend Don John. The features
were pinched and severe. I was so shattered by the
grotesque sadness of it that I broke down hysteri-
cally. I 'd have given anything at that moment not
to have looked, but to have kept the memory of his
face as I last saw it alive that day we sat on the hill
and talked.

I cried so that I thought I should never be able
to stop. But touching his books helped to calm
me, and after a while I went back and began to
tend him, taking the pennies from his eyes and
untying the handkerchief, for which I could not see
the need any longer. I stayed a long time in his
room, then went out and got some Christmas roses
—he had no flowers, of course—and put them in
his hands, and again I sat a long time beside him.
I didn't feel sorry for him any more. Dying seemed
much the best thing he could have done. The
more I thought, the more distinctly I understood
the meaning of his life, and his death seemed to set
the seal on it. He had failed in life, but he had
stood for something more precious and important
than success, and now his humiliation and misery,
which I had often felt so bitterly, ceased to count.
Instead, his plain and unpretentious truthfulness

appeared like a star and showed me my own falseness. I knew then where my place was. I knew—
though I hate and fear failure—that I would rather
end like Don John than succeed on the lines that
marriage with Duncan would inevitably lay down for
me.

When I got home I was thankful to find that
Aunt Harry was out at a meeting. For the first
time I was glad that Ronald was away. I could
not have borne to talk to any one or to hear any one
speak to me. I tried to make an entry in my
journal, but found I could not write more than a few
lines, so I went to bed and almost immediately fell
asleep.

Next day I went to see the brother. He is a
good deal older than D. J. and handsomer—very
dignified and handsome and religious-looking, with
a large gold cross on his waistcoat. He and I were
at daggers drawn from the first. He said nothing
exactly harsh, but made me think all the time of old
Mr. Dudgeon with his ‘a sad business, a very sad
business!’ while his thoughts were clearly on much
more mundane matters. He kept telling me—as if
I needed to be told—how gifted D. J. was, and how
he had deliberately thrown away and wasted his
gifts. In all he said I was sure that his real feelings were simple irritation and anger against D. J.
for not having acted according to *his* standards.

' So-and-so,' he said, ' with half my poor brother's
talents, is now a Monsignor in Rome.' I tried to
tell him how I admired, indeed revered, D. J., what
he had stood for to me, how he had helped me, but
this he brushed aside as a mere impertinence. At
the moment I was almost ready to allow that it was,
but later I saw that it was no such thing. Mr.
Barnaby—the brother—would have it that D. J.
would have done far more good in the world if he
had remained in a position of influence, however
false to himself that position might be. But is all
the influence of a false attitude worth a fig ? And
how can any one measure or limit the good that must
flow unseen from an attitude of simple but determined honesty ? D. J.'s wisdom and worth are not
trumpeted abroad. *He* got nothing out of them.
But in some way they are bound to be made known,
and his having so wonderfully helped an unimportant
person like myself to be honest is surely at least a
proof of his usefulness in the world ? His failure—
that he could not stand up against a besetting
weakness after discarding a false start — is but
another pointer to his virtue. For he had nothing
to gain, everything to lose by choosing to be honest.
Yet he chose honesty and never once complained.

When Mr. Barnaby told me that there seemed to
be ' a sort of will ' written on a half sheet of paper
the day his brother died, and that by it *I* was to

have 'possession of D. J.'s manuscript and books,' I
hardly knew what to do for surprise and gratitude.
Here is the will :—

'. . . subject to the satisfaction of such claims
as my family may make in respect of my funeral
expenses, I leave to my young and dearly loved
friend Ellen Carstairs my collection of books, knowing that she will value them, and to her also I
bequeath my manuscript writings and the copyright
therein absolutely, giving no direction as to their
publication, which I leave to her unfettered dis-
cretion.'

Mr. B. was clearly reluctant to tell me about
this, but he could not very well get out of showing
it to me. He was specially vexed about the manuscripts, but tried hard to suppress his vexation, and
assured me many times that I should find nothing
in his brother's writings worthy of preservation.
He wanted to have them destroyed on the spot, but
I need not tell you I have them all safely at home
and regard them as my chief treasure. As yet I
have not been able to do more than just glance
through them (there 's a great heap), but even with
my unlearned eyes I feel certain there is valuable
work in my keeping. I mean to consult the best
judges of such matters in London. Who knows but
that D. J.'s name will yet become famous !

By this time the body had been removed by Mr.

Barnaby's order to St. Ignatius's, a Roman Catholic
chapel not far from Endrick Street. I went there
by myself. It is a low-roofed, bare shed of a place,
being, I think, only a temporary church till a proper
one can be built. It was empty except for a verger
who knelt to one side of the altar, and dark but for
two candles that were nearly burnt down. The
coffin lay on trestles near the hardly noticeable altar,
and though the lid was on, it was not screwed down.
The verger (I think he was asleep) never looked
round or moved when I raised the coffin lid a few
inches. I was greatly astonished to find that they
had dressed Don John in priestly vestments, all
white but for the black biretta on his head. I suppose having once been ordained, even though he
afterwards became a renegade, this was his right in
death. I rejoiced in the fitness of this. Even as
a priest should, he had pointed out my way to me,
and I felt sure he would not have refused to be so
robed if he could have chosen. In the shadow of
the biretta his face looked calm and satisfied. I
too, though I knew what I had to do, felt calm,
looking at it. I could not look long, however, for
the lid was fearfully heavy to hold up, also I was
afraid the verger or whoever he was (clearly not a
priest, merely some kind of attendant whose duty it
was to wait a few hours in the church) might wake
and find fault with me. I went then and knelt

down, and the course I must take was clear before
me. I offered up thanks from the bottom of my
heart for having met Don John. Very soon the
verger got up, yawned, stretched his arms, sniffed
out the two long candles, and only then seeing me,
came over and told me in a husky, cross voice that
he had to lock up the church as it was sunset.
They had allowed Don John his robes of office, but
in all other ways he was to be treated without ceremony, and his body would be left alone in the
locked, unlighted church until the time of the
funeral the following morning. What after all
did this matter? So the verger bundled me out.

I did not go to the funeral next day. After
lying awake all night I felt very ill and shaky in the
morning. But in the afternoon I went down town
and took the train to Loch Lomond. I just caught
the last steamer to the place I wanted, and from the
pier, walking along the shore road, I found my way
easily to the little copse and the very patch of
shingle where Duncan and I had sat together on our
last evening. This may sound to you like a piece
of sentimentality, but I don't think it was. A
strong instinct drove me to it, and when I got there
I knew my instinct had served me well. I was
giving Duncan his full chance, letting him speak for
himself, and speak better than he could in a hundred
letters or in much actual speech. If his voice was

truer than Don John's I should not fail to hear and obey. But oh, Ruby, it was not! There I sat, not thinking at all, rather *listening* to all Duncan had to say till it grew dark, and so cold that I was afraid. There wasn't a breath of wind, but it was freezing hard. By this time, though, I knew beyond all question what I had come to find out. Many people must have discovered, as I did then for the first time, with what perfect certainty one *knows* when one returns to the scene of a past emotion. On that second occasion it is impossible to deceive one-self as to the nature of one's feelings on the first visit. And that night I was humiliated unspeakably by the knowledge of my own falseness. The very stones and trees and lapping water of the loch whispered to me how dishonest I had been to Duncan and myself when we last sat there, and all his pleadings were on the side of asking me to be dishonest still. It was no use, I knew. I could never be straight with Duncan except in the act of giving him up.

I had missed the last steamer back, so had to walk four or five miles over the hills to Helensburgh, and at Helensburgh I had to sit for an hour in a dark, very draughty station waiting-room till I could get a train to Glasgow. All the time I kept turning over words and sentences, trying to find the plainest, most final, least hurtful way of telling Duncan.

But when I got home I was too tired to write, besides feeling ill and thoroughly chilled. Again I had a fearful night. The next day I managed to get Duncan's letter written and posted. I also told Aunt Harry, though I don't think at the time she took it in (she does now). And in a sort of frenzy, to make the smash complete, I called at the Bruces' house in the afternoon. As it happened, Madge and her husband were there, just returned from their honeymoon, and Laura also came in. I told them all that the engagement between Duncan and me was at an end, and that Duncan was in no way to blame. At first they pretended to think that it was some kind of a bad joke, but very soon they saw I was in earnest. It was frightfully unpleasant, and I got away as soon as I could and went home to bed. Not one of them has called to ask for me since, though they knew from Aunt Harry at church that I was pretty badly ill. The worst thing in the last fortnight, though, has been the arrival of Duncan's unknowing letters by each Indian mail. I read the first. The others I had to tear up unread. It will be some weeks yet before I can get his answer, if he writes at all after getting my letter.

And now what am I going to do? One thing is sure. I shall leave Glasgow. Even if I wanted to stay, life here has become impossible for me. And

Lord knows I don't want to stay.   Indeed, now that
my health is returning to me in ever bigger waves, I
can't restrain a wicked glorying in the fact that by
my impossible behaviour I have rid myself of the
whole incubus—school friends, family friends, Christian friends—all at once.   (I should have told you
that Miss McRaith is palpably overjoyed—though
of course she pulls a long face at my catastrophe,
also that she is as firmly convinced as ever I was in
her case that Duncan has really been the one to
break off the engagement !   Twice when I was in
bed she played the Good Samaritan and brought
me flowers and grapes !)   I feel fearfully alone and
very much like a shorn lamb.   Still, it *is* fine to feel
free, grand to know that I need trim no longer, that
I am thrust definitely and for ever without the pale.
I have sat long enough on that same pale and was
growing more sick of the balancing act than I
knew.

When Aunt H. hears that I mean to go at the
New Year, she may try to put up a little fight.   But
she was content—Ronald too—that I should go far
away to be married, so at least I need have no
scruples about leaving her by herself.

Where shall I go ?   Much depends on Ronald's
letter in answer to the long one I have written to
him.   I expect to hear from him any day now, and
though I am prepared for the gravest reproof, I

don't think he will forget his own last promise and suggestion. If he wants me I may possibly go out to stay with him for a time at least.

But much too depends on your next letter, Ruby. Do you remember when I was in London, but before I got engaged, we talked over all sorts of plans for both leaving home and sharing rooms together? I should like that if, after all, you would care for my company. Sooner or later I am sure I shall find a job. Meanwhile I have a little money of my very own which, now that I am of age, Aunt H. cannot refuse to let me have. I think it comes to about £80 a year, and up till now it has always gone toward helping with the housekeeping when I was at home. When I was in Frankfort it covered both my living and all fees at the Conservatorium. I know things are a bit more expensive in London, but *I shall manage*. All I need is time to write ! Honestly I have the impulse. I don't feel elated, rather the reverse, but subjects jostle one another in my head and I have the will and the capacity to work hard. Of this I am positive—I am done with music as a profession. Like the rest of my old life that must be let slip. Any wage-earning work I get now must either be itself writing or something to do with writing which will at the same time allow me leisure and strength for working out my own ideas. One room in the most unfashionable neighbourhood will hold me and my books——Don John's books! I am not counting on getting any money from his writings, even if I get them published. But if anything ever *should* come in from them, I shall use it religiously to provide me with more time to work. No one in London will live more economically or more laboriously than I. How glad I am that I am young and strong, that life is before me, that already I have tasted just enough of the sweet and bitter of Reality to make existence seem rich and full of savour! I no longer envy the middle-aged. I know at last to what world I irrevocably belong, and that it is not Duncan's world. I have found this out in time. And just because of it I have the whole of Duncan's world to write about. One can never write till one stands outside.

'Also, vorwärts!' as Zilcher used to say! Let me hear from you soon. If you are not convinced by my *apologia*, suspend your judgment till you see me. Continue to be my friend on trust, as I am ever yours in deed.   ELLEN CARSTAIRS.

THE END

U